Lady Undertaker II:

The Embalmer's Blues

Lisa Branch-Edwards & Lyn Johnson

ISBN: 978-1-66785-628-5 eBook 978-1-66785-629-2

To our mothers, Lauretta Rocke and Ingrid Johnson.

For everything.

Chapter 1

"My Mama Done Left Me"

"**My word—she don't** look so good," whispered Sister Whitley as she shook her head. "Too much makeup and that dress. Lawd have mercy!"

The other women nodded in silent agreement as they all surveyed the open casket of Miss Lula Mae Moore. None really knew the deceased well as she was not a frequent church attendee, but they wouldn't miss a chance to see the funeral of the town's harlot.

"And where is Leona?" inquired another woman. "She's always here early, greetin' folk."

"She's where I'd be," quipped Sister Whitley. "Far away from this mess. No woman should have to bury her husband and then his mistress too!" The woman all snickered sarcastically and continued their idle gossip.

They were momentarily silenced by the opening of the French doors. All eyes were fixed on the center aisle, as Leona Harris Williams, owner of Williams Mortuary, gracefully made her way toward the casket. Leona and her late husband, Jamison Williams, had started the business over forty years ago and turned it into one of the largest funeral homes in the Southeast.

The elegantly coiffed older woman was flanked on each side by her girls, daughter Sydney Samuels and niece Kalen Christina Watkins. Both women were licensed funeral directors and ran the business's day-to day operations. Kalen was a tall, thin, browned-skinned natural beauty who kept her hair neatly tucked into a bun. Her cousin Sydney was her exact opposite— short, plump, and curvy with her mother's light brown skin and a mane of wavy brown hair. As Leona reached the group, she smiled graciously.

"Were you ladies looking for me?" she asked sweetly. "I was serving another family, but I didn't want to miss the chance to see my sisters in Christ." Sydney had to stifle a smirk at her mother's last line. These women were definitely not her mother's sisters. Leona had heard every word spoken through the chapel's microphone system that was piped directly into her office.

"Sister Whitley, how is Brother Whitley doing? You two are in my thoughts all the time," drawled Leona. It was common knowledge in town that Brother Whitley had a gambling problem and had stolen several thousand dollars from his employer. But only Leona Williams could get away with asking about him.

"He's coming along," answered Sister Whitley, eager to end that particular conversation. "Let's go, ladies; we still have to visit Brother Manley at the nursing home. Good to see you, Leona," she said as she and her entourage swept out quickly.

"Those hateful bitches! I can't stand them and that ..." Sydney's tirade was cut short by her mother's withering glance.

"Harris women do not swear, Sydney Michelle, and are certainly not bothered by the gossip of pathetic, slow-witted women. Now where is Rev. Monroe, so we can get this show on the road?"

Leona's no-nonsense tone was the exact opposite of how she felt inside. She hated the fact that her nemesis lay in a casket a few feet away. Lula Mae Moore was the mother of her late husband Jimmy's illegitimate son, Damien. Jimmy and Lula Mae had carried on an illicit affair for over forty years and she was one person in the world Leona could truly say she despised. But there she was in her funeral home, having her home-going service. In spite of the circumstances, she had graciously embraced Damien, a skilled embalmer and funeral director in his own right, welcoming him into the funeral home and her family. The whole situation was stressing Leona out. She wished she could stay hidden in her office, or better yet, at home, away from this circus.

Feeling compelled to protect the aunt she loved like a mother, Kalen Christiana, called KC by her family and close friends, gently offered to take over the viewing duties. "Aunt Leona, I'll stay here till the service begins. Why don't you go back to your office? I would love you to look over the week's schedule and make sure everything is okay."

Relieved and grateful, Leona shook her head and retreated to the safety of her office suite.

"Since when did you need someone to look at the schedule?" questioned Sydney.

"She didn't need to be here, Sydney, with everyone whispering and looking at her with those pitying glances. This whole situation is insane," KC looked at Lula Mae's body critically. "How could one woman cause so much trouble?"

As Sydney moved closer to her cousin, she too was drawn to the sight of the small, emaciated woman. "She didn't do it alone, KC. Daddy brought this on us."

Arriving at precisely the same time, Troy Watkins and Avery Samuels delayed their entrance to the funeral home, preferring to remain in the parking lot, swapping stories. The two men were married to KC and Sydney, respectively, and, along with Damien, had christened themselves "The Three Amigos."

Besides being roughly the same height and married to cousins, the two men couldn't be less alike. Troy was tall, muscular, and chocolate with a bald head and impressive beard. Extremely good looking, he would be most women's fantasy. Avery, on the other hand, was equally as tall, but was fair-skinned with close cropped mixed gray hair, soulful gray eyes, and glasses. His wife often said he reminded her of a sexy science teacher.

"This is total bullshit," exclaimed Troy, KC's husband, who was always ready to keep it real. "I know Damien is our boy and we family and all, but this whole situation creeps me out. I mean, damn, Lula Mae was Mr.

Jimmy's jump-off and Aunt Leona has to act like this whole thing is okay. KC says the place has been tense all week."

Avery shook his head in agreement. "It's all I've heard about. Sydney feels like she's stuck in the middle. After all, Damien's her brother and he just lost his mom, but being loyal to him is being disloyal to her mother. I'll be glad when this whole thing is over with. I wish …." But before Avery could finish his thought, his cell phone rang. Seeing his wife's name, he pushed it quickly to voicemail.

"Let's go, Troy. That was Sydney—she probably knows I'm standing out here." Avery quickly became nervous; his need to please his younger wife was always a joke between the men. Troy often said Avery was the most whipped guy he knew.

"Probably that tracking device she put in your shoe," Troy replied dryly. "Come on man—let's go face the music."

Damien sat quietly at his desk nestled in the back of the storage room in the morgue. The previous head embalmer had positioned his desk in the front of the state-of-the-art facility so that he could oversee all the work, but Damien preferred being tucked in the rear. He felt he had a better vantage point from the back, unseen but always watchful. He knew he needed to leave and join the others in the chapel, but he just couldn't bring himself to leave the sanctity of the only place he really felt comfortable—the morgue.

As if on cue, Damien's best friend and brother-in-law both walked in, interrupting his thoughts.

"Yo, man, what's up?" said Troy. "Everybody's looking for you."

"Okay; what's the deal? A lot of people in the chapel?" inquired Damien.

The two men looked at each other before Troy commented, "Man, I'm going to be honest. There's some rough looking sistahs out there… I thought I might get cut."

"Aw… shut up…those are my mom's peeps from the cannery." His mother was a retired forewoman at the local fish cannery for over 30 years. He turned to Avery and said, "Alright; let's get out there. I'm sure your mother-in-law is having a fit."

Damien was all too familiar with Leona's need for order when it came to mixing with "common folk."

Damien could hear the straining voice of Mrs. Corbett, their organist, who was murdering the final stanza of "Blessed Assurance." Troy and Avery quietly slid into the seats in the rear of the chapel, while he walked toward the available seat next to his fiancée, Clarissa and their fifteen-year-old son Damien Jr., known as DJ, on the first row.

He was touched to see his sister and cousin standing at the head and foot of the casket as this was usually reserved for the funeral attendants. The service was pretty lackluster until the program allowed for remarks from the audience. After an awkward moment of silence, several people stood up and headed for the podium. The first to speak was Lula Mae's oldest friend and drinking buddy, Ms. Patsy Lee Parker.

"Lula Mae was my friend for real. Even when she moved away, we still would get our party on! She was always someone that you could talk to, and she would always help you sort shit out! Ooops… I didn't mean to say that…but for real, she was my girl, and I'm going to miss her crazy ass! I'm sorry! I'm sorry but I'm grievin'. I just think of all those good times…me and Roscoe, her and Jimmy playing bid whist all night long!" It seemed that everyone but Patsy knew the impact of her words as there was an audible gasp among the crowd.

After several low brow comments from her co-workers and fellow bar flies, Damien slowly approached the microphone. "I want to say thank you to everybody who came out today to support my mom. As many of you shared, Lula Mae was one of a kind. While we didn't always see eye to eye, she was my mother and I was her son. I also want to thank my extended family for their support during this difficult time. I truly appreciate everything that was done despite the circumstances."

As Reverend Monroe concluded his eulogy, Damien recalled all the things that his mother said, and more importantly, what she hadn't.

The repast was held at Clarissa and Damien's large but modest home. Clarissa had tried her best to decorate her house, but she wasn't blessed with a sense of style. Hardly anything matched, the furniture was sparse and cheap, and clutter was everywhere. Old mail, magazines, and DJ's videos games littered the living room.

"Dang, didn't she know we were coming over? Could have cleaned up a little," remarked one of Lula Mae's cronies.

"I know that's right. Mm… mm, guess it don't pay to be the illegitimate son—I hear Jimmy's daughter got a mansion big as her mama's," commented another.

True to form, the folks from the cannery stayed throughout the day, eating and drinking up all that Clarissa could put out. Clarissa was in her hostess mode, trying to accommodate two distinct groups of people. Sydney, however, was over the whole situation.

"Pigs in a blanket and sliced Velveeta are too good for these people. She should have set up a trough out back for them!" remarked Sydney sarcastically.

"Hush! They may hear you," hissed KC. "But look at this crowd! Drinking and smoking like we are at a barbeque! Are we forgetting that someone died?"

"That's my little Sunday School teacher!" exclaimed Troy. He lovingly rubbed her shoulder, happy that he had married the nice one.

"Well, I'm hungry and there's barely anything left," pouted a "hangry" Sydney. At precisely that moment, Morgan and Jamie, Sydney and Avery's 12-year-old twins raced into the room full of questions and demands.

Morgan was a typical tween braces and ponytails, thin with coltish long legs. With a smattering of light brown freckles adorning her nose and her father's gray eyes she would one day grow into a great beauty. Her twin brother, Avery Jamison, named after his father and grandfather, also had his father's eyes and mother's brown hair but towered over his twin sister— most people thought he was older than his twelve years. Finding it difficult to have two Averys in the house, Sydney started calling her son Jamie and the nickname stuck.

"Mom, can we please order Uber eats or something? We're starving and this food is like so gross," spoke the twins in unison. Despite the difference in appearance, the twins were so close they moved as a unit, often speaking at exactly the same time. They were a force of nature and often totally overwhelmed their parents. It had been that way since their birth.

"No! Absolutely not! We aren't ordering food to somebody else's house. It's rude. We're leaving shortly, so you can just wait until we get home," Sydney was clearly flustered by their demands.

"Daddy said we could, but you have the Uber account on your phone," Morgan had already started grabbing for her mother's phone. Sydney snatched her phone away.

"Don't try me, little girl! Eat this cheese and crackers if you're starving," Sydney turned and saw her husband sheepishly standing in the corner watching the drama. He adored his children, but discipline always fell to Sydney. He was the perennial good cop.

Their antics were interrupted by the arrival of the newest guest, Leona. While she was the same age as Lula Mae Moore and her cronies, the years had been more kind. Her black Chanel suit, gleaming patent Prada heels, and gorgeous flowing silver hair stood out glaringly among the bad wigs, run-over shoes, and clothing from the Pic 'N' Save. Leona's skin was free from the wrinkles that came with hard living. Stopping only to kiss her grandchildren and without acknowledging the other guests, Leona quickly sought out Clarissa to present her with a basket of homemade gourmet treats.

"Thank you so much, Miss Leona," gushed Clarissa, "I'll put these right out. I'm so glad you could come. I don't think you've been here...," but Leona silenced her with a look.

"No, my dear, why don't you save these for you and Damien? What you have out for this crowd is just fine," responded Leona. "Where is Damien?" Before Clarissa could answer, Leona had moved on, greeting her daughter and niece.

Leona found her stepson alone in the garage, apparently hiding out. She marveled at how much he looked like his father. While not quite as tall, Damien had his mother's light brown skin with Jimmy's chiseled features. But it was his eyes that reminded him most of her late husband, a sparkly brown when amused, and a rich deep onyx when angry.

"I thought things went rather well, don't you?" asked Leona.

"Yeah, sure, as well as could be expected," responded Damien awkwardly. "Listen, I just wanted to apologize...."

Leona quickly cut him off, "What happened between your mother and Jimmy is neither of our concerns. You were a good son and I, a devoted wife. What's important is the future. Take time off if you wish, but we need you at the funeral home in an increased capacity. I need you seeing families, working services, and overseeing the embalmers. I know it's a lot more responsibility, but I know I can count on you."

Leona paused and reached for Damien's hand, "It's time to get you out of the back and up front where you belong."

"Of course, Miss Leona, you can count on me. That's how family works."

"What did Aunt Leona want with you?" grilled Troy as Damien joined him and Avery on his back patio. "We thought you needed to be rescued," laughed Troy.

"Naw; it was cool, man. She just wanted to talk. She offered me some time off, but she really wanted to discuss my new responsibilities. Leona needs me—it's time for me to step up and follow in Jimmy's footsteps. I think we're finally seeing eye-to-eye."

Both men looked at each other but said nothing. They hoped that Damien's assessment of the situation was correct. The three men, while vastly different had bonded over the fact that though they were successful now, they had overcome great obstacles and similar dysfunctional upbringings. They also had in common that they were all eager to please Leona and remain on her good side. Leona ruled her kingdom with an iron hand and was always in control.

As the men drank their beers and sat in silence, each contemplated their relationship with Leona Williams. Finally, Troy parted with some final words on the situation.

"Man, do you. You deserve this chance. But watch out for that Queen Bee. She's got a wicked sting."

CHAPTER 2

Family Ties

DAMIEN, EXCITED IN his increased responsibilities in the funeral home, noticed that the back garage loading area where the bodies were loaded and transported was sorely in need of repair. After calling several local companies, Damien spotted on his way home an older European man who was doing work on a local property. The small wiry man with thick white hair and bushy eyebrows had a thick accent that Damien couldn't place.

"Hey there! That cement work you're doing looks pretty good," commented Damien. The cement driveway and steps were flawless.

"Thank you, young man. My sons and I take pride in our work. There aren't any better cement masons in the whole state," he boasted proudly. "You need some cement work done?" he inquired, always on the look-out for new clients.

Damien explained the work they needed done and the man instantly gave him a price far below the other contractors. Damien was immediately hesitant, but he liked the old man's swag. "Look, the price sounds right, so when can you start?"

"We will start as soon as tomorrow, but I need cash young man, no fuss no muss," Mr. Leander Cordona's company had no formal name, but he explained that he and his sons did all the work and it was guaranteed. Used to doing things off the cuff, Damien agreed, and the deal was made. Mr. Cordona promised the work would take two days, but at the end of the second day they were far from finished.

"What's going on, Mr. C? You said you'd be done in two days," Damien was concerned at the timeline, but he had to admit the back garage was looking good. The work was top notch, but the hassle of re-routing pickup and deliveries was quite an inconvenience.

"Just one more day, Mr. Damien, and we will be done." A frustrated Damien shook his head but agreed. The next morning, Damien noticed that there were no workers on site. He was about to call Mr. Cordona, when the old man appeared, tearful and broken.

"My oldest son, Vano, he died last night. He got in a fight at a bar. My boy fell and hit his head. We were at the hospital all night. But we will start work now." The old man's shoulder's slumped under the weight of his tragedy. Vano ran the crew and always had a cigarette dangling from his mouth and a ready grin.

"No, no, Mr. Cordona, go attend to your family," Damien said. He was truly sorry about Mr. Cordona's loss and all thoughts of the back garage went out the window.

"Mr. Damien, can you take care of my boy? My family would be forever in your debt. We will pay cash." Feeling sorry for the old man and his family, Damien agreed to meet with the family that afternoon. Williams Mortuary occasionally served other faiths and races, but Damien couldn't recall any Eastern European families, where he figured the Cordonas were from. Mr. Cordona referred a few times to the "old country" wherever that was. But Damien definitely wasn't ready for what lay in front of him. When he came back that afternoon from lunch, Leona, KC, and Sydney were all standing in the front lobby looking wide-eyed and concerned.

"Damien, can we speak with you a moment?" asked Leona. They moved into Conference Room A, with Clarissa following behind.

"Okay. What's up?" he asked, clearly aware that there was a problem of some kind.

Before Leona could begin, Clarissa blurted out, "Your new family is in the chapel waiting for you!"

"Why are they in the chapel? You should have put them in here." Still getting used to seeing and families and making arrangements, he wasn't sure what was going on.

Clarissa smirked, "Oh, you'll see." Leona glared at Clarissa and turned to Damien.

"We have a situation with those... those people!! We can't serve them!"

Damien quickly answered, "Mr. Cordona is a good dude. I've got this, no problem. I'm sure they only want a viewing and then they'll send the body back to wherever they are from."

KC and Sydney both still looked concerned but said nothing, trying to be supportive. As he left, Clarissa passed him a small can of air freshener.

"Why are you giving me this?" he inquired, confused.

This time, everyone said in unison, "You'll see!"

Upon entering the chapel, Damien instantly regretted saying he'd handle this situation. There were at least forty people in the chapel, laughing, talking and crying all at one time. Damien thought he even heard music coming from somewhere. There were women in long skirts and lacy veils, children running up and down the aisles, and several groups of men, ignoring the 'No Smoking' sign posted in the chapel's entrance. Not knowing where to begin, Damien went to the podium and addressed the crowd.

"Ah! Hello! I'm Damien Moore." A few members of the crowd glanced at him curiously as Mr. Cordona came to the front.

"Mr. Damien, this is my family," he said, spreading his arms out toward the crowd, who now were staring in rapt attention.

"Wow, all of them?" replied a surprised Damien. "Okay, maybe we should go to somewhere more private where we can talk."

"No, Mr. Damien; it's our custom that we all come to talk about the funeral. The family must all be present."

A confused Damien was trying to act cool, though he was clearly bewildered by the whole scene. "I understand, sir. I'm just curious—where exactly are you folks from?"

Mr. Cordona answered proudly, "We are Romany, but you Americans call us Gypsies. My wife and I are from the Old Country, Romania, and we will bury our boy in our tradition." The next two hours were spent going over their traditions and expectations for the service. Damien listened intently, taking notes for all of the things he needed to do. He stopped, however, when they expressed the need to stay with the body.

"Y'all can't stay here—this is a place of business." Damien knew there was no way in hell, or any other place, that Leona Williams would let a group of gypsies take up residence in her funeral home.

"Mr. Damien, we will pay extra. How about I just give you $15,000.00 for your troubles?" The wife, who had not spoken during the whole transaction, began to pull bundles of money from under her skirts. Several other females started to do the same.

"Whoa, okay!" He hadn't seen this much cash in a long time. Even though $15,000.00 was a good price for a service and burial, somehow Damien felt like he was not charging enough.

"And don't worry about the rest of the work; we finish that for free! My gift to you for letting us stay with our boy." The old man was quite persuasive, but in the end, they came to a compromise. Only ten persons would stay inside with the body, camping out in one of viewing rooms. The remaining family would stay outside in tents behind the building. The family would bury Vano in three days, meaning that they would also be around for three long nights. Damien shook his head. Miss Leona was going to kill him.

Damien knew the girls would not help him, but they never said their husbands were off-limits. Damien called his boys together, and they met at

Troy's office above his garage, their favorite meeting spot, to explain his situation.

"Man, you gotta be kidding! Where the hell are we supposed to sleep?" asked a reluctant Troy. "Them gypsies are crooks. Don't you watch Dateline? They're always moving from place to place, taking folks for their money."

Avery shook his head in agreement. "Damien, can we even trust these people? Sydney said they had to air out the chapel when they left. She said it smelled like goats and garlic."

That was the last straw for Troy, "Aww... hell naw! This sounds like a bad horror movie. Ain't they from like Transylvania or something?" Everybody cracked up at Troy's antics, but eventually agreed to help. Troy was posted outside, watching over the mini tent city, while Avery was the inside man, sleeping in his wife's office. Damien had the day shift and had to endure the tight-lipped Leona who was counting down the days until their departure.

By night three, the men had bonded with the Romany family who shared with them their special mourning elixir, which consisted of bourbon and coffee. During the mourning period, the men of the family where only permitted to drink bourbon, coffee, and water.

Troy, also a skilled mechanic, had fixed one of the men's trucks, while Avery had worked on Mr. Cordona's books. Damien came thru and laughed at them.

"Now y'all friends?" joked Damien.

"They're nice people," answered Avery. "We wanted to help. But man, his books are crazy! I see there's money coming in, but I can't balance anything. It makes no sense."

Troy looked at him and shook his head. "That's cuz they're gypsies!!"

The outside was alive with a party-like atmosphere. There was music and a constant barbeque. Folks drove by just to see what was going on.

Finally, the day of the funeral had arrived and the whole funeral home was buzzing with anticipation and relief. It had been a long week and Damien and the guys were exhausted. The family had two gentlemen to act as security as the mourners passed by the casket dropping money, jewelry, alcohol, and even a cell phone in the open casket. These were supposedly all things the deceased needed for the afterlife. Somehow, during the constant drinking and barbequing, the paving and cement work got completed. As a special touch, Mr. Cordona even gave Damien his own parking spot and a plaque with his name on it that read Mr. Damien's Car. Leona was impressed at how Damien took charge and formulated his own plan to keep order and still serve the family at the same time.

So happy to be rid of the entire situation, she promised her family an extra special Sunday dinner. It was the family's tradition to gather every other Sunday at Leona's Grace Lane home to break bread together.

"Where is my Pandora bracelet!" wailed Tianna. "I took it off last night on the couch and now it's gone!" She frantically tore away all of the sectional sofa cushions, turning KC's beautiful living room into a disaster zone.

Her expensive linen pillows were strewn everywhere, the cashmere throw unceremoniously dumped on the floor. KC gently placed her arms around her stepdaughter and tried to talk rationally to a hysterical 11-year-old. KC had just returned from church and was in a quiet and reflective mood.

"I know your bracelet is here; we just have to find it. But you need to be more careful with your things, Tianna. Let's start looking. Daddy and Tre will help too," KC said as she pointedly glanced over at her husband Troy and stepson Tre, both of whom seemed disinterested in this latest family saga. All hopes of a drama-free Sunday morning were suddenly dashed.

"Ain't nobody wants that stupid piece of junk. Besides you too old to be crying like some baby. You need to man up!" said Tre, cruelly. He threw his lanky six-foot frame into KC's antique dining chairs and continued scrolling through social media. KC rolled her eyes in disgust at his nonchalant attitude. Tianna's Pandora bracelet was her prized possession. Her mother had purchased it for the girl's eleventh birthday and filled it with Tianna's favorite charms.

"My mom gave it to me and she's not here anymore," Tianna started sobbing in earnest, her chest heaving as she struggled to cry and talk at the same time. "I miss my mom so much," she cried.

Both KC and Troy tried to console her, but their attempts were in vain. Only locating her beloved bracelet would make things better. The bracelet had become a security blanket of sorts and had sustained her since her mother's passing.

KC sighed heavily as she continued her search. The last eight months had been very stressful on her marriage. She and Troy had a whirlwind courtship. KC had been engaged to another when she met Troy, but it was all over for ex-fiancé the moment the suave Mr. Watkins held her hand. Troy and his brother Travis owned Watkins Livery and Transport Service. The twin brother entrepreneurs serviced Williams Mortuary as well as other funeral homes in the area, providing body removals as well as limousines and hearses. With Avery's help, Troy had been able to acquire two smaller livery companies in the area, making Watkins Livery a leader in funeral transportation for the living as well as the dead.

Their picture-perfect rustic wedding was the perfect backdrop to what had been a fairytale courtship. The couple was total opposites. Troy was the sexy, street-savvy bad boy turned good, while KC was the pretty, shy preacher's daughter. Somehow, the complete opposites completed each other.

The Watkins' been happily married for over eight years when tragedy struck—Troy's ex-wife Sharisse, with whom he had two children, passed away from an apparent fentanyl overdose. Troy was aware that Sharisse was a party girl but didn't realize she was heavily into drugs. Troy and KC went from occasional weekends with the kids to full-time parents.

Troy III aka Tre was a sullen, angry sixteen-year-old, an average student who often clashed with his teachers and schoolmates—he had been to several different schools in one academic year. He had never warmed to his father's new wife, calling KC a "churchy bitch" who thought she was better than them, but nothing could be further from the truth. Tre was the spitting image of his father, the same chocolate brown coloring but with mane of short locks. He was extremely handsome, but he possessed none of his father's charm.

Tianna was the exact opposite of her older brother, sweet and kind but very needy. She adored KC before but had clung to her even more since her mother's passing. The young girl followed her around the house, always wanting to sit or be near her. She was KC's greatest cheerleader as she struggled with new motherhood. When her futile attempts at hairstyling Tianna's long, thick tresses ended in two messy braids that began to immediately unravel, sweet Tianna still said she loved her new "do." KC had taken to sending Tianna to Sydney's twice a week so her cousin could do her hair.

After thoroughly searching the living and dining rooms, Troy walked in triumphantly. The elusive bracelet had been found!

"You found it… you found it," Tianna shrieked, clutching her bracelet tightly in her hand. KC thought how remarkable it was that the mood of a child could go from despair to euphoria in a few mere seconds.

"You'll never guess where I found it—in the garage of all places. Pumpkin, were you playing in the garage? Maybe it fell off your wrist," Troy inquired.

"No, Daddy, why would I play there? It's so dirty and disgusting in there."

"Crisis averted; your bracelet is safe. I'll check the clasp and make sure it's secure. C'mon and let's get ready for Sunday dinner at Aunt Leona's," said KC, gently pushing Tianna toward the stairs. As Troy followed his daughter upstairs, he looked lovingly back at his wife. One of the things he loved most about KC was the compassion she felt when it came to his kids. Having them full-time was an adjustment, but KC really seemed to enjoy her role as mother, especially when it came to Tianna. Troy secretly hoped that it wasn't too late to have a child of their own.

"C'mon, Tre, that means you too," said KC quietly. She always tried to tread lightly with Tre. She could never tell what might send his mood into a tailspin.

Tre groaned loudly and rolled his eyes. He was definitely not a fan of her family's tradition of gathering on Sunday to share a meal or KC's gentle admonishment.

KC quickly glanced over at the boy before walking up the stairs. She had no doubt he was behind the missing bracelet. He seemed to delight in tormenting his younger sister or anyone he deemed weaker than himself. As her mama often said, "That one bears watching."

As Sydney approached her kitchen, she could hear the raucous laughter of her family. Her two older daughters from her previous marriage, Chloe and Kendall Hudson, were both home for the weekend. Chloe was in her second year of law school at Emory, while Kendall was a senior at her mother and grandmother's alma mater, Spelman College. Standing there watching her older girls, anyone watching might mistake Sydney for their older sister. Sydney at forty-eight had a youthful face with hazel brown eyes and an engaging smile. A former runner-up for Miss Spelman, Sydney was still a beautiful woman, but she struggled with her weight. She vacillated between a size 16 and 18 and was always on some type of diet and was usually cheating on it. Sunday morning breakfast was a Samuels' family tradition with all four children assisting Avery with the cooking after the family returned from church. Unfortunately, the delicious meal left Sydney with a huge mess to clean up.

"What's going on in here? I could hear y'all laughing all the way upstairs," Sydney inquired, taking in the scene. Her spotless white kitchen was littered with pots and pans, spilled flour, and sticky maple syrup. Amid the mess on her marble island was a tripod, which her children and husband were standing in front of, attempting to do an intricate dance routine.

"We're making a TikTok, babe," answered a smiling, out of breath Avery.

"Whaaaat? What do you know about TikTok?" she countered, clearly amused by the whole situation. Avery was twelve years her senior but far better informed when it came to anything that involved his kids, from fashion to music to social media.

"OMG, Mom, this is like Dad's third one. We're trying to go viral!" replied Morgan. Sydney smiled at the thought—Avery's colleagues and clients would be absolutely shocked to see the CEO of one Atlanta's largest merger and acquisition firms dancing on social media.

Sydney and her husband met as the result of a botched fraudulent merger between his former employer, a funeral home acquisition firm, and Williams Mortuary. LHP Corporation was known for buying up family-ly-owned funeral homes and turning them into corporate entities. Jonathan Edwards, Williams Mortuary's former manager, attempted to fraudulently sell the funeral home from under Leona and the family. Avery's intervention and a clever plan between him and Leona thwarted the sale. The result ended in the funeral home's former manager being fired and serving jail time for fraud and embezzlement. The whole fiasco was the catalyst for Avery starting his own tech acquisition consulting firm, which had grown from a simple start-up to being wildly successful. But the only real merger was the union of Sydney and Avery. The couple had been blissfully married for over fourteen years.

Sydney helped herself to breakfast and sat at the other end of the island watching their antics. No one would guess that they were a blended family.

Chloe and Kendall adored Avery, calling him Dad almost immediately after the couple married. Once, when one of Chloe's friends remarked on how cool her stepfather was, Chloe replied icily, "The only steps we have in our house are the ones that go upstairs—he's my dad, period." Their loyalty to him was unwavering and in return he gave them the attention and unconditional love their biological father didn't. Presently, Sydney was snapped out of her reverie when she heard her name being called.

"Mom, should we dance to Megan Thee Stallion or Cardi B?" inquired, her son Jamie. "Daddy always picks Cardi—that's his girl."

Avery looked guilty and started to stammer. "Babe, I just like her music. She reminds me of you. You know, the song about the red bottoms …," he trailed off, knowing his wife wasn't buying it. Chloe and Kendall both were laughing hysterically at this point. Their father's crush on Cardi B was obvious and as usual he was like a nervous teenager around their mom.

"Whatever you're going to do could you do it another room please? I need to clean this kitchen and return some emails before we go to Mama's." She knew the mention of clean-up would send them scurrying. Her husband, the biggest kid of them all, was only too happy to keep the party going. They hurried into the living room, looking for another space for to decimate.

Sydney sighed and shook her head. She could definitely have worse problems in marriage. Her husband was kind, gentle, and attentive. He always listened to her problems, showered her with gifts—Sydney had a handbag and shoe collection that was truly enviable—and still held her hand whenever they entered a room together. Avery rarely raised his voice and any disagreements the couple had ended in him apologizing profusely. He was a good man plus he still made her toes curl in the bedroom! The Samuels were a team as well as couple. But as she started cleaning her kitchen, with the sounds of him and the kids dance-off in the background, she sometimes wished she could be the fun parent who made TikTok videos instead of cleaning up everyone's mess.

Clarissa lay naked in her bed, patiently waiting for her man to get off the phone so that they could engage in their favorite Sunday morning pleasure, hot sex, followed by a steamy shower and more sex. She was fully enjoying her wet and wavy weave. It meant she could get down and dirty in the shower and her hair still looked good. She could hardly wait for the fun to begin. She was wet with anticipation for today's encounter.

Damien entered the room and hastily began to put on his clothes. The look on his face said it all. There would be no play time today.

"What's going on, baby? Where are you going," asked Clarissa, crestfallen at the interruption of their weekly ritual.

"My sister just called; we have a death call and it's a bad one. Car crash in Kennerville two nights ago. Deacon White from First Baptist. He's going to need a lot of restorative work, so I want to get started right away. I'll probably just meet you at Miss Leona's for dinner."

Clarissa hated it when Damien spoke of his family, his sister this or his cousin—that he never even used their names anymore. Like Clarissa or the rest of the world needed to be reminded that Sydney was his sister! Over the years, as the bond between he and the Williams clan had strengthened, it seemed that she and Damien had drifted apart.

"Baby, c'mon you've got time for a quickie," she drawled sexily. No man in his right mind could resist Clarissa Dickson. Her naked body was every man's sex fantasy, large full breasts, a tiny waist and a tight booty that most twenty-year-olds would envy. Most would be surprised to know she was a mother of a teenager and forty-four years old. While attractive but plain in the face, her devastating body was definitely the main attraction and she clearly knew it. Wrapping her arms around Damien's neck she slowly started to gyrate, grinding her naked body to his.

Damien gently pushed her away, unmoved. "Rissa, I got work to do. Maybe later tonight when we get home." His tone clearly indicated his disinterest. In his mind, he was already out the door.

"Yeah, whatever," Clarissa said as she made no attempt to hide her disappointment at the turn of the events. Damien gave her a dry kiss on the cheek and was off to his one and only true love, the morgue. Clarissa lay back against the headboard, covering her naked body with the thin sheet and contemplated her life.

Eighteen years ago, she had started as a part-time receptionist at Williams Mortuary. Her uncle, Norm Dickson was the head embalmer and Jimmy Williams' best friend. Her uncle had arranged for her to get the job. After Jimmy Williams died and her uncle retired, she was promoted to head receptionist and was a full-time member of the staff, ultimately becoming the head administrative assistant.

She met Damien when he took her uncle's place. She was smitten with his good looks and thuggish charms and they soon became inseparable, sharing work gossip and a voracious sex life. The fact that he turned out to be Mr. Jimmy's son was the icing on the cake. Clarissa thought she had found The One. They were both overjoyed to find out about her pregnancy and Clarissa assumed that marriage would soon follow. But almost sixteen years later, she was no closer to the altar than when they'd met. They lived together and Clarissa wore a ring, but it was more promise ring than engagement. Damien rarely spoke of marriage anymore, always saying, "When the time was right."

Her only consolation was her son DJ. A sweet and caring young man, he was the best combination of both his parents. DJ had inherited the Williams' family good looks and charm. He adored his father, was a loving son to his mother, and made both very proud, doing well in school and excelling at sports. But he too was drawn to the glitter of the Williams family, spending most of his time after school hanging at Sydney's with her children. It was as if the family had a magnetic pull on her men. She, Sydney, and KC had once been friends, enjoying girls' night out together, but things quickly changed when she and Damien became a couple. They never approved of the relationship and quickly became distant. They adored DJ but never truly welcomed Clarissa into the fold. But worse of all was the cold shoulder extended by Leona. She saw Clarissa as nothing more than a secretary and baby mama. It was evident in her demeanor and how she treated her. Clarissa believed the older woman's attitude was part of why Damien wouldn't marry her.

Still, DJ and Damien were thick as thieves and she knew Damien would never do anything to jeopardize that relationship and that included leaving her. He was adamant that DJ would grow up in a stable home with two parents, the exact opposite of his upbringing. But for the couple's relationship to survive she needed something to bring them closer and she knew sex alone wasn't enough. She would need to be creative. She needed to get her family from under the spell of the Williams.

Damien slipped into the funeral home through the back entrance and quickly made his way to the morgue. He wanted to avoid having to make idle chit chat with the Sunday staff, folks asking about your weekend or commenting on the weather. The morgue was cool and quiet; the only sound came from the low hum of the air conditioning unit. He strode into the walk-in holding freezer where the newly arrived deceased were held. As the decedents' bodies came in, they were placed there by the removal team, logged in, and tagged. The embalmer on duty then later logged them into a separate computer system where the deceased name and funeral information was entered into the main database. After the embalming process took place, the deceased was thoroughly washed from head to toe, and then placed on tray that ultimately was placed in an intricate cadaver rack in their second walk-in freezer to await dressing and casketing. The clothes of the deceased were held in separate dressing area whose shelves resembled a small clothing boutique. Everything was carefully labeled with names and numbers that corresponded with its' decedent identification tag. Damien had designed the system himself to avoid clothing mix-ups and keep the morgue area orderly. Williams' Mortuary did in excess of 1,500 cases per year, which broke down to 25-30 bodies per week, so order in the busy space was a top priority.

Damien unzipped the blue body bag issued by the coroner's office, and he gazed critically at Deacon Harold White. Mr. White was an usher and served on the Deacon Board of First Baptist Church of Maxwell. He was a complete pain in the butt, always coming up with a new rule whenever Williams had a funeral there. Rumor had it that he received money from other area funeral homes to refer church members to them when a death occurred. How ironic that his family chose the one funeral home that didn't believe in kickbacks.

Damien carefully assessed the restorative work that needed to be done. He was an expert embalmer, but his real talent lay in the restorative arts— he enjoyed the work of making a decedent look like their former selves. He was trained in Houston, Texas, where he joked that he had sewn up more bullet wounds than most ER doctors! Mourners would often lean into the casket trying to spot the gunshot wounds, amazed that they could see no trace of violence that the deceased had endured. Several funeral homes in Texas were interested in him, but his dream was to return home to Georgia and work alongside his father. Jimmy and his relationship were strained—it was hard, knowing you were the product of an affair between your mother and a married man. He often moved between hating the man and wanting to earn his praise. Unfortunately, he returned to town too late for them to work together. Jimmy passed away from a massive heart attack one month before Damien's return. He didn't even attend the lavish funeral for his father, but he did go to the cemetery, watching the horse drawn carriage that held the body of the man he barely knew. He always remembered Sydney weeping openly, being led away from the grave. He longed to feel the emotion she displayed, but thoughts of his father left him empty and bitter.

Finishing his initial suturing, Damien began to prepare to start the actual embalming process. While grabbing the arterial embalming fluid from the closet, he heard his phone ringing from his desk. He hoped it wasn't Clarissa as he was in no mood for a fight. He grinned when saw it was his son.

"Yo, lil man; what's up?"

"Hey, Dad, I'm at Aunt Syd's. She wants to know what time you and Mom were coming to dinner. She said we're always waiting on you guys."

"Tell her when I get there," he said jokingly. "Naw, I'm kidding! I'm at the funeral home, doing a body. I should be finished in about a half hour."

"Cool! Me, Morgan, and Jamie are riding our bikes over to help out Mom-Mom Leona. That way, we get to taste test the food first," he laughed. Both DJ and his father were serious about their food.

"Save some for your old man, alright. Be careful, son. Love ya!"

"Gotcha, Dad! Love you too." Damien and DJ ended every call with those endearments. The love he felt for his son was immense. Damien managed to take all the love he never received from his father and pour it directly into his son.

Thoughts of DJ always lead him back to his complicated relationship with Clarissa. She was the mother of his son and he had mad respect and love for her, but he had long since fallen out of love with her. They were too different, and she had changed after he became close with his father's side. She was always full of complaints about some slight that Sydney, Leona, or KC had done, either real or imagined. Under any other circumstance, they would have long ago parted ways, but he wouldn't dare leave his son and he knew Clarissa wouldn't let him have custody of the boy. Also, they worked together, and he wasn't interested in the whole funeral home knowing their business. Damien figured he had a few more years and DJ would be off to college and he would finally be free. He smiled in spite of his self. Three more years and he would be eligible for parole on what seemed like a life sentence.

Leona sang softly to herself as she chopped the collard greens and started her three-step washing process. Belle had just put on V102's Sunday gospel show, and they were playing one of her favorites, the Clark Sisters' "You Brought the Sunshine." She and Belle were Halleluiah two-stepping all around the huge kitchen. Leona enjoyed cooking her infamous Sunday dinner alongside her sister-in-law, Belle. Belle was Jimmy's younger sister and the two had been extremely close. Belle, her husband Rutherford, and daughter KC regularly visited from Shreveport, Louisiana. This was the reason that KC and Sydney were as close as sisters. Jimmy and Leona were thrilled when KC expressed her desire to become a funeral director and join the family business in Maxwell.

Belle and Rutherford had been a comfort to Leona after Jimmy's death, coming almost every month to visit. Leona was happy to do the same for Belle after Rutherford succumbed to cancer earlier that year. She even convinced Belle to move to Maxwell and take up residence in Leona's spacious guest house.

"Girl, you know that's my song! I remember seeing The Clark Sisters perform that one at the Louisiana Gospel Conclave. They sure were something," reminisced Belle. She had been the first lady of her husband's church for over forty years. She missed him and the church they had built, but even she would have to admit it was good being with her family again.

"Did you ever see the movie they made about them? It was some kind of good. I think it's on Prime Video," Leona asked. "Maybe we could watch it after dinner."

"Oooh, girl, I would love that. Rutherford never liked watching anything on TV. I've missed everything," Belle lamented.

"That's what on demand is for, Belle"

"On demand? Is that a show?" questioned Belle.

"I've got so much to teach you!" Leona laughed and hugged Belle.

Later, with the help of her grandchildren and Belle, everything was done. Leona's table looked like something out of *House Beautiful* magazine. The finest linens and china were set out, along with her mother's crystal and her grandmother's silverware. Fresh flower arrangements and candles completed the look, but the star of the show was the large buffet covered from end to end with the most mouthwatering, delectable food anyone could imagine. Fried and barbeque chicken, prime rib roast, fried catfish, yams, macaroni and cheese, greens, and potato salad. Homemade butter biscuits and corn bread finished off the menu. Plus, the desserts were legendary. Belle always made sweet potato pie, bread pudding, and her famous Hope cake!

Every Sunday dinner was the same, with everyone arriving in the same order. Deacon Richard Patterson, Leona's gentleman friend (as she referred to him) was the first to arrive, always with flowers and a gift for the hostess. As he kissed her lightly on the lips, Richard whispered softly in her ear, telling her how beautiful she looked. Leona blushed like a schoolgirl, happy that Sydney wasn't there to see this interaction. She would have teased her mother all night.

Next to arrive were the Watkins clan. Leona loved Tianna and her sweet disposition, which she found so refreshing. Belle was also smitten with her new granddaughter and was delighted that she asked to call her "Grandmom." Leona was slightly troubled by her niece's demeanor. KC was always quiet and somewhat introverted, but she seemed troubled these days, almost depressed. Leona made a mental note to mention this to Sydney. If there was something going on, Sydney would most definitely know. The two Watkins' men brought up the rear. Troy was his usual charming and jovial self, giving kisses and compliments to the ladies. Leona frowned slightly at the sight of Tre and his low rider jeans and hoodie. His sulky expression and disrespectful attitude didn't sit right with Leona. He barely mumbled hello before heading to the den where the other young people were watching TV. Troy and KC traded glances after the boy's lackluster entrance.

Clarissa arrived next, dressed in a too tight, low cut red dress and carrying a store-bought cake. Leona rolled her eyes to the heavens at Clarissa's inappropriate outfit and dry-looking cake. As Clarissa reached to hug her, Leona tensed up ever so slightly. Everything about the young woman rubbed her the wrong way. Belle, forever the peace maker greeted her and took the offending cake from Clarissa.

"Good to see you, dear. That's a magnificent shade of red," remarked Belle, seeing the women's awkward exchange.

"Thank you, Miss Belle. I hope y'all enjoy the cake." Even after sixteen years, Clarissa had not been asked to call Belle or Leona by any other name but Miss. It was evident that she was not family. Clarissa made her way through the house in search of her son.

"Leona, you have to all least try to be nice to the girl! She's obviously Damien's choice. They've been together for years," exclaimed Belle.

"But he hasn't married her and that speaks volumes to me. I just happen to think he deserves better than a social climbing gold-digger!" Leona was never one to mince words when it came to her family.

The conversation was interrupted by the arrival of the Sydney, Avery, and Leona's elder granddaughters. Her consternation turned to delight at the sight of Chloe and Kendall. She felt as though she barely saw them anymore.

"Here's my babies!" she cried, enveloping both girls in a tight hug. "You look so good! I've missed my baby girls so much," she gushed. Chloe and her younger sister Kendall were both medium height and thin with their mother's complexion and thick wavy hair. Chloe favored her natural curls while her baby sister dyed her hair monthly and always sported the latest hairdo. Today, her hair was a honey blonde.

"Dang! Hi, Mama," joked Sydney. She and Avery stood there, both amused by Leona's histrionics. The girls never missed a dinner or family function, but Leona always acted as if she never saw them.

"I see you every day! Hi, Avery," Leona greeted her son-in-law warmly and kissed him on the cheek, still ignoring her daughter. This was their little game they always played. Leona and Sydney shared a closeness not often found by mothers and daughters. They spoke three to four times daily and usually saw each other physically every day. Sunday dinner could not start until Sydney arrived.

"I hope everybody is here because I'm starving!" This was nothing new— Sydney was always starving!

"Just waiting for Damien and we are ready," Leona glanced anxiously at the door. She moved close to her daughter to share her observations about KC. "You need to talk to KC later. She doesn't seem like herself. I didn't want to worry Belle, but I'm concerned," whispered Leona.

Sydney looked concerned as well and nodded in agreement with her mother. Rest assured she would get to the bottom of this before the night's end.

As the family begun to gather at the table taking their respective seats, Damien sauntered in, taking in the whole scene. He loved coming to Grace Lane on Sundays, his family all together. The scene reminded him of one of his favorite movies, "Soul Food." Damien had always wished for a family like the one in the movie and their traditions. Finally, his wish had come true.

Leona took her place at the head of the table and asked Richard to bless the food.

Richard's strong voice filled the room. "Father God, we are here once again in Your presence for food and fellowship. We ask a special blessing over this food and this family. Bless and keep them, Lord, as they serve others in their time of need. Bless the hands that prepared this feast and keep us all in your loving mercies in Jesus' precious name we pray. Amen."

As the meal commenced, there was plenty of conversation, good-natured ribbing and compliments to the chef.

"Leona, your biscuits are absolutely heavenly," remarked Richard, as he reached for his third one.

"Ooooh, Mama, Deacon likes your biscuits," quipped Sydney. The whole table burst into fits of laughter. The teasing would go on all night with this group.

"They taste better with honey," drawled Leona, causing the deacon to blush.

"You go, Mom-Mom," cheered Kendall. She was glad her grandmother was dating again.

"Yup, Mama, seventy is the new fifty!" agreed Sydney. She too was happy her mother seemed to be open to dating again.

"Hush now, the both of you. Damien, how bad was Deacon White? Will we be able to have an open casket?" asked Leona. Soon, the conversation turned to funeral service, schedules, and industry news.

After dinner, the men retired to the den to watch basketball, while the women chatted and assisted Leona with the cleanup. Sydney used this time to talk with her cousin.

"Hey, Kay-Kay, what's good with you?" Sydney always used their childhood nicknames when they talked one on one. KC looked nervously around before answering.

"Nothing, Syd. Same ole, same ole," replied KC quietly. Sydney saw her cousin's eyes fill with tears, as she turned and quickly exited the room.

As Leona, watched the entire exchange she tried to distract the others while Sydney went in search of KC. She found her in Leona's prized garden, weeping softly near a hydrangea bush. Amidst so much beauty, KC's demeanor seemed almost tragic.

"Okay; spill it! Something is wrong and I'm not giving up until you tell me. You've barely said a word all night. Did you and Troy have a fight?" Sydney was in warrior mode—God help with the person who messed with any member of her family.

"Nooo; it's the kids. I can't take it anymore. Tianna doesn't give me room to breathe and Tre is so mean. He terrorizes his sister, hardly speaks to me, and only talks to Troy if he wants something. Sometimes, I hide in the bathroom just for a break, but when I come out their right there—arguing, crying, or needing something!" KC started to weep again.

"Awww, Kay-Kay; mom duty is hard. Sometimes, it feels like they are smothering us with their 'Mom, this' and 'Mom, that.' Have you talked to Troy about how you're feeling? Maybe Tianna's grandparents could help out." Sydney felt sorry for her cousin, knowing that she often felt the same way herself. Thank goodness Avery was a hands-on dad.

"They take her on weekends sometimes. I tried to send Tre over there too, but he never wants to go. He'd rather sit in his room and blast rap music all day and night. I just need a break. Troy helps out when he's home, but with the business taking off, he's so busy! I barely have time to take care of these kids and he wants to have baby?" KC continued to shake her head in despair.

Obviously, thought Sydney, *this is more than one night's worth of girl talk. This was going to be a whole evening with plenty of wine.*

"C'mon, Kay, let's go inside. We'll work this out. You can bring Tianna to my house on Saturdays so you can get some you time. One more kid won't make a difference," Sydney said with a grin.

KC looked hopeful and gave Sydney a weak smile. "Thanks, Syd. You're the best sister-cousin ever!"

Later that night, after all her guests were gone, Leona sat in her favorite spot in the whole house, the conservatory. The floor to ceiling windows gave great sunlight in the day and a perfect spot to star gaze in the evenings. She liked to sit in the room with a glass of her favorite merlot and reflect.

Tonight, she was drawn especially to the mahogany sideboard where her collection of family photos was prominently on display. Weddings, birthdays, graduations, all of the family's milestones were framed in elegant crystal and silver frames. But Leona was drawn to the framed photo of her and Jimmy, smiling brightly, looking happy and relaxed. The photo was taken on their last Mexican cruise before his death. Not a day went by that she didn't miss him, the smell of his cologne, his cigars, the mess he made in the bathroom…. Jamison Williams had been her soul mate and Leona feared no one would ever measure up. But she knew that she didn't want to spend the rest of her days without feeling love one final time.

CHAPTER 3

Bright Lights Big City

STATE SENATOR BERNARD Adams was one of Maxwell's most prominent sons. After years of working as community and civil rights activist in Atlanta and Washington, DC, he had returned to his hometown and became a living legend. First running for city councilman, the career politician had eventually made his way to state senate with his eye on a Congressional seat in the near future. His battle with heart disease was ongoing, but everyone was still surprised by his death from a massive heart attack. His public persona was that of a stand-up family guy and committed public servant. He had marched with Rep. John Lewis and was personal friends with Al Sharpton.

Williams Mortuary was prepared for a large service with dignitaries from across the state. The service was so large that Damien, Sydney, and KC worked together, each handling different aspects of the funeral. But no one was expecting a call from a woman who identified herself as his mistress and who wished to be accommodated with a private viewing for her deceased lover. Sydney was shocked, especially when the woman threatened to show up at the actual service and reveal herself to the whole town. Sydney immediately knew she would grant her request, even though she was totally repulsed by the entire situation.

Unfortunately, the case hit too close to home for Sydney on many levels. She was reminded of her father's betrayal of her own mother. Jimmy had carried on an affair with Lula Mae Moore, her brother's deceased mother, for over forty years. It was horrible enough when she and her mother found out after Jimmy's death, but they would have been devastated if that vile woman had come to her daddy's service, embarrassing their family. She was determined to save the Adams family that particular trauma. Sydney also knew how it felt to be humiliated by your husband as her first husband Terrance had a PhD in indiscreet affairs.

On the morning before the service, Syd and Damien both came in early to receive the grieving mistress. Damien was silent and slightly hostile toward the woman, not able to hide his feelings. Sydney was more diplomatic and curious about this woman who thought she deserved a private audience. The woman, who only gave her name as Lanice, wore a tight black lace dress, a small black pill box hat complete with veil and a dark mink draped over her shoulders, totally inappropriate for the warm spring weather. She wailed openly and continually repeated the same phrase, "Nobody loved me the way you did." Damien rolled his eyes in disgust and mumbled under his breath, "If he loved you like that, he would have divorced his wife and married your dumb ass." She stood at the casket, smoothing down his lapels and brushing invisible lint off his jacket. All Sydney could hope was that they smell of her cheap perfume didn't linger. When she finally left, the two siblings sipped coffee and reflected on the fact the funeral directors always knew the real deal, no matter what the public saw.

Maxwell, Georgia, population 26,732, was once a sleepy small town, only a blip on the radar as one passed through metro Atlanta on Interstate 20. The town had experienced rapid growth and was added to the list of bedroom communities surrounding Atlanta. Its Main Street was now full of boutique shopping, trendy restaurants and bars, coffee houses, and professional offices. The growing need for housing coupled with city dwellers seeking more bucolic spaces, caused a construction boom like none other. Maxwell still had small town appeal with big city amenities and young urban professional flocked there in droves. The result was an affluent suburb where 84% of African American households had persons who had at least a bachelor's degree and many held advanced or professional degrees. The town was 57% white and 43% Black and Hispanic.

Leona sat on the board of trustees at the local bank and owned several area properties and acres of land. As developers continued to offer top dollar for land, Leona's portfolio continued to grow, making her a very wealthy woman. Avery, too, got in on the action as he was appointed to the Maxwell Redevelopment Council. Both were integral in making Maxwell the next up and coming suburban enclave. Sydney and Leona worked tirelessly to preserve Jimmy's legacy and managed to get the street name where the funeral home was located into Jamison Williams Way. There was even a park named in Jimmy's honor.

With the shift in the socioeconomic make-up of Maxwell came new social clubs and activities geared toward upward mobile African Americans. There were two large golf and country clubs as well as a host of social clubs to accommodate the growing need for social and networking needs. In addition to national staples like Jack and Jill, The Twigs and the Links, new organizations also joined the local scene. The Circle was one of those groups. One of the most coveted female organizations in Atlanta and the surrounding areas, its civic mindedness was the biggest draw, but the fact that some of the most accomplished and successful women in the region were members made it a particularly hot ticket. The women from all over the region sought membership; however, it was by invitation only. The wait list for consideration was at least two years long and there was an extensive application including financial and personal references. Naysayers said that it was worse than applying for a job! A priority however was always given to legacy, the daughters of these illustrious women. The cost of entry into the circle was $10,000 payable upon acceptance, no exceptions. The new members were inducted at the famed Crystal Ball held every spring at The Four Seasons Hotel in downtown Atlanta. New members were presented with an 18-carat gold and diamond circle pendant necklace from Tiffany's.

The upcoming Crystal Ball was a source of constant conversation throughout the Williams family. Leona, Sydney, KC, and Sydney's oldest daughter Chloe were all members of The Circle, while Kendall, Chloe's younger sister was to be inducted at this year's ball. Leona was chairperson of the gala and the event was the talk of the region.

The topic of the ball came up at dinner that week in the Samuels household. The women were chatting excitedly about the upcoming event and what each would be wearing.

"I haven't found anything yet," lamented Chloe. She was the least enthusiastic about the gala. Shy and introverted, Chloe was never comfortable in social situations that included anyone besides her family. Most people mistook her quietness for conceit, her beauty sometimes making others uncomfortable, but that was not case. Chloe would rather be curled up reading a book or watching Netflix with her sister, than at a fancy party. Her sister, however, was the exact opposite.

"Omigod, Chlo, I got two dresses on hold at Saks and a back-up coming this week. You've got to find something. Have you seen Mom's dress? It's so freaking sexy—" But just then, Sydney interrupted her daughter.

"Hello? I was trying to keep my dress a secret." She smiled slyly at her husband, who instantly began to blush.

"I forgot; they act like they going on the prom," laughed Kendall. Her parents' love affair was usual fodder for the rest of the family, but the older girls thought they were sweet as they still keenly remembered their mom's first loveless marriage to their father.

"This is the most expensive prom I've been on. $10,000 for Kendall's acceptance fee, $10,000 for the table, and I don't want to even see this month's Amex bill," commented Avery, only pretending to be upset. He would have easily paid double that amount to see his beloved "girls" happy.

The twins, who had basically been ignoring the conversation, were intrigued with the cost. "That's more the $20,000 for one night," said Morgan. "Seems kind of silly to me, no offense, Mom," she added. Sydney only smiled. She knew she'd sing a whole different tune when it was her turn.

A disgusted Tre was behind the counter of Watkins' Brothers Mortuary Transport silently cursing his father. He hated cleaning the limos and hearses, picking up dirty tissues and dead flowers that the families left behind. "Just clean up after your damn selves," he thought angrily, as he grabbed the keys to the black stretch. It always irked him that he had to do such menial labor; after all, he was the owner's son. He should be driving the limos, not cleaning them. He was about to go back to the garage, when a young man walked in, inquiring about a Hummer rental. Tre was instantly impressed by all the ice he wore, his Alexander McQueen sneakers and his Givenchy jean set. He wondered if dude was a rapper or celebrity, but nobody that cool would be in Maxwell.

"Uh, can I help you," stammered Tre, not used to speaking with customers.

"Hey, young blood; trying to get me a Hummer limo for tomorrow night. Me and my boys are going into the city to some strip clubs! We hittin' Cheetah, Déjà vu 2, and Magic City!! It's gonna be lit!" The young man took out a large wad of bills that appeared to be all hundreds and started to peel them off. "Just tell me how much you need!"

"Uh, I'm not sure how much they are. My dad and my uncle handle that part," confessed Tre, trying unsuccessfully to hide the rags and bucket by his side.

"Damn, young blood; you the clean-up boy and your daddy owns this joint?" he said, taking notice of Tre's work overalls. "You can't be a boss cleaning out no limos. You need—". His advice was interrupted by Travis Watkins' appearance in the office. Travis, Troy's twin brother and Tre's uncle, greeted the new customer by name.

"Yo, Nine; what's up? Ain't seen you in a minute. Business must be good," laughed Travis. The two bumped first and both chuckled.

"Yeah, we've been hustlin'; that's for sure. Taking the boys out to the city for some female entertainment. Gotta keep my boys happy so they can move that product," answered Nine. "How much for the night—we need one of those stretch Hummers. We might bring us some hotties back home."

"C'mom on, man; let's go in my office so we can talk," Travis motioned for Nine to follow him upstairs where the offices and files were held.

"See you around, young blood. And if you want to be baller, come by and holler at me," Nine said and scribbled his info on the back of a Watkins Business card and handed to him.

Tre accepted the card and watched Nine bounce up the steps. With a wad of cash and the gear he was wearing, Nine had to be in the drug game, Tre knew. Tre had heard rumors that his father had been a hustler back in the day but went straight and was now a legitimate businessman. He shoved the card deep in his pocket and grabbed his bucket and rags. It might come in handy one day.

Chloe stuffed her laptop in her bag and hurried out of her Civil Procedure lecture. She was supposed to be home by 6:30 but it was already 6:15, and she had picked today to walk to class from her Druid Hill condo. That was just one of the benefits of living so close to campus. After graduating with honors from Avery's alma mater, the University of Michigan, Chloe had resigned herself to living at home with her parents and siblings while she attended Emory Law School. However, Avery and Sydney surprised her with a luxury condo near the campus. It was a two-bedroom oasis with a balcony, blond hardwood floors, and a modern kitchen. She decorated it in her own eclectic style and her place felt like a home. She loved on the weekends when her sister crashed with her. Kendall still lived in the dorms at Spelman and loved to raid her big sister's fridge and borrow her clothes. Chloe and Kendall had been best friends all their lives; no two sisters could be closer. As if on cue, Chloe glanced at her cell phone and saw her sister's name.

"Why are you calling me? Aren't you supposed to be at work?" Chloe demanded. She knew her sister's schedule as well as her own.

"Hello to you too!!" Kendall sighed heavily. Like their mother, she had a flair for the dramatic. "I didn't feel like going. Working at Saks is fun when I get to use my discount, but other than that it's flipping annoying. I'm thinking about quitting."

"Girl, don't tell Mom; she'll lose her mind. She lives for your discount. Hell, so does Daddy." Chloe didn't care much for shopping, but Kendall and her mother were hard-core shopaholics.

"Who are you telling? He said I single-handedly saved the family at least $3000.00 last month alone," laughed Kendall. "That woman can really shop. I know I'm bad, but she needs a 12-step program! But enough about your crazy mother! Can you pick me up so I can wash my hair at your place? I have a date tomorrow and I can't go with stinky hair."

"Sorry, sis; I have a Moot Court meeting at my place tonight. You can come over tomorrow when you get a break. I'll even flat iron it for you." Chloe knew her sister wouldn't be able to resist the offer of having someone do her hair as it was down her back and extremely thick. Even the most veteran hairdressers were intimidated by her mane.

"Chloe, I love you. You're the best sister ever. See you tomorrow afternoon!" A happy Kendall hung up, excited about Chloe's doing her hair. Chloe, however, felt immediately guilty. She rarely ever lied to her sister, but she couldn't tell her about tonight's plans. She could hardly wrap her head around it herself. Before she knew it, she had reached her place. As she got closer to her door, she could hear the sounds of Nina Simone singing "I Put a Spell on You," which could only mean one thing—Blaze had already arrived. That song was definitely appropriate because that's exactly how she felt since meeting Blaze. She could barely keep her mind on school. Chloe was trembling with excitement as she opened the door.

"Hey, beautiful! How was your day?" Blaze's voice was low and sexy with just a touch of a Cajun accent. Chloe could smell something delicious coming from the kitchen. Blaze was from Louisiana and spoiled Chloe with the best Creole cooking she'd ever tasted.

"It was long and hectic, but at least it's over," answered Chloe. Blaze had slipped behind her and sensually began to rub her shoulders and kiss her neck simultaneously. Chloe softly moaned and turned to face her lover. As their eyes locked, she knew why she was nervous and excited at the same time. Chloe was falling in love with this woman.

Sydney was in her office, complaining to KC about her monthly business meeting with her ex-husband Terrance regarding the gym that she owned, and he managed. While they were married, Sydney's father Jimmy had purchased the building and started the gym as a way to give his unemployed son-in-law a job. Terrance named the gym Fit4Life and made it quite successful. When her father died, he left the gym and all its' contents to Sydney. Unfortunately, she and Terrance were just as bad as business partners as they were a couple. Things only got worse once she and Avery married. For tax purposes, Avery converted all of their investment properties and the gym into one holding company called Jamison Morgan Holdings, LLC, which the couple owned jointly. The once tense meetings had become truly uncomfortable with the two men trying to out-do one another.

"I'm sick of both of them, KC. Terrance is at his worse, flexing and throwing shade about Avery's age and arguing with me about everything else. But Avery's no better, always trying to make Terrance feel small talking about money and business, and he always mentions the girls, which kills Terrance since they barely answer his calls." Sydney looked defeated before the meeting even started.

"Terrance has always been jealous of Avery, even though you can't really blame him. You essentially left him for Avery," replied KC. KC never being a fan of Terrance's, Sydney was surprised she would take his side.

"I left Terrance because he got his underage towel girl pregnant and stole from my girls' trust account," stated Sydney, slightly indignant. She hated the fact that she was still married to Terrance when she and Avery first met. They had carried on an illicit affair until Sydney finally divorced Terrance. If there was anything that she and Avery could change, it would be the circumstances under which they met.

"No, Syd; I'm just saying: Terrance is insecure. Avery took his wife and made her happy; he raised his kids and became their dad, plus he's freaking rich and successful. That would make any man insecure. As for Avery, Terrance will always have two things over him. One, he's the girls' biological father and two, he had you first." KC's simple logic was something that Sydney admired. Her cousin had a way of breaking complex situations apart that made them more manageable.

"Look, cousin, treat this meeting as what it is, a meeting between business associates with one goal, which is to make money. No more, no less. Terrance will always try to antagonize you; don't let him take you there. He needs to see you and Avery as a unit, a strong confident couple. That will shut him up for sure."

Taking her cousin's advice, Sydney came dressed to hilt and confident. Clad in a pale gray suit and her signature Manolo Blahnik heels, her Hermes Birkin in the crook of her arm, she very much exuded confidence and poise. As she exited her black Range Rover, she was surprised to see that her husband, who was waiting casually by his car, had dressed in his gray Saint Laurent suit. She was also struck afresh about how attracted she was to him. He had a mature confidence, especially when it came to business, which turned her on.

"Hey, gorgeous!! Look at you, almost on time," joked Avery, as he kissed his wife. Sydney's lateness was constant joke in their family.

"Hi, my love!! Look at us matching in gray—you were gone before I got out of the shower. We must be psychic," she laughed, happy that their styles complemented one another.

"No; we're just always in sync. I know you hate these meetings, but let's make the best of it. Always know I support you one hundred percent. I promise. I'll be a good boy this time," he quipped, an indirect reference to his on-going feud with Terrance.

Syd smiled and kissed her husband warmly. He always knew how she felt and the right thing to say and when to say it. They really were in sync.

"That's why I love you."

Terrance waited patiently inside while his ex-wife and her new husband played kissy face outside. He hated these meetings as much as they did, but he was grateful that they were fair with the profit-sharing and anything business-related. He begrudgingly admitted that Fit4Life had become far more successful since Avery had come on board. He reduced the taxes, got them on a better payroll system, and increased the gym's visibility on social media. The result was increased profits and more business than Terrance could handle. He'd just hired three new personal trainers and a general manager due to the increased work-load.

Terrance wished that they would sell the gym to him—he practically begged Sydney for years, but to no avail. Then, he wouldn't have to see them together. For Terrance, it was like pouring salt on an old wound. He didn't realize he loved his ex-wife until she found love with another. He lost everything, his wife and his girls, and it was all his fault. Terrance had cheated on Sydney throughout their twelve-year marriage, but it was when he got his teenage employee pregnant that was the final straw.

However, it was far easier to blame it all on Avery. Terrance knew he was better looking. Terrance had black curly hair, a café au lait complexion and a disarming smile. His movie star looks had grown better with age and he kept himself in top shape. Most women couldn't resist the charm of Terrence Hudson, but that's where it ended. He didn't have a pot to piss in or the proverbial window to throw it out of. His car was a used clunker, he had no savings to speak of and most of his earning went to child support for his youngest daughter Alyssa that he had while still married to Sydney. But his nemesis, Avery Samuels was rich, not just got a couple of dollars in the bank rich, but stinking rich. Terrence had read an article about local black millionaires and sure enough, Avery was on the list. Even Terrance couldn't compete with that.

Sydney and Avery entered the gym, hand in hand, laughing. Terrence cringed but tried to remain civil. The financial part of their meeting always went well since the gym was making crazy money. Terrance went out on a limb and unveiled his plans for expanding the gym in a medi-spa with services like Botox and facial peels, expanding the juice and supplement bar and his most exciting idea yet, adding guest trainers who happen to be social media influencers.

"That's a great idea, Terrance. Do you have anyone lined up?" answered Avery, clearly interested in this particular plan.

"Actually, I have a few, but I want to get Chardonnae Jenkins to offer her classes first. She does this twerking yoga class in the city that is constantly sold out. I slid in her DMs and she liked my ideas," countered Terrance, clearly surprised that he wasn't being met with resistance.

"You slid where? What the hell does that mean? I don't like the way that even sounds!" Sydney shook her head in disgust.

Avery and Terrance both cracked up. "No, babe; sliding in her DMs means he sent her a direct message on Instagram," Avery gently explained. "I think we should do it, but be prepared; we may have to expand."

"How should we pay for these upgrades?" asked Terrence. "Do we need to apply for a bank loan?"

"No need to do that; we can finance this project in-house. How much do you think you'll need?" Avery was all about business.

"Fifty thousand?" Terrence was hoping that he hadn't asked for too much.

"Babe," said Avery to Sydney, "write the man a check."

Clarissa was in her car outside of Williams Mortuary, detoxing. It had been a hell of a day, with seven different services at various churches and in the funeral homes' chapels. That meant staff, limos, paperwork, and personalities clashing all at once. Sydney had snapped at Clarissa twice, once because she couldn't find a burial permit and the other time because Clarissa got the lunch order wrong. She had to smile at that memory. She had purposely left off Sydney's cheese fries with bacon since she clearly didn't need them. She just kept complaining about the order being wrong, which served her right. That heifer needed to order her own lunch.

She had purposely avoided going to the back to speak to Damien. Clarissa didn't need him asking about dinner. She had planned to tell him she was going to her Aunt Hattie's tonight to check on her and Uncle Norm, but that was far from the truth. She had other plans tonight, something that might change the trajectory of their lives.

Clarissa shot Damien a quick text with her story about visiting her family. But instead of sending her back a text, Damien called.

"Hey sexy, what's up," she drawled, hoping that being nice might make him less suspicious. "Did you get my text?"

"Yeah, I got it. What about dinner? And who's picking up DJ? He has basketball practice tonight." Damien was always particular when it came to his son.

"Can't you do it? I really need to check on Aunt Hattie and Uncle Norm," she asked, knowing fully well he'd say no.

"I know you saw those five cases that came in today and we got four services tomorrow. My morgue is a mess and three of those cases are autopsied. I'm gonna be here all night as it is. Just pick up DJ and take him with you. And bring me a plate if Miss Hattie cooked."

A frustrated Clarissa wasn't interested in being late. "She's not cooking; I'm taking them dinner and I have to pick it up. Just ask your sister if she can pick him up. She owes me that after the way she rode my ass today."

"What did you do?" he asked.

Clarissa was so angry, she exploded. The weight of the day, her nervousness about tonight, and Damien always assuming the worst of her was too much. "I didn't do anything but my job, but that wasn't good enough for the Puffy Princess. I swear—" She had to stop before she said something she regretted.

"You know what, don't worry about it. I'll pick MY son and take him to MY sister's house were he'll get a proper meal and help with his homework. Do you, boo!" The call ended and Clarissa sighed. At least she didn't have to worry about being late.

Clarissa arrived at Eddie's Bar and Grille in Kennerville in record time. She'd been there a few times for their "meetings." Eddie's was a typical southern dive bar, complete with the requisite blues music, soul food, and plenty of patrons with gold teeth. Clarissa made her way to the rear where Coley was seated. Coley Smith was a full-time embalming assistant at Williams Mortuary. As an embalming assistant, he helped wash and prepare the bodies before the licensed embalmers started the embalming process. He also dressed the bodies and helped with final preparations before the services. He had been employed there for twenty-five years but was never able to complete mortuary school despite being a fairly skilled embalmer. He was a large man, with neat locks and a well-manicured beard. Coley had never married and lived at home with his mother and sister.

"Hey, Clarissa! How you doing?" asked Coley, smiling broadly. He had a slight crush on Clarissa.

"I'm tired and fed-up. That damn Sydney always snapping at folks like she queen bee," said Clarissa angrily.

"Aww, Ms. Sydney is always sweet to me, and so is Miss KC. I just wish they'd give me a chance to show my skills. I started prepping a body the other day because I was trying to help Damien out and he went off. Yelling and saying I didn't have a license to embalm. I used to always help Mr. Jimmy out." He sighed and quickly looked at Clarissa. "I don't mean any harm. I mean, I like Damien and all, but he didn't have to get all nasty."

Coley's story was interrupted by the arrival of the rest of their crew. Tyriq, the young man who worked in maintenance, his girlfriend Dorinda, an office assistant, and Layla, a funeral attendant rounded out their group. After greeting each other and ordering their first round of drinks, the "meeting" officially started.

The group of disgruntled Williams Mortuary employees had started meeting a few months ago to complain about their employers and commiserate about how badly they believed they were being treated. Not originally welcomed to attend their weekly session as she was the boss' baby mama, Clarissa had quickly assured them that she was as dissatisfied as they were with the Williams Family and shared as much gossip as she could about Sydney, Leona, and KC. They loved the nicknames she gave them—The Puffy Princess (Sydney), Bookworm (KC), and Cruella DeVille (Leona).

But mostly they talked about how things would be if they ran their own funeral home. Convinced they could do a better job, they fantasied for hours how their business would be different. Dorinda said the first thing she would change was "that stupid Mourning Basket." Williams Mortuary provided each bereaved family with a basket of snacks, paper products, and baked goods, aptly called The Mourning Basket.

"Don't nobody want all that crap. You can get all that stuff at the dollar store," Dorinda remarked sarcastically. "Folks need cheaper services, day-care for their kids while they are at the funeral, maybe a gift card to the market—stuff like that."

Each member of the group had ideas about what could make the funerals better and more modern. Williams' traditional services were without the fanfare and showiness that some newer firms offered. They didn't post on social media or television, just the occasional radio commercials. They advertised on billboards throughout the region, but most of their clients were repeat customers or referrals.

"Cruella hates if anybody posts on Facebook or Instagram! Don't she know that's free advertising. If we was running things, we'd be blowing up social media. Posting services and our work," Layla said and looked pleased, happy with her contribution. They continued to swap ideas and stories as the drinks followed freely. Clarissa carefully took notes of all their ideas and gave them updates on potential properties that could be used for a new funeral venture. While the group enjoyed their dreaming sessions, little did they know that Clarissa had plans to make them a reality.

KC, Troy, and Tre were seated at their dining room table, having a discussion regarding the purchase of a car for the teenager. At the time of Tre's sixteenth birthday, his father had promised him a new car. As time progressed on, Troy became hesitant about his son driving. KC wasn't sure about the car or whether Tre's constant bad attitude deserved to be rewarded with a vehicle.

"It's not that we don't want to buy you a car, but this is a bad time for young Black men and the police. You might get stopped and I wouldn't want you to have any interaction with law enforcement," commented KC.

Tre looked away and rolled his eyes. He couldn't understand for the life of him why she was even part of the conversation. It was his dad's money and his decision.

"Son, KC has a good point. These racist cops out here stopping young brothers over nothing, and then arresting them or worse. I'd have to kill somebody if they laid a hand on my son. Maybe we should wait a little longer, till things get better."

Tre leapt to feet, angry at the way the conversation had turned. "Damn, Dad! Can't you make any decisions without listening to her?" He angrily pointed toward KC. "She ain't my mom, so it shouldn't matter what she thinks. I'm sick of you always taking her side. I'm your blood!"

Troy stood up also, moving so close to his son that he could feel his breath. "Boy, you better sit your narrow ass down somewhere, before we really have a problem. KC is my wife and your step-mother and you will respect her, understand? You keep acting like this and you won't have to worry about ever driving!" Troy stepped back and shook his head, hoping that after a moment of cooling off, he'd be able to get this discussion back on track.

"Naw, Dad; it's all good. I see how this is goin' down. I'm outta here!" Tre grabbed his jacket and stormed out of the house, leaving the front door open.

A shaken KC sat at the table, tears running down her face. She knew that Tre was not her biggest fan, but the venom in his voice felt a lot like hate.

"Baby, it's okay," Troy said as he stood rubbing her shoulder, attempting to comfort his wife. "He'll be back; he's still grieving for his mother and adjusting to a new life. Just be patient with him."

KC said nothing, keeping her thoughts to herself. Tre needed more than just time to grieve; he needed anger management and therapy.

Tre had walked for an hour, angry and hurt that his own father would take KC's side. He had promised him for years that he would get him a car, but he turned out to be just like every other adult in his life—full of shit, never keeping their word. His mom had said she'd stop taking the pills and take better care of him and Tianna, but she never stopped. He remembered how scared he'd been the day she died, trying to wake her up, calling her name over and over. Presently, before he realized it was standing outside Nine's house. There was loud music and people on the porch, drinking and smoking, the pungent smell of marijuana hung in the air.

Nine stood in the middle of the crowd, staring at him. "Hey, young blood; you coming in?" he asked. Tre shook his head and then slowly walked up the steps.

CHAPTER 4

When a Man Loves a Woman....

THE GIDEONS, STELLA and Thomas, had been married for seventy-five years. They had met in grade school, married before Thomas left for WWII and had stayed in Maxwell all their lives, raising their four children in the home they still shared. Both in their mid-90s, they remained active in the church and their community. The adage was "Where you saw one Gideon, you saw the other." When Stella's health started to decline, her husband and children took care of her at home as Thomas refused to put his first and only love in a nursing home. "My baby won't do well away from me. She'll die in this bed next to me, God willing," he always said.

The Gideons' dutiful granddaughter, Yolanda, came in each morning before work to fix her grandparents' breakfast and stay with them until their aide arrived. She was surprised that morning her grandfather wasn't up yet because he usually met her at the door with a cheerful grin. When she found him, he was at his wife's side holding her hand.

"She's gone," he whispered. His beautiful wife had passed away peacefully in her sleep. Yolanda gently led the elderly man to his bedroom chair.

"Granddaddy, are you going to be okay?" tearfully asked Yolanda.

"Yes, Landa, I'll be alright, I just need a minute. Please call the family and let them know," responded Thomas.

She quickly left and called the family to share the news. When Yolanda returned to the room, she saw that her grandfather had slumped over in his chair. The paramedics, who'd been originally called for her grandmother worked to revive Thomas, but it was too late. The family was devastated but eerily calm as they informed the Williams Mortuary that they would need their services for both Stella and Thomas.

Troy, who received the transport request, was visibly moved. "Bro, you ain't gonna believe this one—wife and husband died within an hour of each other. Is that crazy?" Travis and the team had several questions. It was unusual that they would have more than one removal at a private home. After some discussion on the logistics, the men decided that they would bring two hearses to pick up the couple and that they would travel out personally to make this removal.

Each car had their equipment and staff. Before arriving at the Gideons' home, they decided to stop at a local florist and pick up two single stemmed red roses to place at their bed sides. The family was truly impressed with the care and sensitivity that the men brought to the removal. The staff was clearly moved by this ultimate love story.

All week, the tale of the husband and wife circulated through the funeral home and Maxwell. The couple was placed in beautiful caskets—hers a beautiful silver, his, a stately bronze. The family spared no expense for their services, from the elaborate booklet program that chronicled their life together to the lavish flowers that decorated the entire church. The couples' son gave a moving tribute of how his parents had never spent a night apart, with the exception of when his father was in the army. They would even stay together during hospital visits, with one sleeping in the chair next to the other. Even the site of the two hearses traveling to the cemetery moved the onlookers, with some of the gentleman removing their hats in respect. At the cemetery, the two caskets sat together, the couple in death exactly as they lived their lives—side by side.

That night, the men met up at Avery's favorite cigar bar called Stacks. Located in the neighboring town of Sunner, the cigar bar had an anti-quated feel to it. Decorated in muted grays and overstuffed leather chairs that swiveled, Stacks allowed the men to retreat, bond, and compare notes. Over drinks and good cigars, the men discussed the Gideon ceremony. It made them think about their own marriages and the ups and downs they each experienced in their relationships.

"Man, I don't know about me and Clarissa. I'll be honest with y'all; I'm just not there anymore," offered Damien, choosing to start this particular conversation.

"Where?" quipped Troy. "Not up for some sexual healing every chance you get. Is there a problem? Not from where I'm sitting!" Troy and Avery agreed in unison with a high-five.

Avery interjected, "What's it been, fifteen years? That's a long time to be together. What's the deal?"

"If I'm real, and yes, I know it sounds crazy, but I want more than sex. I'm not getting any younger and after all that heat, I literally just want to talk to someone. She's got a one-track mind and it's the same whether she's happy, sad, or angry. Does that make any sense?" Damien sipped his whiskey and braced himself for their response.

Both Avery and Troy had to admit, that while they may have been receiving less sex, their relationships did have more substance.

"All I know is that I want to honor my commitment to my son and give him what I didn't have. Once he graduates and heads off to college, I will feel more comfortable with us splitting up," said Damien. The conversation grew quiet as the men contemplated the impact of their friend's words. "And for the record guys, this is and NPT situation," emphasized Damien.

"NPT?" queried both men.

"Non-Pillow Talk! Y'all know y'all fools are weak. Try and keep this one to yourself," said Damien pointedly and staring right at his brother-in-law.

The men laughed, but both agreed. They knew how persuasive their wives could be for good intel.

"While it's great to know what you want and don't want, D, I'm worried if I'll be around for this family that Syd and I have created." At sixty, Avery was pre-occupied with his life span. He worked out every day, rode his Peloton religiously, boxed twice a week in a gym, watched his diet and slept a minimum of eight hours per night. He loved his vibrant life with his wife and kids. In fact, he had never felt more alive. However, he was focused on his DNA history and recalled that there was little longevity for the men in his family. Both his father and grandfather had died in their early fifties and this made him self-conscious.

"I want to walk all of my girls' down the aisle and meet my grandchildren," he said, sadly. After a long sip, his friends encouraged him that he would achieve what he wanted.

"Man, I look at you and my sister and I see a perfect couple. You will do it because it's what you both want," commented Damien.

Troy, who was a bit slower with his thoughts, added, "Man, I have to admit, even though Syd gets on my last nerve, you ain't gonna die till she tells you to!" The three cracked up at Troy's comment.

"From your lips to God's ear," said Avery ruefully.

"Naw, Ave, I mean it," responded Troy. "There's nothing better than being in sync with your partner; it just makes everything better. I thought KC and I were on the same page—about kids, our lifestyle, and getting the best we can afford. But I gotta say, marriage is work! I want more kids, but I'm not sure my wife does. She really came through for my kids when their mom died. We were used to just getting them every other weekend; now, they are with us full-time. She's the real MVP. She and Tianna are close, but it's been a struggle with Tre. I have to figure something out for him so the two of them can get closer. He needs a little more nurturing."

Damien and Avery glanced at each knowingly. The subject of Tre was always a touchy one with Troy, but Avery decided to take a leap and offer a suggestion.

"Hey, what about more responsibility at the garage? He can get a closer look at what you do and consider it for his future," suggested Avery.

"Mos def! I want my boy right by my side. He needs to see his dad and uncle grinding. I need him to see that nothing worthwhile comes easy. Hopefully he'll appreciate that," Troy added.

"Dawg, you gotta look at that temper, too. Don't know if you see it, but he acts like a ticking time bomb," offered Damien.

"Yo, what the hell you talking about? My son ain't crazy," exclaimed Troy hotly.

"Man, I didn't say that," countered Damien. "But he does have an anger management problem. Have you seen him with the other kids?"

Troy abruptly stood, the change in the mood apparent. "Maybe you should watch your situation and I'll concentrate on mine." Troy reached in his wallet, threw several twenties on the table and exited, leaving a stunned Damien and Avery.

"Well, that's the end of this night," said Avery. "D, you know you can't talk about anyone's kids."

"He shouldn't have opened the door. He knows that boy is aggressive. I really don't want him and the boys to hang out," Damien added, referring to DJ and Jamie.

"I know, I'm concerned too. Sydney says he gives KC a bit of trouble. I hope Troy can handle this situation." Avery stood up and gathered his jacket.

"I'm just glad I rode with you tonight," laughed Damien. "Cuz, I ain't into walking!"

Meanwhile, across town, the ladies gathered at Sylviana's for last minute alterations to their stunning dresses. The prestigious locally owned shop catered to the couture needs of the wealthy women of Maxwell. Sipping champagne provided by the owner, the ladies had the boutique to themselves. Sylviana's offered a personal touch, making sure their patrons had privacy when trying on dresses and never selling two women the same dress for the same affair. Ladies paid a hefty price for this concierge level service. The three women looked like a singing group out of a magazine shoot, each looking beautiful in their own right.

"Mama, that dress looks amazing on you! It's hitting you in all the right places. Deacon is going to love it," exclaimed Sydney as she watched her mother studying herself in the full-length mirror.

"Auntie, she's right," confirmed KC, "you look like a million bucks."

"Thank you, my darlings. I'm so happy we will have our whole family here for the Crystal Ball. Just then, the Hudson sisters walked into the shop. Chloe and Kendall had been at two other stores but decided to come and see if Sylviana's had anything to offer. Kisses and hugs abounded as the girls joined the dress search.

"I don't really know what I'm looking for, but I'll know it when I see it," explained Kendall as she browsed discontentedly through the racks of expensive dresses and gowns.

"Chloe bug, what about you?" asked Leona, using her childhood nickname. "Have you chosen a gown for the ball?"

"Oh, Mom-Mom; I hate picking out stuff." She grabbed the second dress she saw off the rack. "This looks okay, doesn't it?" asked Chloe with little enthusiasm. The dress was an old-fashioned mother of the bride dress, with large silver sequins and a bolero jacket. The group groaned in unison.

"Chloe, you have such a beautiful figure," commented Sydney. "You need something hot and sexy to show it off." Sydney immediately started to scour the racks in search of the perfect dress for her oldest daughter. Choice after choice received a chorus of no's from Chloe—if her mother had her way, she'd have a dressed in two Band-Aids and a thong, thought Chloe.

"Why are you acting like a fifty-year-old woman," asked Sydney, exasperated with her daughter's conservativeness. "If I had your body, I'd definitely show it off. You'll never get the guy's attention looking like a nun." Even at forty-eight, married with four kids, Syd was still man-crazy.

"Speaking of gentleman, do you ladies have escorts for the evening? Kendall, most of the other Circle inductees are either being escorted by their husbands or fathers, so Avery can walk you in. But, Chloe, what about you? I'll need your escort's name for the Maxwell Gazette. They always do an extensive write up on all Circle events." Leona eagerly awaited her granddaughter's response.

"Mom-Mom, I, I…," Chloe stammered, unable to answer her grandmother and mother expectant gaze. Her eyes darted around the room, as she looked for a way out of the uncomfortable moment. Sensing her niece felt cornered, but not fully understanding why, KC quickly changed the subject by producing a dress that she thought would be acceptable to all.

"Look, Chloe, what about this dress?" KC said brightly. She held up a gauzy Grecian style gown that covered up enough for the modest young woman but left her shoulder bare, which mollified Syd. It was an ivory color and a slightly see-through—the perfect boho gown for Chloe.

"Oh, Aunt KC, it's absolutely beautiful. I love it," exclaimed Chloe, grateful to her aunt for helping her out of the hot seat. She did like the dress, but it wouldn't have mattered if it was a full-length straight jacket, she would take it to end this particular situation.

Sydney happily gave the salesperson Chloe's gown and her own so that payment could be made for both dresses.

"Wait, Mom! I have two dresses too," Kendall held out two form fitting gowns for her mother to purchase.

"Kendall, two dresses? Really? As I recall, I paid for a dress at Saks that you said was for the ball. Did you return that one?" asked Sydney.

"I'm being inducted, Mom! I'm going to have to changed midway before the actual ceremony. The other dress was for the after party," smiled Kendall sweetly.

"Yup, she's definitely a chip off the old block," laughed Leona wickedly.

As the ladies finished their purchases and continued to talk about the upcoming event, Chloe quickly said her goodbyes and slipped into the cool night air, relieved to not be the center of attention any longer. She truly loved her family, but since her sexual awakening, she felt like two different people. There was Chloe, dutiful daughter, sister, and granddaughter, an anxious overachiever who always felt it her duty to be perfect vs. the Chloe who was involved in Blaze, who loved her passionately and wanted to be accepted for who and what she was. She wished there was a way to reconcile the two. Her ride back to Atlanta was long and distracted. Chloe was glad that Kendall had opted to spend the night at home so she could brood in peace.

Chloe's anxiety grew as she approached the entrance to her condo. She secretly hoped Blaze was either not there yet or asleep so that she could slip the dress into her closet and avoid all talk of the Crystal Ball. But that was not to be, as Blaze greeted her at the door, covered in paint, but happy to see her woman. She smiled sexily, asking, "Is that something for me?" Blaze's smile and sexy, piercing eyes always made Chloe's stomach flip-flop.

"Nooo," Chloe drawled, enjoying their flirting. "This is just a dress for a silly family event." She tried to move past Blaze to put the dress away, but she stopped her.

"Let me see," Blaze asked. She stared at the dress, careful not to get paint on the delicate fabric. "This is a beautiful dress, so your style. But this is for more than some family function," she remarked.

"What's going on, Lee?" Blaze had decided to call Chloe "Lee," a nickname for Leona, her middle name. It usually was cute and playful, but at that moment, it felt accusatory.

"So, the dress is for the annual Crystal Ball given by The Circle," Chloe answered.

"What the hell is The Circle; sounds like coven or something," Blaze said.

"No, worse. It's a coming-out party for Black society." Chloe was always embarrassed by some of things her family deemed important. She had hated going to Jack and Jill and cotillions as a teenager. Her plan had been to join The Circle to please her mother and grandmother, but never attend the meetings or functions.

"Well that's perfect, I'm black and I already came out," she joked. "So, do you want me in a tux or just a suit?"

Chloe felt a flash of heat and put her head down. Her silence was deafening. Blaze knew undoubtedly at that moment that she was not to accompany Chloe to the ball and that they were in two different places.

"Wow, so I guess I'm not invited, am I?" Chloe, who was immediately ashamed, went to reach for her hand, but Blaze recoiled.

"Baby, I thought you were comfortable with us," Blaze questioned.

"I am, sweetie. Here in the city. I'm from a small town and people are small-minded. I don't want to expose you or us to that mentality. It's actually embarrassing how country we are. I'm thinking of you." Chloe was hopeful that her explanation would be enough. It wasn't.

Blaze turned and began to disassemble her easel and collect her various paints and brushes. As she stuffed her apron angrily in her large leather satchel, Chloe knew how truly upset she was.

She finally turned to Chloe and stared directly at her. "No, you're thinking of you. When you're comfortable with yourself, holla at your girl." Blaze kissed her on the forehead and left. Chloe was devastated, collapsing in tears, with the dress still in her arms.

CHAPTER 5

All That Glitters ....

WILLIAMS MORTUARY WAS abuzz with activity amid reports that the body of Michael Darrow aka Baby D, an Atlanta rapper, was due to arrive from the DeKalb County Medical Examiners at any moment. Baby D, a native of Kennerville, had been gunned down after leaving a gentlemen's club called Skins. He had made the fatal mistake of calling out another rapper on social media. The beef went back and forth until a member of Baby D's entourage put the rapper's location on Twitter, daring his rival to come and "step to him like a real man." The confrontation ended with two men in Baby D's group injured and the young Grammy award nominated artist being killed.

The Darrow family came to the arrangements with the remaining members of his entourage, his fiancée, his manager, and lawyer. The group inspected the premises with the manager taking pictures and notes. KC and Leona, who were meeting with the family, were both intrigued and annoyed at the same time.

"Is this all the space you have? We gonna need a lot more room for the viewing," stated the manager, a fast-talking New Yorker who clearly was unimpressed. "And we gonna need a lot of power for the lighting and sound system."

"Young man, our main chapel seats 500 guests, which is bigger than most churches in the area," answered an indignant Leona.

"Can't we rent out the Fox Theatre or something? That will hold at least 5,000—" the manager was going on, but he was interrupted by Mrs. Darrow who had been quiet since their arrival.

"My son will be buried here in our town at this funeral home where we buried my parents and his father. He might be Baby D to you, but to me he's Mikey, my baby boy. Y'all do whatever else you want, I don't care," Mrs. Darrow became overcome and excused herself, her family members following behind to console her.

"Okay, so y'all heard Mrs. Darrow; this place it is. But we are going to need some things. First, we'd like one of those clear caskets and we definitely need the one with the lights inside. His outfit is being custom-made by a designer and we want him to shine. Also, we'll need space for the DJ to spin Baby D's hits. Our lighting and sound guys will be here to hook everything up. Yeah, and let's spell out his name in lights above the casket. This shit gonna be dope."

KC had been mentally tallying up the cost of all of their "needs." "Who will be taking care of the costs of the service?" she asked meekly.

The blond-haired lawyer, who hadn't spoken since they had arrived, reached into his Hermes briefcase and pulled out a leather checkbook and a large envelope bulging with cash. "Would you prefer cash or check?" he asked dryly.

After a long week of changes, specialty items and fans camping out in front of the funeral home, Baby D's homecoming was finally about to take place. There was a line of luxury cars that stretched two blocks long. Clarissa was literally bouncing in her seat with excitement. According to the program, one of her favorite R &B singers, Deanna S. Garrett was supposed to be singing a solo. As she attempted to make her way to the chapel, her plans were foiled by Leona.

"Clarissa, exactly where do you think you're going? This office is a zoo. You'll need to man the phones and get some order in here." Leona stood tapping her foot, a sure sign she was losing her patience.

"I just wanted to see Deanna Garrett. She's my favorite singer. I was hoping get a picture of her singing for my Instagram."

"Exactly why you need to stay in this office and focus on your work," Leona admonished her about her lack of discretion when it comes to celebrity clientele. "This is a young man's funeral not a media event. No matter how these people act, we will conduct ourselves with dignity and class." Leona turned and walked out leaving a clearly upset Clarissa once again thinking how out of touch these people were in terms of the services folks really wanted.

After countless hours of planning, prepping, and primping, The Circle's Annual Crystal Ball was being held at the Four Seasons Ballroom in

Midtown Atlanta. The lavish hotel had hosted the event the previous year and Leona was determined to outdo the previous chair's work by adding small extra touches to the already extravagant event. The ballroom's magnificent staircase was flanked on each step with a beautiful white floral arrangement. The attendees would ascend the stairs a la The Met Ball and were to be photographed at the top by the official ball photographer. Directly outside the ballroom, attendees were then given their swag bags, which included a Mont Blanc pen set, a Waterford crystal picture frame, gourmet treats from a local black-owned bake shop, and a beautiful Swarovski crystal ball shaped paperweight made in commemoration of this year's event. Once they received their bags and table assignment, each guest was escorted to their seats by a member of the host committee. Leona had added the swag bags and the personal escort this year after seeing it on a show about the famed Met Ball.

Upon entering the grand ballroom, guest were greeted to an opulent scene of dazzling white floral on tall crystal pedestals with hanging crystal accents, beautiful place settings, and a sea of bedazzled accents from the Swarovski crystal napkin rings to mirror chargers that the plates sat upon. No expense or attention to detail was spared. There was jazz band playing dinner music, which would later make way for an R&B cover band and DJ combination to get the party started! On the stage, there was also a large screen that would feature a slideshow of each of the women who were being inducted that evening.

The list of members and guests were impressive on its own. The newly elected mayor and her husband, two senators, numerous politicians and even a former recording artist were slated to attend. Tonight's gala was more than an event for the beautiful people to showcase their fashion and wealth, several local charities including a women's shelter, Voting Rights campaign, and a community group aimed to stop gun violence would benefit from the funds raised at the event. Attendees paid a whopping $1,000 per ticket or $10,000 per table. Corporate sponsorship started at $10,000 and Leona, Troy, and Avery's companies were all sponsors.

The ladies had all gotten luxury suites at the hotel so that they could leisurely get ready for their big night. Even the younger ladies were staying at the hotel. Leona was in her suite, getting ready as she was expected to be on site early for any last minute details. As she was adding the finishing touches to her light makeup and elegant up do, she heard a discreet knock on her suite door. Smiling, she opened it wide for Richard, her escort for the evening.

"Hello, beautiful," said Richard, greeting Leona with a sexy smile and a kiss. He was partially dressed for the evening in conservative Hugo Boss tuxedo, his jacket and tie still in the suit bag he carried over his arm. "Mmm, mmm, mmm, you sure are looking good, Leona!" Richard openly admired Leona's silver beaded dress, with its modest side slit and deep v neckline, which showed a bit of cleavage. She finished the look with her diamond circle pendant necklace and exquisite drop diamond earrings.

"You don't look so bad yourself, Deacon," she teased. "And you're just in time to finish zipping me up." Leona coyly turned around, exposing her partially zipped gown.

"I'm much rather help you unzip it," he quipped.

"Deacon!! Don't make me tell Pastor," laughed Leona. Richard slowly zipped up the gown, letting his fingertips linger on her bare back. "Besides," she continued, "we don't want you starting anything you can't finish!" She smiled sexily at him as she continued to get ready. It was definitely going to be a good night.

Love was also in the air in the Watkins suite, as Troy puts the final touches on his look for the evening. Not one for conservative dressing, Troy had purchased a Brioni tuxedo with a brocaded jacket. He'd seen it in a magazine and knew it would be perfect for tonight. He was looking forward to spending an evening alone with his wife. The Four Seasons' suite was perfect for baby-making!

KC came out of the bedroom shyly and did a half twirl in front of her man. She was not one to wear a lot of makeup, but Sydney had convinced her to go full glam. The makeup artist had expertly applied the makeup to achieve a glamorous but natural look. KC loved the result, but the eyelashes took some getting used to. She kept blinking hoping they'd feel more comfortable. She also loved her form-fitting dress with its low cut back and subtle beading. The dress showed off her well-toned body and runway model height. Instead of her usual bun, she had decided to wear her shoulder length hair out tonight. The result was quite dramatic.

Troy let out a low whistle at the site of his wife. He thought his wife was pretty, but she was more reserved when it came to sex appeal. However, tonight she had transformed herself and she was positively hot.

"Damn, girl, you make a brother wanna do some things," he exclaimed. He didn't want to mess up her makeup, but he knew he had to kiss her.

KC was excited at Troy's reaction to her look. They began to kiss, tentatively at first, the kiss turning more passionate by the moment. The spell was broken by the ringing of KC's cell phone.

"Do you have to answer that?" sighed Troy. *It's probably just Sydney calling,* he thought ruefully. But as he listened to KC's side of the conversation, he knew it was Tianna and he could tell that there were tears.

"It's okay, baby, just tell Jamie and DJ that they have to share the television," she answered. KC looked at her husband, exasperated. "No, we can't come and get you until tomorrow. Please let me speak to Grandma Belle."

The conversation between KC and Belle continued for a few moments, with KC asking to speak to Tianna again. The little girl must have been calmer, with KC telling her she loved her and would see her tomorrow.

"What was that all about?" inquired Troy. There seemed to always been some drama whenever they tried to spend time away from the children.

"Tianna and Morgan were upset because the boys won't let them watch videos," she sighed. "I asked Mama to referee but she seemed a little overwhelmed. I told her to let them watch TV upstairs, but apparently that wasn't good enough."

Troy chuckled at his wife's sarcasm. "Kids—there's always something going on with them. That's what happens when you're parents." He turned back toward the mirror to check his appearance before they left.

KC frowned and mumbled, "Yeah, that's the problem."

"Dang, Tianna, why'd you go and call Aunt KC? Snitches get stitches," teased DJ, grabbing at his cousin's ponytails. He and Jamie always messed with the girls, but it was all in fun; the four cousins genuinely loved each other and got along most of time.

"Whatever, DJ! It got you off the game, didn't it?" laughed Tianna triumphantly. They were now watching a movie on Netflix.

DJ checked his phone and saw that he had a message from Tre asking if he wanted to come over. He apparently had a new vape pen and some beer and wanted to party. Not really a fan of either, DJ hated to appear uncool so he texted back that he would come and asked if Jamie could come too. It would be easier to tell Aunt Belle that they both going over to the Watkins home. Tre reluctantly agreed.

The two convinced a gullible Belle that they were just walking to KC's for some more video games that Tre was planning to lend them. She was reluctant at first to let them walk in the dark, but the Watkins' home was a mere four blocks away in their gated luxury enclave. The whole Williams family lived in the quiet safe neighborhood within walking distance of each other.

"You two be careful and come right back," cautioned Belle. Both boys assured her they would, knowing full well Belle would be fast asleep and never know what time they returned.

DJ and Jamie made record time and were soon absconding from the Watkins' comfortable family room, amid the twirling smoke of Tre's vape pen. Tre had passed out beers to the boys as soon as they arrived.

"What flavor is that?" asked Jamie. Though he was a novice to vaping, many of his friends at school were into the trend and he had heard of the many flavors.

Tre laughed heartily his eyes already glassy. "Naw, lil' man; this here is cannabis! They call this blend Girl Scout cookie!" He continued to crack up and offered the vape to Jamie and DJ. Both reluctantly took a drag, with Jamie coughing violently after his puff. He was asthmatic but didn't want to seem like a little kid.

"Damn, what the heck is this stuff," exclaimed DJ. As an athlete, he stayed away from drugs and alcohol, but like his young cousin he didn't want to seem uptight. He'd taken a sip of his cousin Kendall's wine once, but this was his first experience with marijuana. He felt like he was floating, and everything seemed really fuzzy.

DJ looked over at Jamie, who was laughing, but nothing appeared to be amusing. "What's so funny, man?" asked DJ.

"I swear that picture of my mom and your dad keeps looking at me," he drawled, talking very slowly. The family room was fully of family pictures and heirlooms. DJ understood what Jamie was saying. The cozy family room that they had spent countless hours suddenly felt weird.

Tre had gotten up, presumably to get more beer, but returned with a large black backpack. He opened and revealed its' contents—two large bags of marijuana and another bag full of small baggies. He meticulously began to separate the drug into piles and began the bagging process. The younger boys were silently mesmerized until DJ finally spoke up.

"Cuz, are you selling weed now? What if your folks find out?" he questioned, concerned for Tre.

"Look, my dad started out selling, and then he went legit. I'm going to do the same thing. Shoot, DJ, you need to get in on this hustle too. Hell, lil' man, those middle school kids at y'all fancy school are all smoking! You can recruit me some more customers." Tre was in mogul mode. He checked his phone, quickly texted back a reply, and packed up his supplies.

"Gotta go make this money. It's getting late anyway and y'all better get back before the old biddy realizes and starts calling everybody."

Avery and Syd were in their suite, with Avery in the familiar position of waiting for his wife to finish getting ready. A veteran of seven Crystal Balls, the routine was the same. He would always arrive there first, check into the suite, and wait for the whirlwind that was his wife's late arrival. This usually gave him time to dress, have a scotch, and read the financial news on his phone.

The Crystal Ball always gave Avery secret anxiety for several reasons. The number one reason was the sheer amount of money spent on one night. Deep inside, Avery still felt like the poor kid from Detroit, not the wealthy man from Georgia that he'd actually become. Dropping almost $30,000 in one night, even if it was a charitable tax write off, was enough to give anyone sleepless nights. But probably the most troubling fact was that despite the expensive Prada tuxedo, the Cartier eyeglasses and expensive BWM, he always felt like folks considered him Sydney's sugar daddy—a middle-aged guy trying to recapture his youth with his younger wife.

In the bedroom, Sydney took a look at herself in the full-length mirror, equally as critical of her appearance. Her plan to lose twenty pounds before the ball had failed miserably, only netting a loss of a mere eight pounds. She was, however, happy with her dress choice this year. She had picked out a stunning ivory colored Carolina Herrera one shoulder gown with a slightly risqué thigh slit and dramatic train, which she was pleasantly surprised came in size 16. The dress showed off her legs and the Jimmy Choo crystal encrusted four-inch heels. She had endured spending all day at the hair salon getting her hair straightened. It now hung as a curtain down her back. From her sexy underwear, daring dress, and sexy shoes, she had crafted the look for one purpose, which was to dazzle and seduce her husband. He would never know that most things she did were for his benefit.

Sydney exited the bedroom for her grand entrance. She was struck how handsome Avery looked in his tuxedo. "Okay; I'm ready," she announced, holding her breath for what she hoped would be a slew of compliments. Avery looked up and smiled. He was taken by her look, but a little unnerved by the sexiness of her outfit. She looked phenomenal, which made all his insecurities come flooding to the surface.

"Awww, babe, you look at you!" He kissed her chastely on the check. "I was just thinking, maybe we should have brought the kids along, they could swim in the hotel pool and we could have had brunch all together at the restaurant downstairs. I think it's called Park 75."

A disillusioned Sydney stared at her husband in disbelief. A dry kiss on the cheek and then this crap about bringing the kids. Was he kidding?

"Avery, they have a pool at home to swim in and we eat breakfast together almost every weekend. This night was supposed to be about us. All

I've thought about all week is being with you." She looked crestfallen. "Obviously, we had different visions of this evening."

Avery started to protest, but the look on his wife's face made it evident that anything he said would have sounded like a lame excuse. As she turned and walked out, he followed, knowing he was definitely in the proverbial doghouse.

"Chloe, I swear if you make me late," threatened Kendall, clearly annoyed by how long it was taking for her sister to get ready. "I mean, damn girl, you don't wear makeup, all you have to do is zip up the damn dress and put on your shoes." Kendall was a glam princess like her mother, with a full face of expertly applied makeup and her hair dyed a rich brown with bronze and blond highlights. It was curled in intricate halo that was swept to the side. Her lame gown left little to the imagination. To top off the look, she had "borrowed" a pair of her mother's crystal Louboutin heels.

Chloe's look while not as striking as younger sister, would still turn heads. Her white gown was gauzy and ethereal, a perfect complement to her earthy personality. Her natural curls were shiny and beautiful, thanks to the insistence of Kendall that she get highlights and Kérastase treatment. As an ode to the formal occasion, she had twisted up one side of her hair and added an antique barrette that belonged to great grandmother, Elise, and finished the ensemble with delicate strappy heeled sandals. The look was vintage Chloe.

"I wish this night was already over," lamented a forlorn Chloe. She was upset at the fight that she and Blaze had regarding the Ball and more importantly, the fact that she was not "out" to her family. She and Blaze had spoken a few times, but things were still tense for the couple.

"What's going on sis?" asked Kendall, immediately concerned. Her sister had always hated formal affairs and crowds, but there was something different, almost sad about her expression.

"I'm going to tell you something, but you can't tell anybody else, not Dad or Aunt KC and especially not Mom." Kendall was all eyes now, for she, Chloe, and their mother shared almost everything.

"Okay, Chlo, spill it," responded Kendall.

"I, I have a girlfriend. Her name is Blaze and she's an artist. We've been seeing each other for a few months. Kendall, I think I love her." Chloe's words all came out in a rush. She stared intently at her sister, waiting for her reaction.

"A girlfriend…, girlfriend? Omigod, are you a lesbian?" Kendall looked shocked, but not upset.

"I'm not comfortable with labels, but I'm definitely attracted to her."

"Did y'all, you know, do they do?" Kendall asked, eager to get the details.

Chloe looked down, suddenly shy. "Yes, Kendall, we made love. It's different than being with a guy—gentler and loving and very intense." She smiled brightly, "I had my first orgasm with Blaze."

"You got to be kidding! You and Rashawn Knox were hooking up on the regular. I can't believe that fine ass boy wasn't breaking your back," she laughed.

"He did break my back and that's all," Chloe said ruefully. "But Blaze is mad at me. She wants me to come out to the family. I'm definitely not ready for that."

"Girl, Sydney and Leona will have a fit. You're their Golden Girl. Just tell her to be patient with you. I had a friend who came out to his parents and he wasn't ready. It didn't go well and him and the guy ended up breaking up. He ended up marrying some girl from his hometown. The parents didn't even come to the wedding. All that drama for nothing. C'mon, girl, let's go before Mom-Mom calls looking for us. Hey, maybe they'll be some cute girls for you," she teased. She grabbed her sister's hand and squeezed it hard, the small gesture showing that she accepted and loved her unconditionally.

"Whatever, Kendall!" Chloe said and smiled in spite of herself. Her sister really was her best friend.

Clarissa hung up her phone in disgust. Damien had just phoned to tell her he was meeting her at the ball. He explained testily that he had waited as long as her could for her, but he didn't want to miss Kendall's ceremony. *Always something with his sister or her bratty kids,* thought Clarissa. As she stood in their bedroom, smelling his Creed cologne and looking at the tags from his new tuxedo he carelessly left on the floor, she grew angrier by the moment. The Fendi tuxedo (picked out by his sister, she figured) cost almost $4,000.00. She knew this was Damien's first ball, but nothing in Clarissa's wardrobe cost even a fraction of that amount. As she expressed her displeasure about being left behind, Damien came right back at her with his own complaints.

"You were gone for nearly six hours at Kareema's Kuts, getting your hair done. Who knew when you were coming home? This night is important to me. If it was important to you, you'd have been here on time so we could walk in as a couple."

Clarissa knew he had a point, but she also knew it was worth it. She had gotten her lashes done and her hair was looking good. She quickly hung up with Damien and began to get dressed. As she slipped into her hot pink gown with the side cut-outs (all the rage said the girl at the store) and the revealing crotch split (glad she got a wax too) she hoped that this would spark something in the bedroom because things had been a little cold in there lately.

The gala had begun, with a welcome speech by Leona and her committee and opening prayer by Rev. Dr. TB Newberry, pastor of one the largest mega churches in Atlanta. As the jazz band played tasteful dinner music, Leona made her rounds, greeting dignitaries and making sure everything was running smoothly. She was especially proud of how beautiful and poised Kendall looked as she made her way to her seat at the table with the other inductees. Leona also had to laugh at the female heads that turned when Damien made entrance his sans Clarissa. His designer tux fit him like a glove, and he was so mysterious with his shades and black shirt while all the other men wore traditional white.

A sudden commotion at the door, commanded Leona's attention. When she arrived at the welcome table, she saw the reason for the confusion. Clarissa had arrived in her hot pink dress and one of Leona's committee members inquired if she was aware that it is customary for women to wear white or silver to the ball. The woman blocked Clarissa's entrance until Leona arrived. Clarissa looked scared and humiliated at the same time. Not once had Damien or anyone else shared that any specific color was worn at the event. As she looked into the room and saw all the women dressed in various shades of white and silver, Clarissa was completely mortified.

Leona remembered all too well the same scene many years ago when the men in her family did the same thing to Jimmy. Leona's family had taken Jimmy to get fitted for a tuxedo, never mentioning that they always wore black to this particular dance and he had spent all his money on a handsome white dinner jacket. He stood out like a sore thumb but handled himself with more class than anyone in her family ever possessed.

"Hello, Clarissa," said Leona smiling brightly. "Don't you look lovely tonight? You will definitely bring some color to this sea of vanilla. This is Clarissa Dickson, ladies, my step-son's fiancée. Come along, dear; let me show you to our table." The women were wide-eyed but dared not come up against Leona Williams.

Leona ushered her in amid the whispers of the women and gawking stares of the men, daring anyone to say anything. This was the kindest thing Leona had ever done for her and Clarissa was near tears. When she arrived at the table, Damien kissed her perfunctorily and both KC and Sydney complemented her on her dress, but Clarissa was unsure if this was part of their inside joke.

The boys walked home slowly, stopping twice for DJ to throw up in the neighbor's bushes. He was sick from the beer he drank. Jamie continually kept coughing; the vaping having caused his chest to grow tight. When they arrived at Grace Lane, he realized that he left his inhaler at home. A concerned Morgan heard her twin in distress and confronted the two boys who looked guilty at each other.

"What happened? What were y'all doing? I smell alcohol on you," Morgan was like a cop, interrogating a suspect.

"Morg, we had some beer at Tre's and then we used his vape pen," answered Jamie, immediately starting a coughing jag. "I left my inhaler home, but I'll be okay."

Morgan looked at him doubtfully. "We need to call Mom and Dad. You sound pretty bad."

"No!" said both boys simultaneously.

Morgan shook her head, but she reluctantly agreed. She and her twin were extremely loyal to each other. The boys went to their room, hopeful that they both would feel better in the morning.

Kendall was delighted at her moment in the spotlight. There was a professional slideshow that was more like a movie, featuring family moments as her sister read aloud her many accomplishments. The slideshow's musical accompaniment was a recording of Kendall playing classical piano. The final video was of father and daughter playing the piano together. Avery had taught all of the kids to play, but only Kendall had his talent and love for the instrument. The close of ceremony changed the mood of the gala and everyone was encouraged by the band to come out and dance.

KC and Troy, followed by Damien and Clarissa, made their way to the dance floor to enjoy the band's rendition of several popular R&B hits. Even Leona and Richard strutted their stuff, but a hurt Sydney remained chilly to Avery; he had asked her twice to dance, but she politely declined both times.

Standing in line for the bar, he encountered his daughter Kendall, who grilled him about her mother's mood.

"What's wrong with Mom? She's in a crappy mood tonight. She didn't even get excited when dessert came out," she joked.

"I think I blew it. I didn't say she looked nice and then I said something dumb about how we should have brought the twins. I don't know, Ken; I feel like I keep messing up," he said regretfully.

"Okay, Dad, look, she spent a shit load—oops, crap load—of money, time, and effort for tonight to impress you. Mom has some self-esteem issues because of Terrance." Like Chloe, they always referred to their biological father by his first name. "He messed her up badly. I wish she would have gotten some therapy," Kendall sighed. She was a psychology major and thought the whole world needed therapy. "But she is crazy in love with you, that's for sure."

"I love your mother more than anyone or anything in this world. She knows that," answered Avery genuinely.

"Of course you do, but sometimes you got show her better than you can tell her," explained Kendall. "You messed up, so do something grand! She's just disappointed. She kept asking me and Chloe if we thought you didn't like her dress or if she looked too fat. Mom acts like she got it together, but all that designer armor hides who she really is—an insecure human like the rest of us."

Avery hugged his daughter tightly, grateful for her advice and insight. "How much do I owe you Dr. Hudson?" he joked.

"This month's credit card bill will make us even," she quipped with a grin.

Sydney watched from across the room as her husband was deep in conversation with their daughter. The two hugged and he wandered off toward the dance floor. Was he going to ask somebody else to dance? She felt herself tear up—this night was quickly going from bad to worse. She wasn't sure if should just go find him and apologize for being cold all evening or maybe just go upstairs and order Uber eats. Right as she was contemplating her next move, the lead singer of the band announced that they were slowing it with something for the lovers. As soon as she heard the first chords of Robin Thicke's "Lost Without You," she felt Avery's hand on her shoulder.

"Please dance with me, Syd. You can't say no to our wedding song," he said gently.

Sydney smiled as he led her to the dance floor. One of things that the Samuels did extremely well as a couple was dance. It was all the hours they would spend dancing around the house together. As they swayed together in perfect step with one another, Avery whispered in his wife's ear.

"You are absolutely the love of my life, Sydney. There's no one I would rather be with than you. You look beautiful tonight, but I think you always look beautiful. I wish you'd see yourself the way I see you." His words were heartfelt.

"I love you too, Avery. I'm always anxious that I'm not attractive enough, that I'm too fat—."He silenced her with his finger.

"The only one who cares about your weight is you. I love you just the way you are. Have I ever acted like I wasn't attracted to you? Asked you to lose a pound? If you want to lose weight for you, that's one thing, but I like my women thick and you are my dream girl!"

Sydney tightened her arms around her husband's neck and kissed him passionately, not caring who saw her. The evening had just gotten infinitely better.

With the 2021 Crystal Ball firmly in the books, the night ended on several distinctly different notes for each attendee.

Leona and Richard had planned to celebrate her perfectly executed event in her suite with a bottle of champagne. As they made their way to the hotel elevators, a Circle Member who also happened to be one of the church's trustees, cornered the couple, asking Richard if the Pastor would be bringing the message on tomorrow morning. Both Richard and Leona looked uncomfortable while he chatted with the woman. After she had moved on, Leona shook her head regretfully.

"I guess we should call it a night. Too many prying eyes and wagging tongues. Can't have the church folk talking about us," said Leona, her voice tinged with disappointment.

Richard was also disappointed but understood. Both were people who cared deeply about their reputations and felt no need to give folks more to gossip about. "Goodnight, my love. It was a wonderful evening. I'll call you when I get home."

Leona watched his retreating figure. She had to admit she had been looking forward to Richard joining her in her suite and what might come next.

The Hudson girls and some of the other younger Circle members decided to keep the party going at the Penthouse Rooftop Club. Neither girl was much of a drinker, but both had more than a few drinks and were feeling no pain. Kendall had caught the eye of the DJ and spent the rest of the night dancing provocatively in front of his station. He was amused by her antics and continued to play all her favorite songs. But the surprise of the evening was Chloe who ended up making out in the lap of a handsome young lawyer whose mother was a member of The Circle. Kendall did a double take when she saw her strait-laced sister giving the guy her bumbling version of a lap dance. Kendall laughed to herself and thought, *I guess she's not a lesbian anymore.*

KC and Troy arrived in their room with romantic intentions after flirting and kissing all evening. KC was thrilled because it finally felt like the old days of their marriage before the kids and the stress. But it was Troy who this time spoiled the mood with talk of having a baby. He clamored on and on about how a child would bring the whole family closer together. KC felt herself shrinking under the stress of starting a family. When Troy made the comment, "You know Janet Jackson had a baby and she was 50," the headache KC planned to fake suddenly became real. Talk of pregnancy and babies made KC's love turn cold.

"Honey, I'm sorry, the champagne is giving me a migraine," she said softly, holding her head. She was prone to migraine headaches.

"Oh, my poor Boo. Did you bring your meds? Don't worry. I'll get you some ginger ale," he said and quickly grabbed the ice bucket and went out in search of soda and ice. KC felt bad for lying to her husband, but she knew she had to have a real talk with him very soon.

At the other end of hall, however, things were about to heat up for the Samuels. After Avery's romantic gesture, the couple quietly slipped away from the gala just before its end. As soon as they hit the door of their suite, they were all over each other like horny teenagers. Her fabulous gown lay in a heap by the bed, his expensive tuxedo jacket thrown over a chair. Sydney was sure glad she wore her sexy underwear, not that they stayed on that long anyway. Lying naked in bed with just her crystal heels on, neither she nor Avery was worried about extra pounds, age differences, or kids. They were caught up in the perfect ecstasy of each other.

A furious Clarissa started screaming at Damien the moment they arrived at home. She blamed him for the humiliation she endured at the ball as well why he had purchased such an expensive tuxedo.

"That suit cost more than my first car," she yelled angrily. "Why didn't you get me a dress from Fendi?"

"I didn't pick out the damn suit. Avery and I were talking, and he suggested that I try it on. Maybe if you had time, we could have gone together. I haven't worn a tuxedo since my prom. Besides, what does it matter how much it cost? You don't pay a bill in here. I take care of everything and give you whatever you need. I bought myself something nice. So what?" Damien challenged.

"It's just everything, Damien. Your sister and cousin purposely didn't tell me to wear white or silver. I looked so stupid wearing the wrong color. Even the girls in the band had on silver."

"Whatever, Rissa! I'm not going to stand here all night and argue about a dress. You looked good, so what does it matter? I'm going to take a shower, so argue with yourself for all I care." He left the room and she soon heard the shower running. Clarissa took off the offensive dress, which had looked so pretty and chic in the store, but now looked cheap and tawdry in light of the past few hours. No matter how hard she tried, it felt as though she and Damien couldn't get on the same page.

A hung-over DJ awakened to the sound of his cousin struggling to breathe.

"Jamie, are you okay," cried DJ, terrified because Jamie had turned pale and couldn't really speak.

DJ ran to wake up Morgan. She ran into the room and finding her brother in the throes of an asthma attack, she knew what she had to do.

"DJ, go and get Aunt Belle and tell her we've got to get Jamie to the hospital. I'm going to call my Mom right now." Morgan grabbed her brother's cell phone and quickly apprized her parents of the situation. They said they would meet them at the hospital.

A distraught Belle and DJ helped Jamie to the car, and they sped off to the ER.

Belle and the children were sitting in the waiting room of ER when Sydney and Avery rushed in with KC and Leona right behind them. Troy and the girls stayed behind to pack up the rooms and check out before making their way to the hospital. Avery spoke with the doctor while Sydney checked on their son. Jamie was receiving a breathing treatment and tried to explain that he and DJ were fooling around, and he got winded and forgot his inhaler. The doctor said he would be fine and should be able to leave as long as his oxygen levels stayed up.

Sydney and Avery were in the hall after the doctor left, holding hands grateful that their son was okay. Jamie's asthma has always frightened Syd. But mostly they were blessed that Morgan was so responsible when it came to her twin. Right know she was in the room with him, making sure he was okay.

When Damien came to pick up DJ, he detected the smell of last night's beer on the teen's breath and clothes, but he decided to talk to him later about the situation. He hoped that whatever had happened last night was not the cause of his nephew's asthma attack.

At home, a disgruntled Clarissa was sitting in her living room watching Netflix. Of course, Damien had rushed out when one of his sister's precious off-spring was in distress. She actually liked Jamie and hoped he was okay.

He was the only one who called her Aunt Clarissa and was a regular in their home. It just seemed like Damien was at their beck and call. Clarissa grabbed her phone and sent a short text on her crew's group chat—"Y'all, its time."

CHAPTER 6

The Thrill Is Gone

LOCAL TRACK STAR Ma'haalea Jackson (nickname Lia) was a phenom on and off the field. Lia, who half Filipino and half African-American, was a Maxwell high school track-and-field athlete with Olympic potential. She was also a cheerleader, president of the debate club, and an honor student, beloved by both teachers and students. At the state finals, she collapsed shortly after running her signature 400-meter race. Medical personnel attempted to revive her, but they were unsuccessful, and Lia died right in the arms of her teammates, her devastated parents watching from the stands.

Her mother, Liezel, who was Filipino, insisted that she be buried in their customs of her family. In the Philippines, the deceased sometimes wore brightly colored lavish gowns. Liezel wanted her daughter to wear an elaborate, handmade outfit that was based around her track unitard. Lia's aunt, a skilled seamstress had designed the one-of-a kind gown that highlighted her Filipino heritage and the sport she loved. The family's only other request was that she not be viewed in a casket, but that she be posed sitting in an ornate gold chair.

Leona was initially hesitant when the girls and Damien sat down to explain the family's wishes.

"They want her posed in a chair?" Leona questioned. "How would that even be possible? I understand they are grieving the loss of their baby, but this sounds like something you see on YouTube."

"I know, Miss Leona, but this is cutting edge. I've been to several seminars on alternative casketing and viewings and I think I can do this and make the family happy," answered Damien. He had been studying techniques and watching videos since Sydney and KC had approached him regarding the case.

"Mama, this is definitely different, but I felt for the Jacksons. They couldn't bear to see their daughter in a casket. If this makes this tragedy easier for them, does it really matter what we think? I know Daddy would have tried." Sydney's words resonated with her mother. Jimmy always wanted to help his families. It was why they kept coming back.

Damien worked for several days to perfect the young woman's layout. He set up the ornate high-backed chair in a scene with living room furniture. Damien has posed the deceased young woman, before embalming her, making it easier to place her in the chair. Her body was secured by a series of ropes tied to the chair, which were not visible to the public. Lia was posed in the chair with her hands folded. Her trophies and awards where strategically placed on the tables and mantle in the viewing room. There was also a beautiful family portrait in a frame on the table next to the body. The Jacksons and their family who had traveled from the Philippines took turns posing for their last family picture. In Filipino tradition, young children in the family wore red to protect the children from "ghosts." The family was eternally grateful that the funeral home went the extra mile.

Clarissa decided to call an emergency meeting of her "business partners" to plan their strategy. Instead of meeting at their usual spot, she asked them to meet her at an out-of-the-way coffee shop where it was quiet. She needed everyone to concentrate and not be distracted by music or alcohol.

With all of the players assembled, Clarissa shared that she had saved enough capital to start their venture. Over the years, she had amassed $75,000.00 in an effort to save for Damien and her wedding. Disillusioned that those plans hadn't materialized, she had decided to use her nest egg to fund her dream. Clarissa hadn't planned on being a funeral director, but she had always wanted to own her business and to be a "boss." Carefully watching Sydney and KC make arrangements made her supremely confident that she could meet the needs of grieving families. She pulled out her computer and folder full of notes, clippings, and projections regarding the new venture.

Everyone was impressed by how thorough and well organized she was. Coley was the first to speak.

"Clarissa, you got some good ideas and you're a genius with those numbers, but what we need is a building," stated Coley matter-of-factly. He was a man of few words, mainly because of how unsure he was of himself. The others nodded in agreement.

"You're right, Coley; we do need a building. That's why I called this meeting. I have an appointment tomorrow afternoon with the owner of Spencer Funeral Chapel on Dumont Avenue," she said and smiled like the cat that had eaten the canary.

"Ewww, isn't that the creepy run-down place near the woods? That building hasn't been used in years since the owner died," stated Dorinda, clearly not impressed with this location.

"Yes, that's the place. After Old Man Spencer died, his son kept the property intact. Prep room, chairs, office equipment—it's all there. But the son happens to be strung out on heroin and crack. He went through all his father's money and is looking to rent the building. It may be old, but it has everything we need, and he's willing to throw it all in—just needs some cleaning.

"How much is the rent, Miss Clarissa?" asked Tyriq, the youngest of the group. He was Muslim and very respectful, always calling her "Miss" or Ma'am."

"$3,750.00 a month for everything," Clarissa saw the shock in their eyes, but she knew with her money she could easily cover the rent for a whole year.

"That's a lot of money without no funerals. I'm not sure about this," said a hesitant Dorinda. Her negative attitude was starting to get on Clarissa's last nerve, but she was a great office worker and a good funeral attendant.

Clarissa ignored the negative commentary and continued laying out her plan. "Dorinda, you'll be office manager and work viewings and funerals. We'll need you to carry the phone in case any death calls come through."

"Dang," interrupted Dorinda, "I ain't never managed nothing."

"Coley, you'll handle all the embalming, dressing and services. Tyriq, you'll do all the driving, removals, and work the services. Do you still have your Suburban?" she asked Tyriq.

"Yes, ma'am. I just got new tires," he answered proudly. "But I don't have a stretcher, Miss Clarissa."

"No worries," she replied brightly. "We'll just borrow one from Williams. They'll never notice."

Layla, who had been quiet throughout the whole meeting, finally spoke up. "So, exactly where are we getting these bodies that Tyriq is picking up? And what am I supposed to be doing?

"You and I are the most critical people to this funeral home," Clarissa said, ignoring Dorinda's eye rolling and mumbling, and continued her explanation. "I do intake for death calls during the day at Williams and, Layla, you are the nighttime receptionist. Every death call that's a referral to Williams will come to us. I will make all the arrangements myself. If it's a longtime Williams' client or someone who mentions Cruella, Bookworm, or the Puffy Princess by name, it stays with Williams. Referrals won't know the difference, especially when I tell them that we are a subsidiary of Williams Mortuary." Clarissa's plan took some time to understand and sink in, but they were all fully onboard. No one in this crew felt any remorse at stealing a case from their employer.

"But this is the most important part. We are never ever to mention the new funeral home at Williams, not to your friends there, not to our coworkers, nobody!" She said this part with emphasis. One slip and the plan could go south.

"So what's the name of our funeral home?" asked Coley.

"Guiding Light Funeral Home," Clarissa proclaimed proudly. "Let us guide you and your loved one on their final journey." Quiet at first, the group let the name sink in. They all agreed that this was a new journey for everybody, and they hoped to guide their bereaved families into a more modern type of funeral service. But mostly, the new venture made everyone feel that they were finally being seen and valued.

Tre was at the garage cleaning out the flowers from the two hearses that had just got back in, when his father drove into an empty bay in a brand-new Dodge Charger black on black. Tre wondered why his dad needed another car; he had a black Suburban, a convertible Audi, and Ford F150. Troy got out and proudly handed the keys to his shocked son.

"Awww, hell naw, Dad, is this mine?" he asked excitedly. The teenager was lovingly gazing at the car, checking out the interior. Tre looked like a kid on Christmas morning.

"Yes, son; this is yours. I know this year has been rough for you, but I want you to know that I love you and everything I'm trying to do is for you and your sister. I want to give you so much more than my father ever gave me. I always wanted a car when I was your age. Just be careful, okay?" He hugged Tre hard, happy to see his son so excited. He hadn't seen him this happy in a long time

When Travis came to inspect the new ride, he too was hyped about the car.

"Yo, nephew, this ride is dope. All you need is to get these windows tinted and maybe an extra speaker in the trunk, so the hotties can hear you coming," laughed Travis.

Troy looked at his brother in disgust. "No, we won't be doing none of that."

Tre was barely paying attention to his dad and uncle as he sat in the driver's seat of the sleek, new car. He couldn't help but think how much this would help his side business. Making pickups and deliveries either on his bike or on foot was starting to get old. He'd be able to move more weight and service more customers with his own car. Tre asked his father if he could leave so he could show his cousins. Troy agreed happily. It made him feel good that his son would show the new car to his in-laws.

Once his son had driven off, Troy confessed how good he felt to do this for his son, but how nervous he was about KC's potential reaction to the car.

"Man, I know she's going to be pissed. She was against buying him a car in the first place." Troy knew he probably should have at least told her before he picked the car up from the dealer, but a small part of him didn't feel that he needed to justify buying something for his son with his money.

Travis looked at his twin and shook his head. "Bro, you gonna definitely need to order flowers."

Clarissa was slightly apprehensive as she drove thru the run-down gates of the trailer park where Rickey Spencer, son of the late John Spencer and current owner of Spencer Funeral Chapel, called home. Clarissa navigated her car in a vacant space next to a ratty couch, which obviously served as Ricky's outdoor furniture. She was greeted by a dirty mongrel dog, which barked incessantly and looked like he had an advanced case of rabies.

A scraggly blond came to the door, scratching her neck and drinking a beer. Her t-shirt was dirty and full of holes and Clarissa couldn't help but notice that her arms were full of needle marks. The sounds of rock music blared from a rusty old radio on the counter by the door.

"Whatcha want, missy?" she snarled as she swigged her beer. She inspected Clarissa as if she were a bug, taking notice of her sapphire ring and leather purse. "If you from the county? Don't waste your time—my kids live with my mama now."

Clarissa silently thought, *Thank God!!* She cleared her throat and began to speak. "No, ma'am. I'm here to see Mr. Spencer about a business matter." She smiled politely.

"Rickey!!!" she screamed, "it's a bill collector out here to see you!" She let the screen door of the trailer slam in her face, leaving a shocked Clarissa standing outside.

Rickey peeped out the door tentatively but was relieved when he saw it was Clarissa. "Hey, Clarissa, how's it going?"

"All is well, Rickey. I just wanted to come over and sign all the paperwork. I also have your deposit, like we agreed."

Rickey's eyes lit up at the mention of the deposit. He looked toward the trailer knowing that his companion was probably on the other side of the screen listening. "Let's sit in your car and talk things over."

Clarissa stared at Rickey in quiet disbelief. Rickey Spencer had been a star football player in high school but was now a shadow of his former self. Badly in need of shave and haircut, he had a mouth full of rotten teeth and red pockmarks all over his body. Like his companion, he constantly scratched at invisible bugs and his pungent odor was permeating Clarissa's car. Clarissa, eager to get the transaction over with, pulled out the contract she had downloaded from the Internet as well as the cashier's check for six month's rent and the five thousand dollar cash deposit he had insisted upon.

Rickey quickly scribbled his name on the documents, barely glancing at their contents. He handed them back, greedily awaiting the cash. Clarissa instinctively knew that the cash wouldn't last more than a few days and the check only a moment more. He looked as if was salivating over the crisp new hundred dollar bills.

"Okay, so can I get the keys? I'd like to stop by the funeral home and get started with the clean–up," said Clarissa, who was eager to get to the funeral home, but equally as eager to get away from Rickey and the trailer park from hell.

"Sure, Clarissa," said Rickey, flashing what he thought was his mega-watt smile. "I got them right here." He began fumbling through the pockets of his worn jeans but coming up empty. "Just a sec; they must be in the house." He exited the car in search of the missing keys. Clarissa sighed in relief and immediately rolled all of her windows down.

More than fifteen minutes had passed by and Clarissa was fuming. She kept repeating the same mantra in her brain, "I will kill this crack head if he doesn't find these damn keys," when a triumphant Rickey returns, keys in hand. Clarissa left and drove directly to the building.

The old converted three-story building was in need of landscaping and a bit of cosmetic work, but all in all, not in terrible shape. As she let herself in the oak doors, she finally got excited. The main chapel was so dark that Clarissa had to open the dusty burgundy curtains to let in some sunlight. It was a typical southern funeral home, full of antique furniture and dark carpeting. This building was a far cry from the marble floors and modern opulence of Williams Mortuary. Rumor had it that when Leona renovated the funeral home after her husband's death, she spent over $300,000.00 on the fancy upgrades. But Clarissa liked her new digs, it was comfortable and a fully operational funeral home. A little elbow grease and they would have the place looking decent in no time. Clarissa finally sat down gingerly on one of the ancient high back chairs and smiled. The words of the song she had wanted played at her wedding came to mind. "At last," she said. At last.

Saturdays after working services usually went the same for KC and Sydney. They changed clothes in their respective offices and left out to spend the afternoon together. The cousins would either go shopping or run errands and then they'd have lunch before going home to spend time with their families. During this catch-up time, there was only one unspoken rule— no funeral home talk. This day after their errands, they decided to visit their mothers.

The older ladies were excited by the impromptu visit and expertly prepared a delicious lunch out of leftovers for the girls.

"Told you it was a good idea to come to Mama's instead of going to a restaurant," exclaimed Sydney as she happily munched on Leona's fried chicken and potato salad. Belle had just put a pie in the oven to take to the church on Sunday, but the way her niece kept asking about when it would be done, she knew she'd be making a replacement.

"So you two just came here for our food," teased Belle, happy to see her two favorite girls. Belle had been reluctant to leave her close-knit community in Baton Rouge after her husband had died, but her daughter and Leona had convinced her that being near family in her golden years was better than being with her church members and friends. Belle was glad she'd made the move because she and KC had missed out on a lot of mother–daughter moments due to distance. They had a lot of catching up to do.

The four chatted about local events, finally giving Belle a blow-by-blow description of the ball. They hadn't had time to reflect on the evening due to Jamie's trip to the emergency room. Belle felt badly that her nephew had gotten ill in her care, but Syd quickly assuaged her guilt by explaining that Jamie often had attacks and left his inhaler behind. This had served as a good lesson about his being more responsible when it came to his condition and his medication. Belle was just relieved that he was doing well.

"So what else happened at that fancy party? Did you and Richard have a good time, Leona? I saw y'all pictures in *The Maxwell Gazette*. The two of you looked some kind of good together," gushed Belle. Though she adored her brother Jimmy, she knew Leona needed to move on and find love again. After all, Jimmy had been gone for over fourteen years.

"Yes, we had a fabulous time. I wanted us to celebrate with some champagne in my suite, but some of our nosey church folk started talking to him and we didn't feel comfortable going upstairs together," sighed Leona.

"Leona, you let that fine man go home all alone? I'm disappointed in you," joked Belle. Everyone laughed, surprised at the former first lady talking about going home with a man. Widowhood had changed Belle.

Sydney couldn't wait to steer the conversation to Clarissa's fashion faux pas. Belle shook her head as Sydney's described the reaction to Clarissa wearing the absolute wrong color.

"Was that such a big deal? I feel sorry for Clarissa. Seems no matter what side that girl is on, it's always the wrong one. I hope you ladies were kind to her," admonished Belle, looking in particular at her niece. She loved Sydney like a daughter, but she knew she wasn't a fan of Clarissa and could be unkind to the young woman.

"Auntie, I was nice. I complimented her on the tacky dress. But Mama was her BFF that night. Leading her into the room and daring anyone to say anything." Sydney was surprised by her mother's action as she had never been Clarissa's biggest cheerleader.

"Stop it, Sydney!! I just did what was the kind, Christian thing. It wasn't her fault that no one shared information about the ball dress code. As I remember, Sydney Michelle, you and Avery took Damien shopping for his tuxedo. Maybe you could have taken the time to help Clarissa also. That goes for you too, Kalen Christina." Leona was too ashamed to relay the story about Jimmy and her family and what had happened at that dance so long ago. Both girls hung their heads in shame. When Leona used their full names, she was definitely not happy with them.

Belle knew the two cousins were thick as thieves, but it was unusual for them to both have such negative feelings about someone. Especially KC, who usually saw the good in everyone.

"So, girls, why don't you like Clarissa?" asked Belle gently. She knew that Leona didn't see Clarissa as marriage material when it came to Damien, but she was curious why the younger women didn't care for her. "If I remember correctly, you all used to be close."

"Mom, Clarissa is okay, but I don't always trust her motives when it comes to Damien. She'd be happier if he didn't associate with the family at all. At first, I thought she was just a little overwhelmed by everything, but she told one of the girls at the funeral home that we were snobbish and cruel to her. We used to hang out, but it all changed after we got close with Damien. She tells everything we say or do at Sunday dinner to the whole staff. She talks too much and she calls us cruel names behind our back." KC hadn't wanted to talk about any of this, but now it was out in the open.

"Dang, KC, I knew about her big mouth, but what names does she call us?" questioned Syd. She looked like a tiger ready to pounce.

This was exactly why KC hadn't wanted to say anything. "No, I'm not telling you. She's silly and immature. The best thing she'd ever done was produce DJ. Leave it be, Syd," KC warned.

Before Sydney could protest, Leona intervened. "It doesn't matter what she calls us; we are better than that. As Michelle Obama said, when they go low, we go high. No more talk of Clarissa and her antics." Leona's tone made it evident that the topic was no longer to be discussed.

At that moment, Sydney's cell phone rang, and she saw the familiar number of their weekend answering service. She immediately grabbed a pen and paper and left the room. A few moments, they heard Sydney giving her condolences, indicating that this was indeed a death call. Leona started clearing the dishes and preparing dessert.

Belle decided to change the subject and inquired about how her daughter's relationship was going with her stepson. "Sweetie, are things getting any better? Tre seemed really sulky the last time he was here for dinner. I was hoping he would come over when the kids were here, but then the boy's walked over to see him…"

"The boys were at my house? Tre never mentioned that to us at all. See what I'm talking about? He's sneaky. I heard Troy telling him about Jamie and he never said a word. I try so hard to bond with him, but he's so angry. He's constantly doing things to Tianna, mean things like hiding her bracelet or book. If I mention it to Troy, he agrees with me but then goes back and rewards Tre with something—new sneakers, concert tickets. It's so frustrating, Mom." KC always approached situations with logic and fairness, but this tactic never worked with her stepson.

"You have to keep trying, KC," counseled Belle. "Your father and I didn't raise you to be a quitter. Keep it in prayer. God will turn his heart of stone to a heart of flesh, just like the scripture says. If you don't bridge the gap between you and him now, he may get in the wrong crowd and be lost to you forever. Also, all this strife can't be good for your marriage."

"That's an understatement," replied KC dryly. "Things were good between us before the kids came. We're just trying to get back to that good place, but it's not easy. Romance and spending quality time with kids is so hard," she lamented. "At least tonight we have some alone time. Tianna is with her grandparents for the weekend and Tre is usually at his friends during the weekends."

Sydney and Leona had both rejoined the conversation at the tail end. While Belle's pie was being sliced, Sydney chimed in about romance and children.

"I know it's hard, KC. Before the ball, Avery and I hadn't had a complete night alone in forever. Since Mama started dating Deacon, I lost my week-end babysitter. I wish Avery's parents were alive. I could use a twin-free weekend," she joked.

"That's what happens when old folks have kids," countered Leona, laughing. "You and your husband could have had an empty nest, but you were so hot and heavy on that European honeymoon of yours. Should have named those twins Paris and Rome. Now Mom-Mom is getting her groove back. So sorry." They all laughed at that and continued to chat long into the afternoon.

Tre pulled into DJ's driveway, eager to show off his slick new ride to his cousins. Both DJ and Jamie were mad impressed by the fast car.

"C'mon, let's go for a ride," said Tre, ready to ride past the park and to his old neighborhood.

Clarissa, who had come in as Tre drove up, was reluctant to let the kids go with Tre, but the look of excitement on the boys' faces made her change her mind.

"Okay, but only for a little while. DJ, your dad will be home soon and Jamie your mom is coming to get you by 6. Tre, not too fast, and everybody put on your seat belt. Please be careful, Tre," she admonished lightly.

"No problem, Miss Clarissa. I'm really a good driver," said Tre and grinned, like butter would melt in his mouth.

The boys waved to Clarissa, as Tre slowly pulled out of the driveway, the model driver. When he was safely out of the subdivision, things quickly changed. The powerful car went from 30 mph to 70 mph in a matter of seconds. Both boys were nervous about the speed but said nothing. DJ tried to play it cool, but as he saw his younger cousin wide-eyed in the back seat, he knew he was terrified.

"Yo man, slow down!! You late for something?" joked DJ. He was hoping that Tre would take it down a notch.

"Whatcha talkin' 'bout? A car like this is meant to go fast. It's the Hemi engine," Tre said, expertly.

Tre's cell phone rung and he picked it up immediately. DJ wondered how he could even hear over the driving bass of his radio. DJ could tell from Tre's side of the conversation that his "boss" was asking him to come and make a pickup. Tre quickly explained that he had his younger cousins with him. Nine told him it didn't matter—bring them too. They could all "get this work." Tre steered the car toward Nine's home across town. DJ was definitely not interested in being a part of anything drug-related after the last episode and especially didn't want to expose Jamie to anything illegal. His Aunt Syd would kill him!

When Tre arrived in front of Nine's house, he got out to talk with the crew. All the other guys were impressed with his new whip. A scared DJ and Jamie remained in the car, watching nervously from the window.

"Damn, young boy, this car fly as shit. You coming up son," remarked Nine. The other guys nodded in agreement, giving Tre high fives and fist bumps.

One of the young men jokingly made a comment that Tre must be making more than them, if he could afford a car like that. He laughed at the end of the statement, but Nine's silence illustrated that he didn't find the joke funny.

"Whatchu say, punk?" growled Nine, enraged at the comment. He definitely felt disrespected in front of his crew.

"I didn't mean nothin' by it." But Nine struck the young man violently, who lost his balance and fell to the ground. Nine then proceeded to kick him, and blood began coming from his lip as he was kicked repeatedly in the mouth. As they watched in horror, some of the young man's teeth appeared knocked out and he writhed in pain, saying he was sorry over and over again.

Nine stood over his bleeding employee, breathing hard and screaming. "I bet none of you other bitches better ask me about no money. Or you'll end like this sorry muthfucka here." No one dared to move or offer aid to their injured friend.

Nine looked down on the battered young man, actually just a mere boy of seventeen. "Get up and go make my money before I change my mind and shoot ya monkey ass," he spat.

He turned to Tre and the rest of the crew, who were visibly shaken. "That's what happens to disrespectful punk ass bitches, young bloods. Remember that." Then Nine called Tre over, gave him his assignment, and walked away, followed by his frightened but still loyal crew.

DJ and Jamie were silent as Tre delivered his package. Jamie wasn't sure which had unnerved him more, the brutal beat down or the fact that they could be stopped by the police. DJ finally spoke up.

"Tre, are you sure this is what you want to be doing?" He was genuinely concerned for his cousin's safety. "That whole thing back there was really intense. I mean, you don't have to do this. You have a good job at the garage or maybe my dad could get you a job at the funeral home."

Tre glanced at DJ with disgust. "I don't want to work in no damn funeral home around dead folks. That shit is creepy as hell. Besides, man, our fathers were in the life when they were young. They've seen all this and probably worse. We becoming men." Tre too, was scared by Nine's actions, but he didn't want to let it on to DJ.

Jamie was in the backseat, taking the whole conversation in, but he knew one thing. His dad, with his glasses and business suits, had never seen anything like that in his life. The trio rode silently back to DJ's house, everyone in their own thoughts.

Sydney and the boys arrived at the same time. She was floored to see her son hopping out of the back seat of a car driven by Tre. Syd and Damien both waited until Tre was out of ear shot, before they both commented on the new vehicle.

"I bet KC doesn't know about that," remarked Damien, as he shook his head. "A car is the last thing that boy needed."

"I know that's right. I don't think the boys should be riding with him. I don't trust him," said Sydney, perplexed as to why Clarissa even allowed them to go with Tre.

"Tre's family and all and don't mind them playing video games but riding in his car is a whole other ballgame. I'm going to talk to Rissa about this."

"I got bad feeling about the whole situation. See ya tomorrow, bro," Sydney got into her SUV in which Jamie was already sitting, staring into space. He was uncharacteristically quiet on the way home. Usually, he badgered his mother to change the radio station, but tonight they sat in silence, her smooth jazz station playing in the background.

Sydney decided to bring up the subject of Tre and his car. "Jamie, I don't want you riding around with Tre, okay? He's not that experienced a driver and I'd feel better if you guys didn't ride with him." She was expecting her son to put up an argument. He usually wanted to do whatever DJ was doing. It was okay when they were younger but it had grown increasingly more difficult as the two got older.

"I'm okay with that, Mom," replied Jamie, relieved that he had a reason to not ride with Tre.

"Okay," said Sydney, surprised and relieved too that it had been so easy.

Whenever something different, scary, or exciting happened, the first thing Jamie would do is run it by his twin. But he couldn't share tonight even with Morgan. He'd have to deal with his feelings on his own.

KC pulled onto her street, excited to spend the evening with her husband. She had already decided to order takeout from a local seafood restaurant. Troy was crazy for anything from the sea! KC didn't want to go out this evening for she didn't want to share her man with anyone. As she pulled up, she spotted a strange car in driveway. She maneuvered her Cadillac Crossover next to black car, wondering who was there. She hoped it wasn't her brother-in-law. Travis changed cars like most folk changed their underwear, and never knew when to go home.

As she walked up her front walk, her husband and stepson both came out of the house.

"Hey, babe, do we have company?" she asked Troy as she gestured to the car.

A triumphant Tre quickly answered for his father. "Naw, it's mine. My dad got it for me." Tre was jubilant at the look on KC's face. He knew instinctively that he had won this particular battle.

KC ignored Tre completely and looked directly at her husband, and then silently walked up the stairs. Troy knew without a shadow of a doubt it would be a long, sleepless night.

CHAPTER 7

Taking Care of Business

A SOAKING WET Sydney ran from her en suite bathroom to her bedroom to grab her ringing phone. Almost slipping on the marble tile and banging her knee on her nightstand, she thought angrily, *This had better be a death call!* Seeing her cousin's number made even angrier—they were going to see each other in less than an hour.

"What, KC!! I was taking a freaking shower!" Sydney wrapped her towel tight and rubbed her bruised knee.

"This is worth interrupting your shower. Guess who died?" KC was always one for guessing games when Sydney was clearly not in the mood.

"You if you don't hurry up. I'm going to be late for work fooling with you," answered an exasperated Syd.

"If you're just getting out of the shower then you're already late. Anyway, since you're cranky this morning, I'll just tell you—Eloise Hanks!" She delivered the news with a flourish and awaited her cousin's response.

"Old lady Hanks? Didn't she die like years ago? I know she had to be at least ninety!" Sydney sighed, not at all impressed by KC's "news." "When's the service? We can send flowers."

"That's just it; they called us to handle the services! I'm already here in the office and I took the call. It's such an honor for the family of a fallen funeral director to pick us to handle her home going. Miss Eloise was a funeral service icon. Funeral directors from all over the country would want to attend. She was the first female president of Georgia Select, an officer of the National Funeral Service Association and she was the first African American to serve on the Georgia State Board of Funeral Service." KC spoke with such reverence that Sydney had to stifle her laughter. Her memories of Miss Eloise weren't so rosy. While Eloise Hanks was indeed a pioneer for women in the business, she was also a fussy cantankerous biddy who liked to hear herself talk. She had once mentioned casually to Sydney after she had spoken at a local Georgia Select Funeral Meeting that her speech was too long and her skirt too short. Eloise spoke her mind and was not at all bothered how her thoughts were received. Young or old, male or female, no one was unscathed by her iron tongue. She was feared and respected by all.

"Did you tell Mama yet? She's not going to be happy. You know she doesn't like all the pomp and circumstance of these services. All the directors trying to be important, hating because they aren't in charge—it's just too much!" Sydney knew her mother wouldn't be interested in the extra responsibility of a well-known funeral director's service. It was customary for one's local colleagues to assist in handling the funeral arrangements so that the family and funeral service staff could act as mourners. This was further complicated when the deceased was a distinguished member of the local and national funeral director associations. Funeral directors from all over the region and the country came to pay their respects to a colleague. There was also a good amount of socializing and fraternizing all in the name of camaraderie.

But with all the glitz and glamour came a great deal of work and responsibility. Lodging and logistics were crucial when handling out-of-town funeral directors—they needed to be picked up, put up in the finest hotels (with the requisite bar and hotel lobby), chauffeured around, and suitably entertained. The family would also need to be taken care of; there was always a need to please the family of a person who spent a lifetime taking care of the dead.

Sydney's thoughts on her mother's attitude were spot on. "Why on earth did they call us?" exclaimed Leona. The girls had shared the news of Eloise's passing and the subsequent request for their services.

"Plenty of other directors knew her better than we do. Who wants the headache of dealing with all those out-of-towners? We're going to need extra staff, limousines, supplies for the hospitality suite." She sat down at her desk wearily and held her head in hands. Leona was clearly overwhelmed already by the high-profile service.

As the week played out, the entire Williams staff was inundated by phone calls, emails, and special requests regarding the Hanks service. Eloise Hank's had a small family who required big things, a full-time attendant at the family home to receive guests, floral deliveries and cards, a full day of viewing as well as an evening viewing at her church, five limousines, two vehicles for flowers, and the always popular horse drawn carriage.

The service itself lasted four hours with dozens of association members, officers, and local politicians making speeches about her years of dedicated servitude to the funeral industry. Over one hundred six funeral directors from Georgia and beyond marched into church behind the family, all wearing the colors of their respective local associations. After they had viewed her open casket, the members stood lining the walls of the church at attention. When the final director had viewed, they all began to sing "It is Well with My Soul." While not a particular fan of excess pageantry, even Leona admitted that the sounds of their voices all in unison around the church was a moving tribute.

Williams Mortuary sponsored a special repast for the funeral directors at the Marriot Marquis in Atlanta, which had served as the host hotel. The dinner for fifty was a raucous affair, with plenty of good food, drinks, and laughter.

Two of the most senior females recalled a story about their first time asking for a stipend for the cost of their rooms at a national convention. "We submitted our report, asked for reimbursement and waited," explained one of the women. "The acting treasurer looked everything over and then asked why we didn't share a room. Eloise told him that we didn't think we had to since the men never did. He looked at her and said, 'That's because they are men—men don't share hotel rooms with other men.' Eloise had looked him straight in the eye and asked, 'What idiot came up with that rule—I know it was probably some man.'" Everyone at the table laughed at the story, knowing that Eloise was a feminist before it was even popular.

Over the course of the evening everyone swapped stories recounting Eloise's service to her colleagues and community. In such an unusual profession, directors had a small circle of folks who understood their lives and weren't uncomfortable talking about the business of death. The dinner lasted long into the night.

The week-long service kept KC, Leona, and Sydney so busy that it made things easy for Clarissa to be away setting up the new funeral home. She pinched off hours each day to run multiple errands and oversee deliveries to Guiding Light. After leaving her day job, she would go directly to the new building to clean, paint, and set-up her office. Clarissa "borrowed" several items from Williams—casket catalogs, photos of flower arrangements, office supplies, and the like. What she couldn't appropriate from Williams, she ordered on her personal credit cards. Clarissa never realized all the things needed to run a proper office and how much these things would cost. But her excitement at getting started outweighed her frustration and her plans were coming along quite nicely.

Her only regret was the toll this took on her personal life. On this particular, evening, wearing a scarf tied around her precious weave and drenched in sweat from washing windows, mopping, and vacuuming, she received a call from her son. As she answered the call, she noticed she missed several calls from him, Damien, and one from Sydney. She hoped all was well—she and Damien usually just texted and Sydney never called her after hours.

"Hey, sweetheart, what's going on? Are you okay?" asked Clarissa.

"Mom, where are you? I can't believe you missed my game! We played the Bulldogs! It was really important," replied DJ, clearly disappointed at his mother's absence. DJ played basketball, ran track, and played football for Langley Academy, the prestigious private school he and his cousins attended. He was extremely talented, the only freshman who played on the elite varsity teams.

Shit, shit, shit, thought Clarissa. In her excitement to get the funeral home in working order, she had totally forgotten about the big game. DJ and Damien had spoken of nothing else for the past couple of weeks, with Damien spending hours outside in the driveway helping his son with his lay-ups and free throw shots.

"Oh, baby, I'm sorry. I got busy at work and lost track of the time. Is your dad there? Did you guys win?" Clarissa was truly devastated. She was known as the Gatorade Mom by DJ's teammates, always at all the games and practices to cheer her son on. Clarissa had impressively never missed a game or school activity since DJ had started pre-school.

"Of course, we won," he answered excitedly. "I scored fifteen points, two assists, and I didn't miss any free throws! It was my best game this season and you missed it!" DJ's voice wavered a bit on the last sentence. Clarissa could hear the disappointment in his voice. "Dad was here but he left to go back to the funeral home to embalm. Aunt Syd and Uncle Avery and the twins are here. Aunt KC and Tianna came too. We're about to go to eat at Kathy's Diner. Dad's coming when he's done. Are you going to come?"

The last thing Clarissa wanted to do was further disappoint her son, but she needed to get the place in shape. She was expecting someone from the state board to contact her or come by any day regarding the funeral home's required inspection and she needed to be ready. Besides, an awkward evening with the Puffy Princess and company wasn't the way she wanted to spend the remainder of her evening.

"I'm so sorry, honey, but I still have a lot of work to do. But I promise we'll do something special this weekend to celebrate, just the two of us. Maybe go the Sneaker World and get those new Jordans you want so bad!" Clarissa hated the thought of bribing her own son, but she could hear how upset he was.

"The Retro green ones? Dang, Mom, they cost like $279.00! Are you sure?" The mention of the shoes that he'd been begging for totally changed DJ's mood.

"Yes, the Retros. It isn't every day that you beat the Bulldogs and score fifteen points. I'm so proud of you, DJ." The emotion in Clarissa's voice was genuine. Her son was the greatest joy in her life.

"Mom, you're the best! I guess I can forgive you for missing this one game but just don't do it again! I might get a triple-double and you would miss it!"

"I promise I'll be there." When Clarissa hung up, she sat down and looked around the chapel at all her hard work. She certainly hoped that this would all be worth the sacrifice.

Later at Kathy's diner, the Moore and Samuels families sat watching as a number of DJ's "fans" stopped by the table to give their congratulations on the team's big win and his performance. Kathy's was a throwback to the '50s' malt shop with great burgers and comfort food. Complete with red leather booths and the requisite juke box, the restaurant had been around for years and was unofficial after-party for the local high school's athletic competitions. Everyone went to Kathy's!

"Where's Clarissa?" asked Avery when the kids were out of ear shot. "She never misses a game."

Damien's face frowned at the mention of his partner's name. "The hell if I know. She gave DJ some bullshit story about being at work, but she left at 3:30 today. I thought she was going to get stuff for the game, and then she doesn't even show. She's been acting funny lately."

"KC said the same thing. She's been away from her desk at lot too. You don't think she's dipping out on you," commented Sydney, instantly concerned for her brother.

"Sydney!" Avery shot his wife a warning look. This definitely not a conversation that needed to take place at that moment.

"It's okay, Avery," laughed Damien. "I'm used to my sister saying exactly what's on her mind. No, I don't think it's anything like that. Hell, if it is, then dude can't be hittin' it right because she's hounding me day and night."

The three all laughed at Damien's remark, but he was curious about what had gotten into Clarissa as of late.

"I don't know what she's doing but I'm keeping my eye on her. I thought maybe she was looking for a new job—caught her on the computer a few times and she'd change the screen when I came into the room." Damien recalled in his mind how nervous she had seemed, talking too much and shutting her computer down immediately.

"Best news I've heard all week! I will give her a glowing reference," commented Sydney dryly.

Avery shook his head at his wife's comment. Sometimes, Sydney said things that she should only think.

Two weeks later, Clarissa and Coley met at Guiding Light to have a meeting concerning the morgue and the upcoming inspection by the Georgia State Board of Funeral Service. As the two went over the preparation room supplies and chemicals needed, Coley decided to ask Clarissa some questions that had been on his mind since the venture began.

"Clarissa, how are going to get the embalming fluid and supplies? I need suture, fluid, embalming powder—all we have here are instruments and that old ass embalming machine." The previous owner had left an ancient rusty embalming machine in the closet. Coley tried his best to clean up the old machine, but it still looked nothing like the state-of-art machines used at Williams. He hoped that it at least still worked.

"Look, Coley, it was free, so we got to make it work. Once we pass inspection, we can open up an account at one of the funeral supply companies and improve on this equipment. But that's going to take time and money. We got to get some cases first. You gotta walk before you can run." Clarissa wanted all the bells and whistles too, but they had to pace themselves.

"I got you! When will we get the papers from the state? Don't we need somebody with a license to sign stuff? Miss KC is always talking about having a licensed person on every service?" Coley's knowledge of the business and funeral service law was rudimentary at best. This was a plus for Clarissa because if he knew more about the subject, he would never go for what Clarissa was about to purpose.

"Well, that's kind of what I wanted to talk to you about. Between you and me, I asked Damien if he would let us use his license for $1000.00 per month. He agreed so I got everything together, but he can't be here for the inspection. Since the inspector has never met him, I thought you could sign for him. After all, you're going to be doing all the embalming and you are his number one man in the morgue." Clarissa knew she was laying it on thick. Damien thought Coley was a wannabe who couldn't cut it in embalming school. He had often expressed wanting to get rid of Coley and hire some more competent help, but Coley was a hold-over from Jimmy William's era and Miss Leona was loyal to those who had served alongside her late husband.

As expected, Coley perked up at the perceived compliment, but was still apprehensive about forging his boss' signature. "I'm not sure about that, Clarissa. Isn't it illegal to impersonate someone and sign their name?"

"Only if they don't authorize it. Damien knows all about it and he's cool with it as long as nobody at Williams finds out. Just keep it on the low and everything will be cool. I'll do all the talking, and then you show up at the end and sign off on everything. But if you don't want to do it, it's cool. We can just tell everybody we are delaying the opening. Of course, we'll lose all the money we put out." Clarissa was calling his bluff because she knew that they all wanted this as badly as she did, but this was going to be a test to see what he was willing to do for his dream.

Coley was definitely not interested in losing his small investment as it equaled basically his whole savings, five thousand dollars. But moreover, he didn't want to lose the sense of purpose and pride that he'd gained over the past few months. Guiding Light meant more than money to Coley. He felt like somebody for the first time in his life.

"No worries, Clarissa; I can handle this. Just tell me what time and what to say and I'm all in." Though he still felt unsure, he figured Clarissa was Damien's girl and he was certain that she wouldn't do anything that he didn't want. At least, he hoped she wouldn't.

A week later, Clarissa was at Guiding Light, dressed in her best black suit and Michael Kors pumps that she splurged on for just this occasion, awaiting the State Board representative's arrival. When she saw the plain white car pull into their driveway, she knew it was show time. The skinny bespectacled white gentleman inspected the funeral's home sign and then rang the bell.

"Good afternoon. I'm Ronald Krause from the State Board of Funeral Service. I'm here for the facility inspection. Is Mr. Moore available?" He produced a card and showed Clarissa his credentials.

"Good afternoon, Mr. Krause. I'm Clarissa Dickson, the funeral home manager. Mr. Moore is running a little behind and asked me to show you around until he arrives," she answered, smiling broadly and extending her hand.

"That's fine. I can start the inspection, but it won't be completed until I meet with Mr. Moore. I see from my records that his current license hangs at Williams Mortuary. Has he started the paperwork to get that changed to this facility?"

Clarissa panicked slightly at the mention of the paperwork. She had submitted the request online but was concerned that notification of the change would be sent to Williams. "Yes, it was submitted online a few days ago. Mr. Moore hasn't informed his former employers of his new venture. Will they get anything regarding the change?"

"Why heavens no! Just as long as he's not the supervisor at that facility, they won't receive anything from us." Mr. Krause's answer caused Clarissa to almost openly sigh in relief.

Clarissa led the inspector all through-out the facility as he checked boxes on his state-issued tablet. He didn't say much as Clarissa showed him all the different parts of the funeral home. Once they left the small preparation area, he looked at his watch and sighed.

"No disrespect, Ms. Dickson, you've been thorough and diligent in your tour and provided me with all the necessary documents, but you're not a licensed director. Have you heard from Mr. Moore? I have two other inspections today and I can't keep those folks waiting. Should we reschedule?" Mr. Krause was clearly impatient regarding the appearance of Damien. If almost as on cue, Clarissa heard the front door open and Coley made his grand entrance as "Mr. Moore". Decked out in what was clearly his best black suit, a nervous Coley greeted Clarissa and the inspector, apologizing profusely for his lateness.

"It's good to meet you, Mr. Moore. As I explained to Ms. Dickson, I needed to talk to you before we could proceed. Everything looks in order, with the exception of the front sign. You will need to add your name to the sign or at least on the door."

"We are working on that this week. We have a sign company coming to add the lettering," added Clarissa quickly.

"That's fine, Ms. Dickson. This would in no way stop the state from going through with your licensure. Just get it taken care of as soon as possible. Mr. Moore, if I could get your signature on these documents, we'll be all finished."

A nervous "Mr. Moore" quickly scribbled his signature on the papers, as Mr. Krause entered information into his tablet.

"You will receive your official licenses in the mail in about ten to fifteen days. You will be able to operate as a licensed funeral home after 12:00 am tomorrow. Congratulations, Mr. Moore, and good luck." The two men shook hands as Coley thanked Mr. Krause for his time. The whole thing had gone off without a hitch. It wasn't till they both saw his car pull out the drive that they both began to celebrate.

"You did it, Coley! I'm so proud of you. He never suspected a thing. I can't believe it we are finally legit! Time to start burying some folks!" Clarissa couldn't remember being this happy ever, except at DJ's birth. Her dreams were finally going to become a reality.

KC sat in her office, checking her personal email for the tenth time that day, looking for an email from the Georgia State Board of Funeral Directors. She hadn't shared with anyone, not even Sydney, that she had applied for a vacant seat on the Board. Her application had been approved and references received, she was just awaiting the governor's approval and she would become a member of the illustrious board. KC genuinely loved her profession and wanted to further her career in teaching mortuary science as well as playing a role in the politics of funeral service. Making policies that would make life easier for consumers and funeral directors alike was her main goal for obtaining the position. She also wanted to elevate her profession and make sure that unscrupulous people didn't invade the profession she loved. Her thoughts were interrupted by a surprise visit from her husband bearing gifts, her favorite coffee and doughnuts, a throwback to the days of their courtship.

"Hey, baby. How's your day going?" Troy smiled his sexy smile and kissed his wife softly on the lips. Things had been tense in the Watkins household since the purchase of Tre's car. Troy had tried to talk to KC about the situation, but she had brushed him off. This was his last ditch effort in calling a truce.

KC returned his smile with a weak one of her own but was truly happy to see him. She had grown weary of giving him the cold shoulder but didn't quite know how to break the ice. "My day is going well. You must be a psychic because I was sitting here thinking how much I'd love a doughnut." She selected her favorite kind and began to munch happily.

'Baby, I'm sorry about the car. I should have consulted you. I also need and want your advice and input regarding everything, especially the kids. We wouldn't have made it through this year without you. Please forgive me. I just wanted to give my son something that I wanted when I was his age. I know he needs some work on his attitude, but he just lost his mom and I think he's just trying to find his way. Don't give up on him or me, okay?"

KC listened to her husband's impassioned speech and had two thoughts. He sounded sincere and she knew he was truly sorry but wasn't sure that given the same set of circumstances he wouldn't do the same thing again. But she needed her man, so she smiled and told him that all was forgiven.

"I would never give up on you and I will try to give Tre the time and space he needs. I love you, Troy, and I love our family. I just want us all to be happy."

Troy smiled, relieved to be back in sync. "Speaking of our family and expanding it, maybe we need to take a weekend getaway. We could go to that little bed and breakfast you like in Savannah."

KC was thrilled at the thought of reconnecting. Having the children in the house full-time had put a crimp in their sex life. Some alone time was definitely in order. She readily agreed about the trip, purposely ignoring the part about expanding the family. Feeling the need to share some news of her own, KC was about to share her possible State Board appointment when Troy interrupted her.

"KC, this is going to be exactly what we need. We need to leave all this work and stress behind and concentrate on us and our family. Maybe you should cut back your hours at the funeral home. With Damien being more hands on, you could dial back. All the stress of seeing these families and working so many services is probably why we are having trouble having a baby. You need to relax a little more. But I got you, babe." He smiled and kissed her again.

Thankfully, Troy's phone went off, so KC didn't have to respond. She waited patiently while he took the information that was clearly for a death call.

"Gotta go, babe; apparently, Sydney just called in a pick-up. I'll see you tonight." He kissed her again and jauntily walked out. No talk of his slowing down or taking time off from his business, just a kiss and some words, and all is right with the world. KC sat back in the chair, her mind swirling with thoughts of the rollercoaster ride her life had become.

Leona and Richard gathered in her kitchen for an impromptu lunch. Leona hadn't seen her man in almost a week and was eager to spend some time with him. As she moved around her sparkling kitchen making all of his favorites, she reflected on the last few months of their relationship. She hadn't realized how much she missed him when they didn't talk and how much she missed the physical affection he gave her. Sydney teased that she was "sweet on him" and she was correct. When she heard him enter the house, she actual got tingly!

"My my my, have I missed you, girl! Gimme some sugar!" Richard grabbed Leona around her waist and spun her around, and then went in for a lingering kiss. As usual his breath smelled of peppermint and his cologne smelled like tobacco and vanilla. When they parted, both were smiling broadly.

"I missed you too, Richard," said Leona suggestively. Something about him made her feel sexy, a feeling she thought had died with Jimmy.

"Then, maybe we shouldn't go so long without seeing each other," he countered.

The couple sat down to the lunch that Leona had expertly prepared. She made all of his favorites, her homemade chicken soup, a chicken salad on a brioche roll, and hand-squeezed lemonade. For dessert, she had made a delectable apple crisp with whipped cream. Richard smiled at the food, but more at the cook who made it. He appreciated that she always went out of her way to make even a small lunch special.

The two talked non-stop about the week's events. Richard shared a story about a fellow parishioner who was very ill in hospice. As a deacon, he often visited sick and shut-in members. Leona shared about Eloise Hanks' service and all the work it had entailed.

"Wow! That's a lot of hours for a woman who's supposed to be retiring," Richard remarked. Leona had been talking about slowing down and backing away from the day-to-day operations of the funeral home. She had planned to stop coming in every day, but her purposed three-day week usually turned into four or five days.

"I'm not completely ready to retire full-time, Richard. The family and the business take up a lot of my time." She could immediately tell that her answer didn't sit well with him.

"Well, maybe it's time that the family and the business take care of themselves," he remarked.

"The business is the family and vice versa. You really can't separate the two. Sydney, KC, and Damien are all capable funeral directors, but I still feel like they need my guidance. And Lord knows my child seems to always need my help in her personal life. KC has Belle, but poor Damien has no one. My grandbabies—"

"Exactly where do I fit in this equation? Your daughter is almost fifty years old with a husband who adores her and is quite capable of taking care of all of her needs. Damien, KC—they are grown folks with their own lives. Even your grandbabies are almost adults. It's time for us to start our life.

I thought that retirement would mean that you would be free to go when and wherever we wanted. We were supposed to go on a few trips this summer, but here it is spring, and we haven't made any plans."

"I know, I know. We're going to go away; I promise." Leona was clearly flustered by the whole conversation.

"Leona, I'm ready to be part of the family—I want us to take this to the next level. I want us to be a real couple. I'm ready and hope you are too." Richard grabbed her hand and looked pointedly in her eyes.

For a woman who always had something to say, she was rendered speechless. Leona had a lot of thinking to do.

The Back Yard Party was a planned annual reunion of the African-American alumni from Georgia area colleges and universities and the traditional HBCU's in the area. It was a weekend event with each school hosting hospitality suites on Friday, a huge BBQ in Piedmont Park on Saturday and numerous parties, but the most exclusive being held that night at the Sky Room at the Crown Plaza Hotel.

Sydney, a Spelman College alumnus, usually didn't attend the event, but this year, her college roommate Didi Roberts insisted that they go and see some of their college crowd. A reluctant Syd finally agreed but had neglected to share her plans with her husband.

That Friday, as they both dressed for work, Avery casually asked what their plans for the weekend were. Sydney knew that it was time to break the news about the party.

"I figured we'd take the kids out tonight like we usually do and tomorrow Didi and I are going to the Sky Room for the alumni party." She rushed the last part, hoping he would focus on their family night and not her night out.

"Do we need to get a babysitter?" he questioned, obviously oblivious to that fact that she hadn't included him in the invitation.

"No, sweetheart, we don't need a sitter. This is a girls' night out. I'm going with Didi and KC. We haven't been out in a long time and Didi just kept begging. Besides, it wouldn't be any fun for you anyway; you won't know anyone."

"Okay; that's true, but KC went to Tulane. She won't know anybody either," he countered.

"KC and I spent almost every other weekend on each other's college campuses. We both know a slew of people at each other's school." Sydney hoped she sounded convincing.

The silence in their bedroom spoke volumes. Avery was hurt that his wife hadn't bothered to share her weekend plans. He ran everything by her, always seeking her opinion or approval, and considering how she would feel about a certain subject or activity. He had taken her a few years ago to his college reunion back in Michigan. She hadn't known anyone either but started up a conversation with a friend's wife. The two women became fast friends and still talked from time to time. Avery couldn't help but wonder if the real reason she didn't ask him to go was based on her being ashamed of him. No matter how hard he tried, Avery always compared himself to Terrance and found himself lacking.

"Hey, I understand. Nobody wants to be stuck with their boring old husband. I'll hold down the fort," he responded with forced enthusiasm. Sydney knew instantly that his feelings were hurt. She wanted to reassure him that was not the case. She was never bothered by his age as she thought him sexy and mature, not old and boring.

"That's not true and you know it. I wasn't really sold on going at all, but Didi insisted that we go this year."

"Well, is Terrance going?" Avery asked. Sydney figured that her ex-husband's attendance was probably the root of the whole problem. "I know he went to Georgia State at the same time and you all know the same people...," he trailed off, hoping she'd say no.

"I don't know, but probably so. He's always looking for an excuse to relive his college glory days. But it doesn't matter. I'm just going to see my old friends and keep Didi company. I'd rather be home with you," she whispered, wrapping her arms around his neck and kissing him softly on his neck, which led to an even more passionate kiss. As Avery began to unbutton his wife's blouse, they heard a commotion downstairs. They only broke apart at the sound of Morgan's voice calling out for Sydney.

"Damn that girl has horrible timing," joked Sydney pulling away from her disappointed husband. She hoped that the kiss and her words reassured him that all was well.

On Saturday night, Troy's gleaming black Mercedes sprinter pulled up in the Samuels' driveway to pick-up Sydney. Avery, determined not be a kill joy, sat in the family room, waiting for his wife to come down. He was shocked when she entered the room wearing skin-tight jeans with several suggestive rips, a gauzy, revealing ruffled blouse and stiletto heels. He had to admit she looked hot, not at all like a forty-eight-year-old mother of four. Avery suddenly got very worried.

"What do you think? Do I look okay?" she asked. Sydney was nervous that the outfit was too young for her. Kendall had picked it out.

"You look fantastic." His response was interrupted by the beeping of the sprinter's horn. Obviously, the girls were anxious to get the party started. He walked with her to the sprinter and was surprised to see Damien and Troy along with the ladies.

Avery quickly noticed that Didi wore a similar revealing outfit like his wife. Besides being Sydney's former roommate and oldest friend, Didi Roberts was a Maxwell Municipal Court judge. But today, she looked like an aging party girl with her short skirt and fishnet stockings. Only KC looked like herself, wearing sensible jeans, a yellow twin set and pearls.

"I thought spouses weren't invited," Avery exclaimed.

"Man, I went to Clark-Atlanta. My whole squad is going to be there. Travis went to the picnic at Piedmont Park. He said it was off the hook," stated Troy, a half-filled champagne flute in his hand. "The party can't start till Big Daddy Troy gets there!"

Damien laughed at Troy. "Yes, I heard that playa. Hell, I'm going cuz I slept with so many Spelman chicks that they should have given me an honorary degree. I figured you were going too bro. Now I got to keep those knuckle-heads away from my sis."

They all laughed except for Avery, who was even more hurt and embar-rassed that he hadn't made the cut. He quickly made an excuse about a conference call, kissed his wife goodbye, and retreated into the house. He could hear them laughing and the music being turned up. So much for Sydney rather being home with him.

After stewing for nearly hour, Avery formulated a plan. He was going to crash the party. First, he called the young college girl that he and Sydney used occasionally to stay with the twins when family members weren't available. She was free and said she could be there in forty minutes. Next, he decided to reach out to his two older daughters for fashion advice. A business meeting or cocktail event would be no problem, but he was genuinely perplexed at what to wear to a real party.

On a hilarious three-way FaceTime, the girls tried to help their father achieve his party ready look. After thirty minutes and much debate, the Hudson sisters proclaimed Avery was ready to make his party debut. As Avery stared at his reflection in the mirror, even he was impressed. Sydney had bought him a pair of Balenciaga jeans that he had never wore, a gorgeous paisley patterned shirt, and pair of Gucci loafers. His Gucci belt and Rolex completed the look. The girls assured him that he would fit right in with the other "mack daddies" who had descended upon the city for the weekend.

Meanwhile at the venue, Sydney was in full swing; all hesitancy about attending the party was long gone. She danced non-stop with her brother and socialized, basking in the glow of looking better than some of her classmates, many of who didn't resemble their former selves. She was also feeling no pain, thanks to the red concoction called Jungle Juice that they had been drinking non-stop since their arrival.

The vibe changed when her ex-husband Terrence Hudson made his grand entrance with a striking young lady on his arm. Chardonnae Jenkins, aka

Curveegirlzsweat69 was an Instagram influencer and body-positive fitness guru. She was a light brown skinned beauty with long dark tresses and enviable plus sized curvy body, which was usually scantily clad in her online workout videos on Instagram and YouTube. With over 2 million followers, she was extremely well-known in the Atlanta area and was a celebrity in her own right. Chardonnae had been giving sold-out twerk yoga classes at Fit4Life for two months. She was obviously providing Terrance with private lessons on the side based on their PDA.

Sydney took a double take when she spotted Terrence with Chardonnae. She happened to know that Ms. Jenkins was only twenty-five years old, the same age as their daughter Chloe! Terrance's boys were all congratulating him on his latest conquest, plenty of high fives and fist bumps going around. One even remarked that she was the young Sydney upgrade! A confident Terrance couldn't wait to make his way over to his ex-wife who was quietly seething at the bar with KC and Didi.

"Hey, ladies, how's it going?" Terrance's million dollar grin was in full affect. "Just wanted to introduce you to Chardonnae. I'm sure you've heard of her," he added needlessly.

The young woman barely looked up from her phone where she was obviously posting something. She was clearly ready to get back to action on the dance floor and her adoring fans, not standing at the bar talking to these boring middle-aged women.

"Where's your old man, Syd?" asked Terrance innocently. "Or was this party past his bedtime? The elderly need their rest." He laughed at his own offensive joke. "Wow and I heard about you and Darrick, Didi. So sorry," he added insincerely. Didi and her husband, Darrick, had recently divorced.

"Whatever, Terrance," Sydney shot back, determined not to be dragged into an argument in front Chardonnae. They all turned away and finally he got the message and hustled his lady love back towards the dance floor.

Didi took it upon herself to order a round of shots, which they all quickly downed in silence. The trio tried to carry on a normal conversation afterward, but it was stilted. Syd outwardly acted as if she wasn't bothered, but she was fuming that he would start another relationship with a woman half his age. The sight of the couple brought back all of the pain and betrayal of their marriage. Terrance's numerous affairs were always with much younger women.

A half-hour later, Sydney was trashed and definitely not feeling like the belle of the ball anymore. KC decided it was time to leave and went in search of the others. Syd sat staring out into the night sky through the wall of windows. From out of the corner of her eye, she spied a guy who looked remarkably like her husband. A smiling Avery spotted Sydney and made his way to her table.

"Omigod, Avery! What are you doing here?" she exclaimed, genuinely surprised and pleased to see him.

"I decided to crash the party. There was no way I was letting you stay here looking this hot," he answered, grinning. "I came to claim my woman."

"You don't have to claim what's already yours. I'm sorry I didn't ask you to come in the first place. I didn't know the other guys were coming and I would have had a far better time with you here. But what I'm really interested in is your outfit. You look so damn fly. I'm really impressed." Sydney thought Avery looked really good. He needed to do casual more often.

"I can't take any credit. My wife has great fashion sense and the work of my personal stylists, the Hudson sisters," he laughed.

"Dang, I used the Hudson sisters myself!" Sydney exclaimed, amused that their daughters had styled both their parents.

KC successfully rounded up the rest of the crew who were all ready to leave the party but not ready to go home. Troy suggested that they do a throwback and go to the Waffle House. As they were leaving, they ran into Terrance and Chardonnae.

"Hey, Avery, see you made it to the party. It's a shame you missed Sydney's antics on the dance floor. She still trying to drop it like it's hot," he joked, obviously trying to get a rise out of Avery.

But Avery refused to take the bait. "Doesn't matter when I got to the party just as long as she goes home with me. Maybe you can show me those moves when we get home, babe," he said with a smile as he placed his hand on his wife ample behind.

"That's right, baby. I'm going to give you the full show," replied a very lit Sydney. Terrance walked away deflated. They'd taken all the wind out of his sails.

Clarissa sat on her living room couch, angrily awaiting Damien's return. It was almost 3:00 am and Damien still hadn't arrived home. He answered her text at midnight saying that he would be home soon but was still out. When he finally appeared at 3:45 am, Clarissa was livid.

"Well, hello," exclaimed Clarissa, sarcastically. "It's good to know you remembered that you have a home!"

"You can miss me with that drama, Rissa, cuz I ain't in the mood. I was out having a good time and lost track of time. Now, I'm tired and ready for bed," saying so, Damien started to head toward the stairs.

Clarissa was not about to let him off the hook quite that easy. "Exactly where were you having this good time?"

Damien sighed, but told her about attending the alumni party with Sydney and company.

"So you mean to tell me that everyone bought their spouses, but you couldn't have asked me if I wanted to go. Hell, you didn't even go to college but if your sister's doing it, then so are you," she retorted.

"You didn't go either, so what's the difference? I went to the party because my friend asked me to go. Besides you can't stand to be in Sydney or KC's presence anyway, so why would I ask you?" Damien knew he was being callous, but it ticked him off that Clarissa always played the victim when it didn't go her way.

"It would have been nice to be asked, but you stopped caring how I feel a long time ago."

"I care how you feel, Rissa. But you haven't been around enough lately to even know what I'm feeling. You've missed your son's game, stopped cooking dinners, and this house is a wreck. I hope if you've got some dude on the side, you're being careful," he added flippantly. Sydney had definitely planted that seed.

Clarissa looked as if she'd been slapped. The last thing she wanted was for Damien to think her absences meant she was cheating on him. Her whole reason for starting Guiding Light was to lure him away from Williams and build something together, not push him away.

"How could you even think that I was cheating on you? All I ever want is for us to be together! I don't want another man, Damien. All I want is you," she said softly, almost near tears.

"Then, where have you been? If it's not another dude, then what?" he probed.

"Damien, it's nothing! I've just had some things on my mind," Clarissa answered weakly. Her explanation sounded lame even to her.

"Don't sweat it, Rissa; we all have to do what we have to do," Damien shrugged and started up the stairs. "I think I'll sleep in the guest room tonight. I got a lot on my mind too."

CHAPTER 8

When Evil Rears Her Ugly Head

CLARISSA WAS AT Guiding Light on her lunch hour, going over the bills and looking at her empty chapel. It had been a few weeks since the blowup with Damien and it still stung. While she had been with this man for almost two decades, she was beginning to realize how different each of them was. She was determined more than ever to succeed whether Damien wanted to be a part of her grand vision or not.

Clarissa was sweating externally from the July heat and internally from the lack of activity at the funeral home. Williams's morgue was full, but no work had come to Guiding Light—every family had either been a repeat customer or had some connection to KC, Sydney, or Leona. Even one of Damien's friends had a death in his family but it went to Williams.

She was really starting to wonder if starting this business venture was truly a good idea when her phone rang.

"Damn, damn, damn," she exclaimed. It was Sydney, asking about burial permits and talking about two more death calls that had just come in. She made a hasty excuse to Syd and ran out the front door, almost running directly into a well-dressed woman and two men who were coming up the funeral home walkway.

They quickly asked if she was open for business as they had just lost a loved one and were looking for a funeral home.

"Well of course, we are," cooed Clarissa, immediately forgetting her previous plans. After a brief discussion, she was introduced to the to the LeBlanc family. They were from Beaux Bridge, LA, and they were burying their brother Evan who was a local pharmacist and had lived in Maxwell for fifteen years. The siblings had rallied together because their brother was the ultimate bachelor and had no wife or children. They just come from another funeral home in the area, but they didn't feel very welcome.

"Our brother was a class act who had a good word for everybody. That other funeral home was too stuffy for me," offered Mark, the youngest LeBlanc brother.

"We need a proper home-going for our brother." The family explained that Evan's coworkers had suggested Williams Mortuary, but the GPS got them turned around.

"Well, I'm sorry you got turned around, but you are absolutely in the right place," said Clarissa as she smiled and introduced herself. "Funny thing; we're actually are a subsidiary of Williams Mortuary and would be happy to assist you."

She ushered the family in and offered them a seat in the conference room. Over the next forty-five minutes, Clarissa expertly customized a ceremony that would celebrate his Creole roots and satisfy their need for dignity tempered with warmth. It wasn't long after that Guiding Light officially had their first case.

"Oooh, dawg! This some good stuff," drawled Aaron, one of Tre's friends. He took another lengthy drag on the blunt he was smoking, and then passed it to his other friend in the backseat. Tre was enjoying his boys from the old neighborhood, Aaron and Tommy. The three had been friends since Little League and definitely rolled as a crew. They were thrilled to learn that their boy had gotten wheels because now they could cruise in style.

"Yo, man! We livin' our best life!!! Hell, I can move in the trunk with all this space," exclaimed Tommy, cracking up at his own joke. Tre was thrilled that his friends approved of his new ride. It had been a minute since he had seen them, and the weed and afternoon drive was just what he needed. He liked Maxwell enough but there was nothing like his best friends from the old neighborhood.

The boys were too busy screaming the lyrics to da Baby's "Real as It Gets" that no one noticed the police car that had followed them for three lights. When the sirens wailed, all the boys freaked out except for Tre. Tight lipped, he instructed the boys to remain quiet and stash the blunt as he sprayed his travel size Febreze, which he kept underneath the seat.

As he pulled over, he turned off the radio and unbuckled his seat belt. His father had prepared him for this moment hundreds of times, but fortunately this was his first police encounter.

"Hello, Officer. Did I run through a light?" asked Tre when the police officer approached the car.

"No," offered the cop, "but your car was reported as a possible vehicle in a robbery. Can I see your license and registration?"

"No problem; just need to get my paperwork. Is that alright with you?" asked an annoyed Tre. He knew he hadn't done anything wrong but knew that it was the tax he would pay while driving Black. After sharing his credentials, the officer took about ten minutes before returning to the car.

"Are you Troy Watkins' son?" asked the officer.

"Yes, sir, I am," answered Tre, hoping for a way out of this traffic stop.

"I know your father. He picked up my aunt's body from her house a couple months ago. He's a good dude. Okay, well I could've booked you for speeding because you were over the limit, but your name is the same as your dads and I figure I'll give you a break."

"Well thanks, sir," sighed a relieved Tre. Now, he just had to get his boys home and he could forget about this craziness.

"However, I do smell marijuana in the car and that's a problem. I'm going to need to take you and your friends to the station. You're going to receive a citation for marijuana possession providing you don't have more than enough for your personal use." Tre was shocked to see that two additional police cruisers had pulled up behind them. The officer had already called for back-up.

"I'll let you call your father and have him meet us at the station as a professional courtesy," stated the officer smugly, like he was doing Tre a favor.

Thoroughly terrified, Tre called his father and quickly explained the situation to him. Troy was pissed but knew that there would be time to discuss things later. He explained to his son that he was in Atlanta, making a house removal and would be tied up for at least another hour or so. He suggested that he would call KC and have her meet him at the police station.

"Awww! Heck, no, Dad! Can't you get Uncle Travis to come and get me? She'll never let me hear the end of this," cried an exasperated Tre.

"Well, you don't really have a choice in the matter do you?" answered Troy angrily. "Your uncle is out on another call and your stepmother is all you have right now. This is what happens when you do dumb shit. But no problem, you can stay there locked up till I get back."

"Alright, Dad, call her," Tre said unhappily. The other officers were already asking his friends their parents' numbers. The joy in this ride had officially ended.

KC was in her office, finishing up the paperwork when her cell phone rang. She was pleasantly surprised to see her husband's number. Troy rarely had time for phone conversations during his busy workday.

"Hey, honey! What's going on?" she answered brightly.

"Babe, we have an emergency. Tre got stopped by the police and needs someone to come and pick him up at the station. I'm in Atlanta and can't get there."

"What happened? What did he do?" asked KC. She clearly was unable to hide the disgust in her voice.

Troy sighed—he felt defensive, but he knew he needed her help. "Look, I can't go into it now, but our son needs our help. Please can you just go get him?"

KC was unable to hold her tongue anymore. "As I recall, I was against buying that car for "our son." Obviously, he did something to warrant being pulled over, so maybe he should stay overnight at the police station. Maybe that would give him time to think about his actions."

"Overnight?" exclaimed Troy. "We are definitely not doing that. I got two words, Sandra Bland! There's no way we're going to leave Tre in nobody's police station overnight. Can you do it or not?" he asked, clearly annoyed at her train of thought.

"Fine; I'll go get him. But we need to have a serious talk with him tonight regarding this mess. I'm on my way." She hung up without saying goodbye and left for the police station.

KC pulled up in front of the Maxwell Police Station and got out of her car apprehensively. In her twenty-five years as a resident of the town, she had never been to the police station. She spotted Tre sitting on a bench in front of the desk sergeant alone, his friends' parents having already picked up their children. Tre sat with head in his hands, not looking at all like the surly, disrespectful teenager she was used to seeing. KC spoke with the officer, signed the citation, and turned to Tre without speaking. He rolled his eyes at her and slowly followed her out to the car.

The two rode in complete silence, both trying to anticipate their perspective arguments. KC had quickly read the police report and realized that Tre had been caught with marijuana and had been speeding, though he was only charged with a citation for the drugs. Forever the preacher's daughter, she knew very little about marijuana or its effects. She had seen Sydney smoke back in their college days but never had any interest in trying it herself. She somewhat naively thought that marijuana was a gateway drug and would lead to bigger sins.

Tre was happy to be away from the police station but was nervous about his father's reaction to the situation. He feared that Troy would take away his beloved car and his freedom. But mostly, he was just glad that he'd left his stash of drugs at home. Nine would be furious if he got locked up with his product.

As they pulled up to the house, Troy's black Suburban was in the driveway. Tre jumped out of the car, eager to get to his father first to plead his case.

Tre stammered, "Dad, let me explain…"

"Son, are you okay? Did they put their hands on you?" Troy was clearly concerned for his son as he put his arm around the boy's shoulders.

"Naw, Dad; they were pretty cool. I thought dude was going to let me go cuz he knew you, but he smelled Tommy and Aaron's weed and that was that." Tre didn't appear at all remorseful.

"Let you go? Exactly why would he do that? You broke the law by speeding and on top of everything, you were smoking marijuana. Why should he have let you go?" KC was incredulous and looked at the two, awaiting a response. She hoped that her husband would be the voice of reason.

"I wasn't smoking weed," Tre shot back.

"Really?" countered KC sarcastically, rolling her eyes dramatically.

"Look, we're getting off track. We need to get the car back and find out how this citation thing works. I may need to call my lawyer. I don't want this to show up on your record. Weed possession is still a misdemeanor. Even though I don't know why—its legal everywhere else and everybody is doing it. Georgia is so backwards," Troy began to scroll his phone for the attorney's number.

"Backwards? No, the offense occurred because he and his ruffian friends were smoking marijuana in his car. More bad decisions being made. What's next? Maybe they'll rob a convenience store next week. Why aren't we talking about punishment, Troy? How is he supposed to learn from his mistakes? Parents are supposed to guide their children…" KC was interrupted by Tre's snickering.

"Well, you don't have to worry about that because you're not my parent," Tre said smugly. His father shot him a look and nodded for him to go upstairs. Tre gladly retreated to the safety of his room.

"That's the second time he's told me I'm not his mother. Well clearly that's true because if he were my son, I would never stand for him having friends who routinely break the law. My father always said you can tell a person by the company they keep. We were obviously raised differently," she said sadly. Her feelings were hurt, not by Tre's words, but by her husband's lack of defense of her views.

KC went to grab for her purse and her keys, ready to give Troy and the situation a little space.

"Oh, so now you're leaving, like you always do. You act like you and your set never do anything wrong. If this were Chloe or Kendall, you wouldn't be so quick to judge. Look, KC, this is a family matter and you need to stay here so we can work this out as a family." Troy was angry, but he wanted to make the situation right.

"No, your son just told me I wasn't his mother. You stay here and work that out yourselves. Me and my opinions are not valued by either of you." KC was near tears but refused to cry in front of Troy.

"Go ahead then. Go over to Grace Lane and tell them all about my thug son and how he's in trouble again. That's typical Williams' behavior, get together, close ranks, and judge the rest of us." Troy turned away as his wife walked out the door.

A tearful Tianna ventured into her brother's room. She had heard her parents fighting and wanted to find out what was going on.

"Tre, what happened? Why are Daddy and KC fighting?" Tianna hated when the grown-ups argued.

"Dad is finally putting that bitch in her place. She needs to mind her business and stay out of my life!" Tre was excited that his father appeared to be standing up for him.

"Don't call her that! KC loves us and she's a good mom! I just don't want her to get mad and leave us." After her mother's untimely death, Tianna had struggled with abandonment issues.

"Whatever Tianna! You so far up her butt, it's sickening. You always trying to act like her and talk like her—reading all those stupid science books she gives you. She ain't our mother!" Tre began to get angry at his little sister and her fixation on KC.

"She's better than Mommy! She doesn't leave us alone in the house with no food and she doesn't take those pills that make her sleepy all the time!" Tianna answered back. She still remembered the dark days of her mother Sharisse's addiction. There were times that the only meals they got were what they had in school and often the electric or gas would be cut off. Neither child would tell Troy because they didn't want to get their mother in trouble.

Tre grabbed Tianna's shoulders tightly and shook her like a rag doll. "Don't you ever talk about Mom like that, you little bitch!"

"Stop it, Tre; you're hurting me," she cried. Tianna and Tre had their share of disagreements, but they had never turned physical. Tre released his sister and she quickly ran out of his room crying. This was the first time that the young girl could say that she was afraid of her brother.

Clarissa sighed as she sat at her desk. It had been a bear of day; the office at Williams had been jumping and she barely had time to take a lunch break for all of the work they had her doing. She sometimes felt hers was the only name that got called upon all day.

"Clarissa, why haven't these insurance policies been processed? I got families calling me left and right about their money?" Sydney was annoyed at the constant complaints coming from families who hadn't received something that Clarissa was ultimately responsible for.

"Sydney, I have a million things going on. I will get to them in a few minutes," Clarissa clapped back, embarrassed to be caught not doing her job. It had been a struggle to get any of her work done at Williams for all the excitement she felt at conducting her first funeral.

Sydney looked at Clarissa, shook her head and rolled her eyes. There definitely was something going on with Miss Thang. Her bad attitude was getting worse every day.

Later, after everyone had left, Clarissa made her way into one of the conference rooms and stole a casket catalog and other materials she needed to finalize the arrangements the following day. She planned to leave early so she would be both physically and mentally prepared for the meeting. Tyriq had texted her that he had picked up the body of Mr. Evan LeBlanc and Coley had already started embalming him. Everything was falling in place.

When Clarissa arrived home, she was surprised to find Damien there. She could hear him and DJ playing a video game, laughing loudly. She smiled to herself. How perfect it would be if they could be this happy all the time. Unfortunately, her happy thoughts were short-lived. When she arrived in the family room, instead of a warm greeting, she received a barrage of complaints.

"Hey, Mom, what's for dinner?" asked DJ.

"Yeah, because I don't see anything in the fridge or in the freezer. When's the last time you went to the supermarket?" questioned Damien.

"And we're out of toilet paper and soap too," added DJ, still glued to the video game.

"Wow! What happened to 'Hi, Mom! How was your day?'" Clarissa was annoyed by their laundry list of grievances.

"Sorry, Mom," DJ, always the dutiful son, jumped up and kissed his mom on the cheek.

"Go finish your homework, son. I need to talk to your mom for a minute," said Damien. DJ left the room, knowing an argument between his parents was definitely brewing.

Clarissa sighed and sat down on the sofa, staring at her partner's handsomely chiseled features. His brown eyes were tinged with onyx and his usually sexy mouth was frowning. She knew his angry was about to bubble to the surface, but she had no idea just how mad he was.

"What the hell, Clarissa! The laundry isn't done; no food in the house. You're off your game. What gives?" he asked.

"I'm busy at work, checking on Aunt Hattie and Uncle Norm, and I could use some help. You and DJ don't lift a finger around here," she retorted, hating to have her back against the wall.

"Are you saying you're the only one busy at work? I'm embalming, working services, and seeing families. Besides, I pay all the bills in this house. I expect to at least have clean underwear and toilet paper!" he shouted angrily.

Now, it was Clarissa's turn to get to get loud. "Your legs aren't broken. You got time for the gym, and hanging out with your family, and anything else you want to do. Go get your own damn toilet paper!"

The two stared each other down angrily, neither willing to change their positions. When Damien finally spoke, his voice was steely and controlled. "I stay with you because you're a good mother and the sex is good but you ain't hitting for shit on either right now." He knew his words were hurtful, but he was angry and frustrated.

"Really?' said Clarissa incredulously. "Well, I'm giving as good as I get."

Damien stared at her and called upstairs to DJ. "C'mon, son; let's go crash Aunt Syd's dinner. I'm sure she has toilet paper." As they left, DJ looked torn between his parents.

KC drove to Syd's. She needed her cousin's sympathetic ear, but she wasn't answering her phone. Avery answered the door, surprised to see KC.

"Hey, Avery! How are you?" asked KC, as she walked into the Samuels' foyer. Sydney and Avery's place was a massive modern home with expansive windows and an open floor plan. Sydney had decorated the house herself in all neutral grays and creams and with beautiful dark hardwood floors. It was magazine ready but the kids' shoes, books, and electronic devices made it feel like a lived in home.

KC was surprised to see Damien and DJ there as well as Jamie and Morgan, all engaged in a midweek gaming marathon.

"I'm good. Looks like Wednesday night has turned into family night," he answered, laughing. Dinner dishes were still on the table and the kids were laughing and trying to out trash talk each other.

"Where's Sydney?" asked KC. She was eager to talk to her cousin.

"Mom's out in her she-shed," answered Morgan. "She goes out there to get away from us—she doesn't even take her phone."

As KC headed out to the patio, Avery stopped her. "Please don't mention we're in here playing Grand Theft Auto. Syd absolutely hates it and forbids the kids to play," he said sheepishly. KC looked at the 72-inch screen with their "character names" Killa A, Mayhem, Dame the Destroyer, Big Papa D, and Morgan Thee Stallion and laughed to herself. Obviously, they'd been playing for a while.

Sydney's luxury she-shed was nicer than most folks' apartments. Formerly, the family's home gym, Avery had it remodeled as a studio and get-away space so Sydney could paint in peace. Floor to ceiling windows, which allowed good light, comfy oversized sofa and chairs, tons of pillows, and super soft cashmere throws made the space super comfortable. One complete side of the building was dedicated to her art with canvas sets, paints, and several easels. The walls were covered with her art. Sydney was an accomplished artist and was thrilled to get back to her passion. The space even had a loft with a bedroom. Music poured out from the state-of-the-art sound system and the wine fridge was always full.

Sydney was surprised to see KC, but the look on her face spelled trouble; Syd poured her cousin a glass of wine, which she quickly gulped down and held out her glass for more.

"Whoa! Slow down, girl! You know you don't drink like that. What's wrong, Kay-Kay?" Sydney sat down next to KC and waited patiently.

"Tre got stopped by the police this afternoon. He and his friends had marijuana in the car, but the officer knew Troy and didn't arrest them. I had to pick him up from the station," said KC sadly.

"What? This kid is going from bad to worse. I'm going to tell Damien about this too. I already told Jamie I didn't want him riding with Tre, but Damien better tell DJ the same. So what did Troy do? Did he take the car from him?" Sydney hadn't been a perfect teenager either, but she had never had any run-ins with the law.

"Troy didn't do anything. He was more worried about how the police treated Tre than punishing him. Then, he started an argument when I voiced my opinion about punishment. Accused me of running to my family and telling you guys what a thug his son has become. Tre has told me twice that I'm not his mother and my opinion doesn't count. Well, his father confirmed that tonight." KC's voice had started to waver, and Sydney noticed the tears forming in her eyes. She quickly poured her another glass of wine.

"Let's face it, KC; he is a little thug. The goal is to make sure he doesn't become a big thug and end up in jail or worse. But you and Troy have to get on the same page. You have to show a united front, or kids will divide and conquer."

"Dang, Syd, you make it sound like we're at war," exclaimed KC. "I didn't sign up for this shit." KC was officially over her alcohol limit.

"Girl, it is a war and you've got to fight to win. Kids will kill you if let them," slurred Sydney as she opened another bottle of wine. The two cousins "talked" well into the night, eventually passing out on Sydney's sofa.

The following afternoon, Clarissa was at Guiding Light, ordering funeral supplies with her personal credit card. Clarissa had left work early, claiming she had to take her Aunt Hattie to the doctor. Luckily, it was a quiet day at Williams, especially since Sydney had come in late and KC hadn't come in at all.

Clarissa was there happily ordering morgue supplies from the local embalming supply house. Since the funeral home was newly established, she had to make all of her initial purchases via credit card. After ninety days of consistent orders, credit would be extended. As she went to the door to retrieve a UPS package, she was startled to see Travis Watkins standing behind the delivery person.

"Hey, girl! What you doing here? Do you know the new owners?" he inquired, definitely surprised to see Clarissa answering the door.

"What's going on, Travis? I'm just helping out a friend of Damien's who's renting this place. They needed someone to help them get things started till they get a full-time manager," she lied expertly.

"Good deal! I was just coming to introduce myself and see if they had someone doing their removals and livery," Travis inquired, always the salesman.

"No, nobody as of yet. They are doing some of the stuff in-house, but they don't have cars," she answered cautiously.

"Well hook a brotha up! Let me get at the owner so we can talk. I know we can beat the price of any local company. What's dude's info?" Travis was eager to bring in a new account on his own.

"Look, I'll do you a solid. You want the account, it's yours." She hoped that this would satisfy him.

"Good deal. Wow boo, you got pull like that? Who is this cat? I might know him; me and Damien have a lot of folks in common from the old days," explained Travis, referring to Damien's checkered past.

"Naw, you don't know him; he's from South Carolina and looking to open up a place in Georgia. We're just helping him out. I even got a couple of folks from Williams moonlighting over here, so don't be surprised if you see some familiar faces. We all are just trying to make this paper." Clarissa wanted to cover all of her bases and knew this would temporarily satisfy his curious nature.

"No doubt. This is business. What about y'all peeps at Williams'? I know they can't be happy about a new spot trying to take their cheddar," mused Travis.

Clarissa was amazed that Travis was even thinking about the ramifications of Leona and company finding out about Guiding Light.

"This won't even make a dent in their business; they'll be fine. But for that reason, I was hoping that you'd keep our involvement to yourself. I don't want Troy running to tell his wife. Hell! Damien might go into partnership with this guy. We got to take care of our family first; you know what

I mean?" Clarissa needed Travis to be discreet. She hoped he could for all of their sakes.

"No worries; I got you. Folks in this town start trippin' if they think you coming for theirs. I'll handle this account personally. Let's get this money. The Williams' ain't the only ones trying to secure the bag." Travis really wasn't a fan of women and business, but he always appreciated Clarissa's ability to keep it real and watch Damien's back. He sometimes thought his brother should have picked a woman more like Clarissa than KC. His brother wouldn't be going through all these problems if he picked a down chick like Rissa.

After days of preparation, Guiding Light's first funeral was about to take place. Clarissa was a bundle of nerves and couldn't sleep for days before. She left her house at 6.00 am on the day of the service, wanting to be the first at the funeral home. Everything had fallen into place perfectly during the week leading up to the service. Coley turned out to be a great embalmer, having had Damien as a teacher. The body of Mr. Larson was perfection and the family had been well pleased. The service was being held at a small church in neighboring Kennerville with interment in Carlington Memorial Park. The icing on the cake was the jazz ensemble she had hired to provide music at the cemetery. The band would provide a front line of sorts to lead the body from the hearse to the graveside, a nod to the family's Louisiana roots.

Everything went off without a hitch, the moment of truth being the burial. As the first notes of "Walk Thru the Streets of the City," a traditional front-line song, was played, the look of astonishment on the attendees' faces was priceless. The family was shocked but began to smile at the familiar tune. Some began to sway and wave their tissues in the air. The atmosphere shifted from somber to joyous and one could close their eyes and literally be transported to the Big Easy. After the service concluded, the family was full of praise for Clarissa and her staff. Clarissa was basking in the glow of the compliments and even saw family members posting on social media. Tyriq's little brother was paid to video the entire burial and post it to their social media accounts, making sure that didn't include any facial shots of the family or staff. Williams didn't bother much with social media, but Clarissa knew this was part of the new face of funeral service. As she sat in car after the procession had gone, she felt a new kind of high, the euphoric feeling of success.

CHAPTER 9

Quiet as It's Kept

"**SANDERS COLLINS, IS** that you?" exclaimed Sydney happily. She was in the reception area when she saw her childhood friend sitting in the waiting area. Truthfully, she barely recognized him; he had aged so much. His black hair was peppered with gray, his face thin and haggard. The only thing that remained from his youth was his striking green eyes. Sanders clothes hung loosely on his thin frame and his eyes were sad and dull. Sydney wondered if he was ill and had come to make pre-arrangements.

"Hey, Syd; it's good to see you," he answered, but there was no joy in his greeting. "I just stopped by to pick up my mom's …." He trailed off, unable to say the word remains. Sanders Collins' mother Olivia had died almost three years ago, but he couldn't bring himself to retrieve her cremated remains and bring them home. Many folks who chose the ease of crema-tion found themselves unable or unwillingly to come and pick the remains of their loved ones. Williams had a room in the basement area that housed said remains until the family came to claim them. Occasionally that never happened, and the room held cremated remains that dated back to Jimmy William's era.

Sydney remembered several times when Sanders made appointments to pick up his mother, but never showed. She noticed his hands were shaking and he seemed distraught. Sensing the immense sadness in her friend, Sydney asked him to go have coffee with her. At first, he declined, but she persuaded him and as the two sat by the window at the local Starbucks, he began to pour out his tale of woe.

Sanders' life had not been easy over the past few years. He and his wife of ten years had gotten a divorce and as a result of the break-up he was forced to downsize. He moved in with his mother when she became ill and took full responsibility for her care. The impact of the divorce as well as his mother's chronic illness began to take a toll on him. He was able to function at work and no one truly knew what he was going through but there was sadness over him.

Sydney suggested that maybe he should try grief counseling. She shared with him how heart-broken she'd been when her father suddenly passed away from a heart attack.

"I felt like my whole world collapsed. Then, Terrance and I broke up. It was really rough for a while. I wish I'd gone to a therapist," she lamented, hoping that she could encourage her friend.

"But you had the rest of your family, your children, to help you through. All I had was my mom and she's gone. The loneliness is like a cancer; it just eats away at me sometimes." Sanders put his head down and Sydney knew he was crying.

"You have friends. I'm your friend. Please call me anytime if you need to talk." Sydney placed her hand on his to offer comfort. When Sanders looked up, Sydney was surprised to see that the tears had dried, but his green eyes looked dead. There was no life, no happiness, no joy—only sorrow and pain. Sanders thanked her for the coffee and the talk and slipped out of the coffee house.

Without a support system, Sanders' downward spiral began to accelerate. Not three weeks later, news of his apparent suicide began to circulate around town. Sydney was devastated and wondered what more she could have done. His instructions were implicit that he wanted no service or memorial but to be cremated and scattered along with his mother via a cremation society. Sydney was confused about her friend's wishes but realized no one really knew what he or anybody else really goes through behind closed doors.

Leona and Sydney were sitting in her office, discussing the upcoming week's services, when Leona got a call on her cell phone. Sydney figured it was Deacon Richard, but quickly heard her mother expressing her condolences to the caller. *Must be a death call,* she thought and waited for her mother to start writing info down on her pad. But all Leona wrote down was the date and place of the service.

"Who was that, Mama? Who died?" she asked after her mother had ended the call.

"My uncle, Meme's brother, Edward, passed away. We called him Buddy. He and his wife lived in South Carolina. You never met him," Leona explained.

Meme was French for grandmother and what Sydney had called Leona's mother. She had called her grandfather Pepe.

"Dang! He must have been pretty old. Meme's been gone for years." Sydney only saw her maternal grandparents on holidays due to the fact that they had never really cared for her father, Jimmy.

"He was Meme's much younger brother. We weren't close." Leona seemed as if she wanted to change the subject, but Sydney was always curious about the family she barely knew.

"We should go to the service, Mama. Where is it anyway?" asked Sydney, down for a road trip.

"It's in Sumpter, South Carolina, where he lived. I may go, but there's no need for you to leave your family to go to a funeral for a man you've never met."

"This is my family too, Mama. I don't want you traveling alone! Besides, I want to meet my cousins. I know all of Dad's folks, but hardly anybody on the Harris side. You're always saying Harris women don't do this and Harris women don't do that—I'd like to see for myself." Sydney was determined not to miss this funeral. As a funeral director, she knew funerals turned into mini family reunions. She was eager to meet her people.

"Well, technically my mama's people were Beaumonts. The Harris' were Pepe's people. I was closer to them."

Sydney was unmoved by the distinction. "Doesn't matter to me; I want to meet them."

Leona knew that it would probably be easier to say yes than to argue for a week about why Sydney couldn't go. Her daughter was so persuasive when it came to getting her way that she thought she might have missed her calling as a lawyer.

"Okay, Sydney Michelle; you win. I'll make the reservations," said Leona, resigned to the trip.

As Sydney and Leona settled into their first-class seats on the plane, Sydney looked over at her mother. She realized that all though they had plenty of time together via work, Sunday dinners and going to the kid's activities, this one-on-one time was very much needed.

"Mama, it was like pulling teeth getting you to allow me to go with you on this trip. But I'm so glad I'm here with you, although for a sad occasion. I'm looking forward to getting to know your side of the family. We always got together with the Williams side, but rarely got to experience yours."

Leona smiled at her daughter, but a grimace was right under the surface as she remembered why she kept her child separated from her people.

It was the early spring of 1965 and Leona, who had just turned eighteen, was preparing for her big celebration. Her mother Elise was one of twelve children of the Beaumont clan who were a rowdy group of partyers, a far cry from Leona's fathers' side, the more refined Harris family. Leona loved their family gatherings for birthdays as they were always full of food, fun, and dancing. She couldn't wait for her turn, much to her mother's chagrin.

She loved her family but wanted her daughter to be a lady and told her as much.

"Mama, I'll be a perfect lady when I get to Spelman. Tonight, I just want to have fun and dance." Leona had been accepted to the prestigious all female Spelman College in Atlanta, in the tradition of the Harris women.

While so many of her cousins on the Beaumont side either joined the military or married and raised families, Leona was different with future plans of attending Meharry for dental school and eventually joining her father's dental practice. But this night, all thoughts of school and futures were replaced with the sultry sounds of soul music and the taste of sweet wine.

After the large family celebration at her grandparent's home, the young cousins crammed into several automobiles and were on their way to Junior's Hideaway. Junior's was a local club and juke joint out in the sticks where the latest music played on the jukebox and there was often a live band on the weekends. Junior's was packed and Leona and her cousins made their way through the throng to the bar where they ordered shots of Junior's special corn liquor. Leona hated the taste of the clear liquid and the way it burned her throat, but after two glasses she was feeling the warm glow of its after affects. They danced the night away, with Leona garnering the attention of several young men. Her uncle Buddy sat at the bar watching the young people dance and flirt, admiring the beautiful young women, especially his niece Leona. It was funny to even think of himself as an uncle, as he was only five years her senior.

As the last sober cousin inquired about getting Leona home, Buddy replied that he would take her. At last call, Buddy made his way to the dance floor to gather his niece, who had had far too many drinks. Buddy, feeling no pain himself, had to just about pick her up to get her out of the club and into the car. He could smell her warm breath on his neck as he placed her in back seat of the car, her dress opened just enough to expose her upper thigh covered by her lacy garter. As he checked on her still form through the rearview mirror, he began to have other dark thoughts. Buddy drove down the dark country road until he found a secluded spot to stop. He quietly slipped into the back seat next to Leona with the intention to kiss her berry-stained lips. When she didn't respond to his touch, he became more aroused and began to remove her panties. As he fumbled with his belt and trousers, a voice in his head screamed how wrong this was, but the lust in his heart took hold. Buddy was sure she was a virgin because as he entered her, Leona's eyes flew open in confusion and pain. He placed his hand over her mouth and continued to thrust, unable to stop. Tears ran down her eyes, but she remained motionless, too terrified and confused to cry out. Buddy thrust himself inside her once more and shuddered in ecstasy and shame. He quickly got up, fixed his clothing with his back to Leona. When he turned around, she appeared to have mercifully passed out again. He hastily pulled down her dress and got back into the driver's seat to begin the journey home.

Leona grabbed the side of the toilet for the third time on the morning of her high school graduation. She was perplexed by her continuing sickness and lack of energy. She figured that all the graduation festivities and college preparation had worn her out. Elise Harris saw her child limp on the floor and began to put two and two together. Since her birthday she hadn't seemed like herself and was particularly quiet. She wondered if one of Leona's suitors had persuaded her to have sex and the result was this crumpled young woman who rarely smiled or joined her parents for meals. This morning was the last straw and she knew she had to confront her daughter. Upon a thorough cross examination and visit to the doctor's office, Elise was devastated about this unplanned pregnancy and the fact that Leona refused to say who the boy was. Elise was determined not to let this derail her daughter's future plans. She and her sister Sarah devised a plan to keep the pregnancy under wraps. Sarah, a school-teacher, in Danville, VA was thirty-three years old, a former freedom fighter whose fiancé was killed by the Ku Klux Klan. She stayed in Danville to be closer to his grave and his memory and had never married. Elise asked her to let Leona live with her in Virginia until the birth, telling everyone in town that she was going to NY to be with her father's side of the family.

Leona and Sarah's time together turned out to be turning point in shaping Leona's personality and life. Sarah was culturally aware and shared many insights and anecdotes with the impressionable young woman. It was during this bonding time that Sarah was able to coax Leona into recounting the night of her eighteenth birthday and the rape. She was unable to provide many of the details, but Sarah heard enough to know that her brother raped her niece and was the father of her baby. Sarah gave her niece the life changing advice asking her the all-important question. "Will you consume this pain, or will it consume you?" she asked her niece thoughtfully.

Sarah returned to Georgia alone to share the information with her sister. The two women confronted Buddy and his wife Bessie in their run-down apartment. Sarah became so agitated that she pulled out her gun on Buddy and forced him to finally confess to raping Leona, which disgusted his wife. She and Elise informed the couple that they would adopt the baby and raise it as their own telling everyone in the family about their future plans to adopt. Elise looked around at the dingy surroundings and knew that she would never let her seed live in such squalor. She arranged for Buddy and Bessie to move to a better home and provided the unemployed Bessie with a job as a receptionist in her husband's dental office. The two sisters vowed to keep a close eye on him and on the baby, making sure it had the best chance for a decent life and was not marred by its conception.

While her departure had been confusing and painful, Leona knew that leaving Roswell when she did was definitely for the best. She attended Spelman and met her Jimmy during the last year of her schooling. She made a life with him and never looked back. She realized those early years made her who she was, but she was glad she had little to no contact with these people.

Buddy and Bessie had relocated to Sumter, South Carolina, to be closer to Bessie's family. Buddy had modest success with a hardware store in the town and they had made a life. Bessie took ill first, ultimately dying from a massive heart attack. Buddy, a lifelong alcoholic, sold his business and slowly drank his self to death. Their dutiful daughter Vanessa looked after both, taking care of them until their deaths.

As Leona and Syd pulled up to the country chapel, Sydney was shocked by the simple country church. She always thought her mother's side was classy and cultured.

"Ooh, Mama! This is real simple. Do they even have air conditioning? I see everyone fanning, and the windows are open." The country church was very modest and small. The immediate family only filled two rows. The other pews were scattered with distant family members and a few townspeople.

The service was very quick and dry with no one giving remarks and very few tears.

The repass, however, proved to be a little livelier, with a few of Leona's cousins greeting her and introductions being made. Leona excused herself to go speak to her Aunt Sarah seated quietly in the corner by herself.

"Auntie, it's good to see you," said Leona quietly, giving the frail old woman a gentle hug.

"Well, actually it's been too long, Leona," said Sarah with a smile. "It must be bitter-sweet coming here for his funeral," she added. Leona had heard that her aunt had moved back to Georgia and was living with a cousin in Alpharetta.

"No, just final. I waited for this day for a long time. I needed the closure that could only come with seeing him in that casket."

"Well, it looks as if I taught you well; you look exceptional. I've seen you in the society pages at different charity events. You've become a powerful and respected woman." The words were a high compliment coming from her aunt.

"Thank you, Auntie. You and Mama taught me everything I know." Leona smiled at the memory of her mother. Though they hadn't seen each other much before her death, Leona was right by Elise's side during the end.

"You know we now have only one order of business left to tend to," Sarah pointed her arthritic finger at the two women across the room. Leona saw her daughter Sydney speaking to another striking woman who reminded Leona of a younger version of herself.

"Who is that my daughter is talking to?" she asked, but already knowing in her heart the answer.

"That, my dear, is her sister. That's Vanessa, your other daughter." Sarah let her words sink in as Leona, stared, mesmerized by the woman. Mother and daughter were about the same height and size. Vanessa's hair was salt and pepper grey and fashioned in grey corkscrew curls that both she and Sydney spent hours getting pressed out of their own hair. She had a light brown complexion, unlined and bright and she looked to be about thirty-five, but Leona knew her to be in her mid-fifties.

Vanessa marveled at how smoothly the funeral had gone. While she had the help of some of her family, burying her father brought up mixed emotions for her. Growing up, her father had been distant and moody. She had often sought his affection without much luck. Her mother was no better and she seemed to avoid her at all cost. Needless to say, Vanessa could have been a bitter child, but she found great love from her aunties Sarah and Elise. They seemed to overcompensate for her parent's lack. They came to all her big events and supported her throughout her life. Even when Vanessa found out that she was adopted, her Aunt Sarah was there to counsel and support her.

As she became an adult, she learned to rely on her quiet introspective nature and found she gravitated toward holistic therapies. Vanessa discovered her calling and became a mind body spirit practitioner as well as a licensed psychologist. She had always had an interest in yoga and nutrition, and this led her to creating pop-up wellness experiences in underserved areas. She wanted her people to experience wellness. She moved to Charleston where she and a business partner opened up a wellness center with a concentration on people of color. She had hoped to extend out to the Atlanta and Washington DC areas.

Syd was in awe of her beauty and skin as Vanessa was a woman who didn't need any makeup. Vanessa was equally fascinated by Sydney, her bubbly and over-the-top personality, making jokes and running commentary on her newly found relations and talking non-stop about her husband and kids. She was a bright spot for Vanessa. Leona observed the two from afar, gloomily about the work that needed to be done.

Leona slipped into the midst of the two women. Vanessa greeted her warmly with a hug. They hadn't seen each other in almost thirty years, since Leona's mother passed away. The conversation was light as Leona showed pictures of her grandchildren and gave updates on all of them. Sydney and Vanessa were delighted to find out that they were all staying at the Hyatt Downtown Sumter and planned to meet for drinks and dinner later on that evening

A distracted Avery was having a quick lunch in Buckhead before seeing a prospective client. With his nose buried deep in the client's prospectus, he barely noticed the couple two tables away engaging in PDA until he heard a distinctive laugh. He immediately recognized the melodic laughter of his oldest daughter. When she was younger, he would tell her tons of corny jokes to hear her distinctive cackle—when Chloe laughed, the whole world literally laughed with her.

Avery looked around and saw that was indeed Chloe, but he was confused. His daughter was holding hands and kissing a young woman. Her partner was striking with a short natural box haircut with a pink streak on the side. She wore no makeup but was attractive in a natural way. Clad in crop top that showed off her six pack abs, a short leather skirt and black combat boots, her look commanded attention. Avery quickly tried to gather his things and leave the table before the couple spotted him but knocked over his water glass, which broke on the floor. Chloe and Blaze both turned toward the commotion and spotted Avery. The look in both of their eyes was one of shame, confusion, and fear. Chloe was scared but got up and approached the table as Avery and the waitress tried to clean up the mess.

"Hey, Dad! Are you okay?" Chloe asked tentatively. He had spilled water all over his papers and his suit.

"Hey, sweetie. I'm ok. Just really clumsy," he joked. Chloe and Avery shared an awkward silence.

"Dad, this is Blaze. Blaze, this is my dad, Avery Samuels." The two said hello and shook hands. Avery was surprised how soft and feminine Blaze's voice was. Blaze was pissed that Chloe introduced her with no title. The trio stood staring at one another, no one able to break the ice.

"Is Mom spending the night in South Carolina? She said she was going to a funeral for Mom-Mom's uncle," Chloe stated for lack of anything else to say.

"Uh, yes! She's spending the night. She'll be home in the morning. Just me and the twins tonight. I better get going. I have to meet a client and I definitely need my suit to dry," he laughed. They said their goodbyes and a troubled Avery paid his check and hurriedly left for his meeting.

When he arrived home that evening, Avery spotted Chloe's white Jeep Wrangler in the driveway. He was greeted by the twins who happily pronounced that their big sister was there and that they had ordered pizza. Avery, Chloe, and the twins ate dinner together. Afterward he sent them to finish their homework so that he and Chloe could have "the conversation."

"Dad, I didn't want you to find out like this," Chloe started, with tears in her eyes. "I wanted to tell you and Mom together, but it never seemed like the right time."

"I wish you would have felt comfortable enough to just tell us. We love you and who you love will never change that." Avery was close to tears himself as he grabbed his daughter and held her tight.

Chloe told Avery the whole story of how she and Blaze met when Chloe was buying art supplies as a present for her mom. She explained that Blaze was a student at The Art Institute of Atlanta and worked part-time in a downtown art supply store. Chloe said that she was never attracted to women, but there was something about Blaze and the relationship blossomed. They soon began dating in earnest and were now a couple.

"How long have you two been together?" Avery asked, interested in every facet of her relationship.

"It's been almost six months. I'm just scared that Mom will be mad when she finds out," Chloe said, worriedly. Her dad was always supportive and easy going but she wasn't sure that her mother would be as understanding. "Mom really cares how things look and this won't play well in The Circle."

Avery defended his wife. "I know how she can be, but she loves you and your sisters and brother more than anything in this world; all she wants is your happiness. If Blaze makes you happy, then it makes us happy. But you do owe it to her to tell her the truth." Chloe shook her head glumly and suggested that maybe Avery could tell her. Avery looked at his daughter but shook his head no.

"You have to tell her, Chloe."

Vanessa and Sydney were happily seated in the hotel bar swapping stories about each other's lives. Sydney shared with Vanessa all about her first husband and what a scoundrel he was and how he still found ways to get under her skin. Vanessa instructed Syd to put her energy in the positive parts of their relationship—their two girls. Getting in a more positive space with Terrance would help make their relationship easier to maintain. She also told her about her brother and the closeness they now shared and her close relationship with KC. Vanessa shared about her business and how much she enjoyed it. Leona heard them laughing as she approached the table and thought about how nice it would have been if they had known each other earlier. Sydney was constantly being robbed of her sibling experiences by her parents' drama.

Leona joined the ladies and they continued their catch-up session, with Sydney talking about her mother's new romance. They were interrupted by Sydney's phone ringing, and of course, it was Avery. She excused herself as she smiled from ear to ear.

"She won't be back for hours," Leona remarked dryly. "The Samuels have separation anxiety when they are apart for more than four hours."

Vanessa laughed at Leona's commentary. "That sounds quite sweet. I noticed when Sydney talks about her husband, she lights up like a Christmas tree. I don't always come across women who are still that in love after four kids and fifteen years of marriage."

"Avery is a good man," Leona conceded. "He's an exemplary husband and father, both to his children and her girls from her first marriage. I couldn't have picked any better for my daughter, except that I would have made him a little younger. Lord knows I don't want my baby to have to go through the pain of widowhood." She had never expressed to anyone that she worried that Avery might pass away and leave Sydney the way Jimmy had left her.

Vanessa sagely offered that his age was probably what made him a better mate. "As we get older, we grow more aware of what really is important in life, leaving little room for nonsense. Sydney says he's an exercise junkie and health nut. He may be here far longer than we think. But even fifteen years of a great marriage is better than the lifetime of heartache she would have had with her first husband." Leona and Vanessa both sipped their wine thoughtfully. "Besides," Vanessa continued "I know you only want what's best for your daughter, no matter how it comes."

Sydney was lying across her bed as she recounted the day's events with Avery on FaceTime. She was so excited to share with him about meeting Vanessa and how well they hit it off.

"She's, like, so grounded and she gives great advice. I can't wait until you meet her! You're going to love her, babe. She's like no other member of our family. She's into fitness and wellness just like you!"

Avery was listening to Syd's every word, but he was still stuck on Chloe and his encounter with her and Blaze. He wanted to tell Syd, but he knew it wasn't his story to tell. Syd and Avery's marriage was based on truth and openness. An early lack of disclosure almost cost them their relationship, and both were committed to keeping the lines of communication open and honest.

"I'm glad you had a good day and I can't wait to meet your cousin. She sounds awesome. Maybe she'll get you into yoga," he said distractedly.

"You only want me to start yoga so you can bend me like pretzel when we make love," she giggled. Usually, Avery would have a snappy sexy comeback, but he seemed like he had something on his mind.

"Okay, what's up? Did something happen at work? Are the kids okay?" She was instantly concerned.

Avery snapped out of his haze. "I just miss you; that's all. The house is not the same when you're not home." He then distracted her with talk of what he was going to do to her when she got home, and before they knew it, their conversation took a whole different turn.

Vanessa suggested they move out by the pool. She loved the night sky and the sound of the bar's sports station was ruining her Zen. As both women reclined on the pool lounge chairs, Leona thought that the time was right for her to start her tale. She began by asking Vanessa how much she knew about her. Vanessa recalled looking at photographs at her Aunt Elise's home and wishing that they could be closer, but it seemed like Leona rarely came home to visit.

"Before I knew it, my family had moved to South Carolina and I rarely saw any of the Beaumont's," Vanessa stated. "I missed Aunt Elise and Aunt Sarah so much, but my mother was happier with her family and my father never wanted to go back to Georgia."

Leona took a deep breath and stated, "There was a reason I didn't come around." She then began to recall the night of her eighteenth birthday and what happened, leaving out exactly who raped her. She told Vanessa about living with Sarah and having her baby in Virginia. Vanessa instinctively knew the child she spoke of was not Sydney. Finally, Leona talked about going to Spelman, meeting Jimmy and starting her life in Maxwell.

Vanessa had tears in her eyes at the pain the older woman endured. "What happened to the baby?" asked Vanessa quietly.

Leona looked pointedly at her. "Buddy and Bessie adopted you and raised you as their own," she answered.

Vanessa was quiet, her tears now following freely. "You're my mother? I knew I was adopted, and I had planned to try and find my birth parents, but it never seemed like the right time. I never dreamed that my birth mother was a relative. Do you mind if I ask who my father is?"

Leona held her breath—this was the hard part. "Edward Beaumont."

Vanessa's face registered surprise, and then horror. "Your own uncle raped you? How could he do something so low? Why didn't the family go to the police?" She was horrified that the man who had raised her, her biological father, was a rapist. She wondered if her mother knew, and if that was the reason she was so distant and cold to her throughout her childhood.

Leona tried to explain the family dynamics the best she could. It was at that point that Leona realized that Vanessa had grabbed her hand when she'd first started talking and had never let go.

"That was another time back then and families dealt with their own drama privately. My mother and father hated what Buddy did to me, but they would never involve the police or disgrace our family. I just wanted to get as far away from him and the Beaumont family as I could. Everyone staring at me, whispering behind my back. A few of the cousins even saying that I seduced Buddy that night. It was too much." Leona closed her eyes and shuddered as all of the painful memories came flooding back.

The two women sat in the darkness lost in their own thoughts.

Finally, Vanessa spoke. "So, this means Sydney is my sister? I felt a bond with her but didn't know why."

"Yes, she's your sister but we need some time before we share this with her. She's had to deal with a lot regarding her parents and long-lost siblings." Leona wasn't quite ready to drop this bomb on her daughter. She's wasn't sure how Sydney would take this revelation or exactly where Vanessa would fit in their lives.

"I agree, but exactly where does this leave me?" said Vanessa, bitterly. "This is a lot to process but we need to tell her because this affects her too. Our family's secrets have changed the course of all of our lives. I missed out on a whole lifetime of having a relationship with my mother and sister. I would love to come and spend time with you meet the rest of my family. My mother's people are a miserable group with few familial ties or even members left. I'm excited to have family. Children, holidays, happy times—there wasn't much of that here." Vanessa seemed flustered as she continually ran her hands through her mixed gray curls.

Leona looked at her regretfully, "I'm truly sorry. I had hoped they would have done better by you. It was not my intention to let so much time pass before telling you the truth, but I couldn't face seeing Buddy."

"I understand, given the circumstances. My parents did the best that they could. They were two broken souls, tied together by shame, dysfunction, and misery," Vanessa replied sadly. "My journey has unfolded exactly the way it was supposed to. We can only move forward. Regrets are bad for the soul."

CHAPTER 10

Calm Before the Storm

THE CARTER FAMILY sat in Clarissa's office attempting to make funeral arrangements for their son, Jahieem. Jahieem was killed after a deadly brawl with his brother Jahmir. The mood was tense as the grieving family tried to make sense of the tragic situation. The two brothers had been close until a recent disagreement over a girlfriend named Brittany. Brittany had dated one brother in high school and years later decided to date the other one. Forever rivals, the two took to the streets and fought it out. Jahmir, the smaller of the two brothers pulled out a gun when it appeared that his brother was getting the best of him during their altercation and shot his sibling to death.

With one in brother in jail for murder and the other in the morgue, tensions were definitely running high in the Carter family. There were lots of accusations and rumors made about who was truly at fault. However, Brittany considered herself blameless. It was rumored around Maxwell that she was proud that her man had fought to the death for her.

The family, half of which was Muslim, wished for an Islamic burial, which according to Sharia or Islamic law, required that there be no embalming but instead a ritual body washing and wrapping ceremony done by the male members of the deceased family, if possible. A funeral prayer known as the Salat al-Janazah would follow and then the body would be buried lying on its right side in the grave without a casket. This whole process was to be done as quickly as possible.

The deceased's mother, who was not Muslim, wanted at least a viewing for her son. "I've lost both of my sons. I need to at least be able to see my baby one more time. This is a nightmare," she sobbed, inconsolably.

The difficult case was referred to Guiding Light by Tyriq's Iman, who was the head of his mosque. Clarissa was reluctant but she let Tyriq take the lead on this particular service because she knew very little about Islamic burials and because Tyriq had also explained that some of the brothers from the mosque would not feel comfortable talking to her because she was female. She did, however, sit in on the arrangements, making sure everything went smoothly. Clarissa was proud of how Tyriq handled himself and looked forward to getting more cases from the mosque.

The turn-around time on the service was certainly shorter than traditional Christian services and fees was much less than Clarissa was used to charging, but there seemed to be more working parts. The washing and shrouding team had to be assembled and she had to purchase a shrouding kit, which consisted of the sheets needed to wrap the deceased. The cloth was cut and measured to the exact sizes dictated by Islamic law. Jahieem's mother wanted her son in some type of casket, so Clarissa quickly researched Muslim customs and found out it would be permissible for Jahieem be placed in a wooden box with no top. The things needed for an Islamic burial were in short supply in the Bible Belt South, but Clarissa managed to get everything she needed in two short days. The viewing was to be held at the funeral home and the Janazah prayer would be held in Guiding Light's parking lot.

On the day of the viewing, Tyriq was in his black suit, directing the washing and shrouding and handling all aspects of the service. Everything seemed to be going well, when Brittany, against the advice of family, had the audacity to show up at the ceremony, complete with her entourage in embellished t-shirts with Jahmir and Jahieem's pictures with angel's wings attached to Jahieem's image. As she approached the body to view, the boys' sister Jaheerah exploded after a week of silently grieving. She literally jumped across the seats of the funeral home, her black hijab and garb making her look like she was flying and proceeded to attack Brittany in the aisle. A complete melee ensued, with chairs crashing and the deceased mother screaming, "Beat her ass," over and over. It took Tyriq and several of the brothers to break them apart and restore order. A funeral attendee managed to catch the brawl on video and posted it to social media. Tyriq was apologetic and concerned about the negative exposure, but Clarissa was delighted. *Everyone in town will know our name now,* she thought. *Good or bad, publicity was publicity.* She wasn't happy with the fight and chaos, but she felt they could expand on doing different types of religions and ethnic groups.

Tyriq was grateful for the chance to prove himself in front of his religious community. He had converted to Islam while serving time in jail for a juvenile offense and had become quite devout, helping with the washings and janazahs at the mosque. Tyriq's uncle had gotten Leona to give the young man a job at Williams Mortuary after he was released. Though grateful for the opportunity, he didn't want to clean up cars and do maintenance for the rest of his life. Clarissa had given him a chance and he was determined to prove to the rest of his family that he was reformed.

Clarissa couldn't believe how much the business had picked up since the jazz funeral. She had received two cases from the church where Mr. Larson's funeral was held, one a full funeral with the jazz band, and the other a direct cremation. She was excited about their business growth, but it did come with problems. Clarissa had to confront her young staff only days later about business cards that they had taken it upon themselves to get printed complete with head shots. Tyriq's read Director of Islamic Services, while Coley's read Embalming Manager. The ladies had themselves each as Directress. Thankfully, no card had been made for her. They insisted that they just wanted to pass them out to family and friends. Clarissa had covered all her bases but hadn't planned for her staff feeling themselves. Passing out business cards with made up titles for jobs that didn't exist was as illegal as it was unethical. There was no such position as embalming manager and most clients would be led to believe that Coley was a licensed embalmer.

Things were looking up for her except in her relationship with Damien. He had permanently moved into the guest room and the two mainly connected through texts and voicemails. She, at one point, had thought about the prospect of having another child—maybe a baby would draw them closer, but they weren't even speaking let alone making love.

She was also struggling with keeping her job at Williams. This was crucial for getting cases for Guiding Light and making sure the Williams Clan didn't find out about her ownership. A few days after the Larson service, she overheard Dorinda talking about the jazz service with another

Williams' employee. It was stressful watching them every minute of the day, like children.

Avery and Troy met at Avery's Atlanta office to finalize the sale of the Harleigh Crematory to Watkins Bros LLC. The historic cemetery was selling their state-of-the-art crematory due to the owners advancing age. They chose to retain ownership in the cemetery. Avery had learned of the sale via his wife and had casually mentioned it to Troy as he knew he was trying to diversify his business holdings. The sale resulted in a big boon for Watkins. Troy purposely hadn't mentioned the sale to KC. He didn't want her questioning his decision. Her conservative attitude towards business stifled potential growth.

"Bro, I gotta tell you; you really looked out on this sale. This is huge for us. I finally feel like Watkins Enterprises is moving up." Troy and Travis recently added enterprise to their business name to incorporate the various new venues they had embarked on.

"No worries; we are family and it's our duty to look out for each other. How did KC feel about it?" asked Avery.

"Well, how about I didn't tell her yet. Things have been a little tense at home lately. I'm hoping it will get better. We really haven't had a chance to talk about anything other than the house and the kids."

"Man, I totally understand, but you've got to touch base with her on these major decisions. This deal is going to put you in a whole different tax bracket." Avery was concerned that Troy hadn't shared something so large with his wife. He knew about the Watkins' marital troubles from pillow talk with Syd. Avery knew far too well how the lack of disclosure could affect a relationship.

"You're right. It's just been really difficult these past few months. KC is perfect with Tianna, but she and Tre are oil and water. I'm going to tell her soon. But do me a favor; please don't tell Syd. I want to be the first to tell my wife."

Avery nodded in agreement. "No problem. Sydney and I keep business out of our marriage. It was something we learned early on."

KC was twirling around excitedly in her chair like a five-year-old. After months of patiently waiting, her appointment had finally come through. She was officially a member of the Georgia State Board of Funeral Directors. She would now be a professional member of the board where funeral laws were made, and funeral directors disciplined. She couldn't keep the good news to herself and ran to tell Sydney who was instructing Clarissa to alter this week's staffing.

"What! KC that's' so freaking awesome! I'm so proud of you. No one deserves this position more than you. We need women of color on that board. Finally, the board will look more like the people it serves." Sydney was hyped for her cousin's appointment.

Clarissa, however, was instantly paranoid. She knew how upset Leona and the girls would become at the mere mention of the state board. She was doubly afraid that KC would learn her secret and confront Damien about his role at Guiding Light. Clarissa knew she had to make a move soon before everything blew up in her face.

Sydney wanted to share with everyone the news of KC's appointment. "We have to put out a statement to Georgia Select and *The Maxwell Gazette*. Maybe even a press release. I think we should host a reception in your honor."

"Slow down, Syd. That's not necessary. Let's keep this to ourselves," KC said and looked pointedly at Clarissa. "I want to wait for the official announcement from the Governor's office."

Sydney agreed but didn't feel that referred to family. "Girl, y'all doing big things in the Watkins household. You're on the state board. Troy bought Harleigh's crematory. I want to be y'all when I grow up."

KC's surprise was evident. "Excuse me? What the heck are you talking about, Syd?"

Sydney explained that while in her husband's office looking for her American Express bill—he didn't know about the Kelley bag she bought from Hermes—she saw the deed and paperwork. The sale had taken place a few days earlier according to the information she had read.

"Troy didn't tell you? Oops. I guess I spoiled that surprise. I just hope we get that family discount when we bring bodies. Harleigh is literally the only game in town. Watkins has essentially cornered the market on cremations. I feel a trip to Hermes in your future," laughed Sydney.

KC didn't want to show her true emotions in front of Clarissa, but she was anything but excited about Troy's latest acquisition. It felt like every major decision in their marriage was sprung on her without her input or consideration for her feelings.

Clarissa was dumbfounded. Troy's purchase of Harleigh Crematory hit extremely close to home. Harleigh was where Guiding Light took their cremations. She was afraid she couldn't do that now that Troy would be running the place. Both Troy and KC's new positions could jeopardize Clarissa's whole operation.

Sydney was staying late at the funeral home that evening when her brother poked his head in her office.

"Hey, Syd! What are you doing here so late?" Damien was stunned that she was still in the office. Sydney took quitting time seriously and was usually out the door at six o'clock sharp.

"Avery has a late meeting tonight and the twins are at Mama's. I needed to catch up on some paperwork. Did you hear about KC's appointment to the Georgia State Board?" She was sure that KC wouldn't mind if she told Damien.

"Wow! That's incredible. Now we won't have to worry if we get written up for a violation," he quipped.

"Whatever, D! I think we should throw her a party or something. What do you think?"

"Sounds good to me, but you know how low-key Kay is. Better ask her first." Damien knew his cousin didn't like anyone making a fuss over her.

"Fine, I will ask her or get Mama to help me!" Syd was always willing to create plan B. "What about you? Shouldn't you be home with your boo? I think the kids say Netflix and chilling?"

"Naw, that's definitely not going down in our house. Me and Rissa have been on the outs for a minute. I've been sleeping in the guest room for weeks." Damien hadn't wanted to admit to the problems in his relationship, but it felt good to confide in somebody how severed the relationship had actually become.

"Dang, D. I'm sorry to hear that. I'm not a Clarissa fan, but I know how it feels to be in a relationship that's run its course. Maybe the time has come for you two to go your separate ways. DJ will be off to college soon and you could meet somebody else and have a real chance at happiness."

While he appreciated her advice and concern, he shook his head no. "I won't abandon my son or have him living in a single parent home. Happiness is overrated," Damien said sadly.

Sydney touched her brother's hand. "Happiness is everything. You need to sit down and have a brutally honest conversation with Clarissa. Most folks think that time invested in a relationship makes it worthy of staying, but it's not true. You deserve everything and then some."

Damien looked reflectively at his sibling. "Do you ever think we have a defective gene that makes us unable to make good choices when it comes to relationships? We all gravitate to folks for the wrong reasons, me and Rissa, you and Terrance, Jimmy and my mom."

Damien's words cut Syd to the bone. She never thought of her poor choices in romance as a family problem. Sydney thought of her parents' union as successful, despite her father's secrets and lies. The fact that Damien saw them as damaged hurt her very much.

Seeing the sadness in his sister's eyes made Damien keenly aware that she was hurt by his words. "Well, at least you got it right with Avery. He's the real deal. Maybe you'll break the curse." He left Sydney deep in thought and more concerned for her brother.

An excited Leona and Richard decided to venture into Atlanta to try a new restaurant recommended by Chloe. The quaint little bistro called Anderson's served vegetarian soul food. After dinner, both Leona and Richard agreed that they were no fans of tofu as meatloaf. But the night was still full of laughter and flirting and when Richard asked her back to his home she happily agreed. She didn't want this magical time to end.

Richard seemed nervous when they arrived in his well-appointed home. He had been a widower for seven years and he had finally learned how to be a proper housekeeper. But his nervousness didn't come from Leona seeing his space, but from the question he was about to ask her.

"Leona, I want to ask you something. We've been seeing each other for over two years and it's no secret how I feel about you. I love you and I want to take our relationship to the next level. Leona, will you spend the night with me? I want to make love to you." Richard gazed at his lady love, anxiously awaiting her answer.

Leona smiled and grabbed Richard's hand. "Richard, I love you too. I wasn't sure I'd ever want to be intimate again, but with you I'm willing to try. Yes, I'd love to stay the night."

"I was going to get down on my knees and beg but at our age that could create a whole new set of problems," said Richard, grinning happily. The two held hands and laughed, both excited at this new beginning chapter of their lives.

Leona was not at all shocked by his profession of love for her and his wanting to have sex, but she was surprised how quickly she said yes. Richard was so different from Jimmy, so open and honest. He always said what was on his mind and was very laid back. He didn't have Jimmy's charisma or charm, but an honesty and warmth that wasn't always present in Jimmy. He was just what the doctor ordered after what seemed like a lifetime of secrets and betrayals.

Richard grabbed her and held her close. She loved the way he smelled and how he made her feel safe. He slowly began to kiss her softly on her neck, which started to arouse her. She could feel the effect it was having on him as his erection bulged through his trousers. His fingers expertly unbuttoned her blouse and in one deft move he freed her breast from her bra and began to suckle on her hardened nipple. Leona moaned in ecstasy, feeling like a young woman again. As Richard's hand began to roam lower, she gently pushed him away.

"Oops! I forgot to ask if you were on the pill," he whispered in her ear.

Leona giggled and said, "No seriously. I need to tell you something. I haven't been with a man sexually since my husband died." Leona had been in a friendship with a local man, Bart Connors, but it was never more than some hand holding and kissing. She wanted Richard with all her heart, but she was nervous. Sex still caused her some anxiety. Richard looked at her with his kind soulful eyes.

"Darling, we'll go slow, but I'm going to make you forgot all about Jimmy."

Leona laughed seductively as Richard lead her toward his bedroom.

Sydney had a Circle meeting that was being held in Atlanta at the Marriot Marquis. She was on a committee, which was starting an art program in inner city schools and she was going to be teaching beginning painting once a week. Her fellow committee members where surprised she wanted to be so hands-on, but art was her passion and she wanted to do something to give back.

She left the meeting on a high. Sydney had never shared with anyone her dream to teach art. Painting and sketching had helped her get through some tough times. Being able to express herself when she didn't have the words was life changing for her. She wanted to share that with children, especially those whose lives weren't as privileged as hers had been.

With intentions on having lunch with her husband, Sydney decided she wanted to share her new project with her girls first. She first tried Kendall, who informed her that she was on her way to Chardonnae's yoga twerk-ing class.

"You're going where? I can't believe you would go to that heifer's class. Traitor," Syd was still salty about Terrance and Chardonnae's romance. She and Kendall frequently stalked her social media looking for glimpses of the couple.

"Mom, we've got to keep our enemies close. Plus, I got to see that butt in person. That booty is big tight and right. This is a mission—I'll go, learn all of her moves and then I'll teach you. Besides, the added bonus is that my presence will make Terrance feel old. I remind him how old he really is," laughed Kendall deviously. She really was her mother's child.

"Whatever, Kendall! Have you talked to your sister today?" Sydney knew her daughters usually spoke daily.

"Nope, not today. Chlo's been MIA lately. We usually get together during the week for dinner or something, but she keeps bailing on me."

"I'm going to call her and see if she has time for her mother," throwing shade on Kendall's busy schedule.

"That's okay, Mom. You'll be begging me to show you these twerking yoga moves."

Sydney ended the call and tried to reach her elder daughter. Chloe's cell phone was picked up, but the call ended as Sydney said hello. She tried again but it went straight to voice mail. Worried, Sydney decided to go Chloe's to check on her, and then meet Avery. She shot him a quick text saying she'd be a little late and quickly drove to her daughter's Druid Hill Condo.

Upon arriving at Chloe's place, she rang the bell and was greeted by Blaze, wearing a men's tank top, boy shorts, and Gucci slides.

"Hey, baby, did you forget your keys again?" Blaze was shocked into silence when she realized that it was not Chloe but a woman whom she instantly recognized from photos as Chloe's mom.

"Hi! Is Chloe home? I'm her mom Sydney." She stared at the young women curiously. She knew all of her daughter's friends. "And you are?"

"Uh, hi, Miss Sydney. I'm Briana, Chloe's girlfriend." Blaze refused to just say friend to mollify Chloe. She was still smarting from the lack of intro- duction when she met Avery. It was time for Chloe to stand up and be truthful about their relationship.

Sydney looked curious, but said nothing, as she glanced around her daugh- ter's apartment. She spied oil paints and canvas, as well as a picture of the two girls, who were clearly a couple. The thing that spoke volumes was the rainbow flag that was proudly displayed on the bookcase.

"I see," said Sydney quietly in response to Blaze's declaration. She looked at the artwork and supplies and asked the young woman if she was an artist.

"Yes, ma'am," Blaze replied. She knew Sydney was an artist too but didn't think this was the time to mention what they had in common.

"You're very talented. Your pieces show so much passion and life." Sydney admired Blaze's work. Her paintings were all full of warm hues and bright colors.

"Thank you, ma'am. I thought that Mr. Samuels would have told you about meeting me," added Blaze.

"You've met my husband?" inquired a flabbergasted Sydney.

"Yes, almost a month ago—Chloe said you were out of town." At that moment, both women turned as they heard the lock turn and Chloe entered the apartment juggling two smoothies and a bag. Her astonishment quickly turned to fear.

"Hi, Chloe. I was in the city for a meeting and I thought I'd check in on you and I've now had the pleasure of meeting Briana." Sydney was staring daggers into her daughter.

"Mom," she stammered, "I was going to introduce you to Blaze but we've all been so busy," she trailed off, knowing her explanation was weak.

"But you obviously had the chance to have your dad meet Briana or should I call you Blaze? I can't believe you introduced your girlfriend to your step-father before you told me—I'm your mother, dammit!" Sydney was hurt and angry.

"Mom, you know I hate that word, stepfather. He's my dad and it wasn't like that. He ran into Blaze and me at South City Kitchen in Buckhead. It wasn't planned or anything." Chloe had known her mother would be shocked, but not this angry.

"I thought you wouldn't understand and be upset," Chloe added quietly.

"Why, Chloe? When have you ever heard me utter a homophobic word, an intolerant thought? What was it about Avery that made him acceptable to share something so important but not me? Obviously, I don't know you as well as I thought I did, and you surely don't know me. Hell, none of you do. Blaze, it was good to meet you, though I wish it were under different circumstances. You're a talented artist."

With tears in her eyes, she nodded at her daughter but said nothing. Sydney turned on her heel and softly shut the door. Determined not to cry until she was in sanctity of her car, she fled the building quickly. Safely in her Range Rover, she let the tears flow freely as she hastily sent a text to Avery canceling their lunch. All Syd wanted to do at that point was go home.

Upstairs, a hysterical Chloe grilled Blaze on what had been said in her absence. Blaze recounted the conversation as Chloe sat with hands covering her face. She was so distraught that Blaze didn't even argue with her about how poorly she handled the whole situation. She left Chloe alone and retreated to the bedroom. Chloe quickly retrieved her phone and called her father.

"Dad," she said shakily, "Mom just left. She knows about Blaze and she's pissed." There was nothing more to say.

A few days later, Damien was at Mitch's Barber Shop waiting for a haircut when he overheard a patron talking about a funeral he recently attended. He was only half interested and vaguely listening when he recognized a familiar name, Tyriq Walker. The young man had a rapt audience as he went into full detail about how the deceased's sister apparently attacked the deceased girlfriend who she deemed responsible for her brother's death.

"Man, you should have seen this shit. Shawty was all garbed up, getting her cry on when she spotted that ho Brittany coming up the aisle. She was fake crying and had some shirt on with both those boys' picture on it," he paused dramatically so they could get the full picture.

"Damn, I heard one brother shot the other. She had both their pictures on the same shirt? Man, that's some rank shit," added his friend.

"Yeah, that's what I'm saying. When shawty saw that—one had the angel wings on his back, but the other one didn't, she just snapped. Jumped over all the chairs and slapped the shit outta Brittany. That heifer fell back and then the rest of them were on her. It was the Muslim sisters versus the thots. Hijabs and hair weaves flying everywhere!"

An older gentleman who had been listening intently and shaking his head suddenly looked confused. "Son, what exactly is a thot and a hijab?

The two young men began to laugh, but quickly explained. "A hijab is the scarf that the Muslim sisters use to cover their hair. A thot means, 'That Ho over There – T-H-O-T'." The whole barber shop cracked up at his explanation.

"What funeral home did all this take place in?" asked the older gentleman. "Never heard no goings on like that around here."

"It was that new spot. I think it's called Guiding Light or something like that. Reminded me of that soap opera my mama used to watch. My boy Tyriq is running stuff down there." The storyteller was next in the chair and so the topic gradually changed to sports.

Damien was intrigued. He knew most of the local funeral directors personally and was sure he didn't know anyone by the name of Tyriq, except for the kid who cleaned up the morgue and the cars at the funeral home. He'd been curious about Guiding Light for a while and in light of this new development, vowed to check it out further.

After leaving Mitch's, Damien headed over to Watkins garage for the guys' monthly hang session. Sometimes, the guys went to a club or restaurant, but usually their best times were spent in the makeshift employees' lounge/office of the garage.

As the beer flowed freely, Damien captivated the guys' attention with the tale he had overheard at Mitch's. When they all had recovered their composure from laughing, Damien asked the Watkins brothers if either knew anything about the new establishment.

Travis looked oddly at Damien. "I thought your friend from out of state was running things over there."

Damien gave him a blank look. "I don't have any friends running anything up here. At least not that I know of. Who mentioned that I knew the owner?" he asked curiously.

Travis knew immediately that Clarissa had lied to him, but he couldn't for the life of him understand why. Not wanting to get in the middle of what might be a domestic problem, he quickly covered himself. "One of the guys who drives for us mentioned he thought you might know the guy. Here's the card I got." He quickly handed Damien the glossy black business card.

Damien read the card aloud. "Tyriq Walker, head of Islamic Burials. Oh, hell no! What is Tyriq, the kid who cleans the morgue at Williams, doing with a business card? I knew he was a Muslim because I saw him reading the Quran, but I know he ain't an Iman and he definitely doesn't have a license to practice funeral directing."

Damien stared at the card and was truly baffled. Tyriq always seemed helpful and responsible, not the kind of guy who would get caught up in some shady mess like this.

"I gotta ask KC to check into this," he remarked. "I need to know if this crap is even legal."

"That's a good idea," offered Avery. "With KC being on the State Board now, she'll have access to all of the licenses and business incorporation information. I know Tyriq; he's a good kid. I hope he's not mixed up in anything illegal again."

Troy looked at Avery in shock. "Since when did my wife get on the State Board? Why didn't she tell me?"

Damien and Avery both looked at each other and shrugged. "I didn't hear it from KC. Sydney told me a few nights ago."

"Of course, she did," Troy said bitterly. "Sydney probably knows how low my nuts swing."

"Awww, man! C'mon, my wife and your nuts in the same sentence isn't cool," deadpanned Avery. The men began cracking up, breaking up the tension in the room.

"But really, bro, seriously, I feel you. The bond between those two is crazy. Right now, Sydney hasn't spoken to me in three days. She's mad because I didn't tell her that I met Chloe's significant other and that he is a she."

"Damnnn!" Travis exclaimed. "Now we got to do some shots." He produced a bottle of whiskey from his desk drawer and poured four shots of amber liquid into Styrofoam cups. They all took their respective shots and Travis started asking questions.

"How did you find out about Chloe? She's so pretty—what a waste!" Travis was never the most tactful person.

"No, it's not," exclaimed Avery angrily. "It doesn't matter who she loves as long as she's safe and happy. I'm sick of everybody making a big deal of it." The men grew silent. The usually mild-mannered Avery rarely raised his voice.

"Man, I didn't mean anything by it. Chloe's a sweet girl. But it's gonna be hard for her in this town. Maxwell can be mean when it wants to be."

Damien changed the subject, but Avery stayed quiet. The men continued to chat but as the hour grew late, they began to wrap, gathering their things to head to their respective situations.

Avery and Damien walked to their cars together. Damien reached out and put his hand on his brother-in-law's shoulder.

"Bro, don't pay no attention to Travis. He can be crass and ignorant. But he is right about some of the folks in this town."

"Damien, it's not just Travis. Sydney is acting so upset. I don't know if it's because Chloe is a lesbian or because I didn't tell her first. She says Chloe and I both betrayed her. I haven't seen her this angry since we've been married." Avery shook his head sadly.

"Give her a minute, Avery. She loves you and she loves Chloe. She'll come around."

Leona hummed to herself as she put the final touches to her impromptu dinner. She had invited Sydney, KC, and Damien to join her that evening to share Richard and her possible future plans and a little news of her own.

She had taken great pains to make each of their favorite dishes. For Sydney, it was Leona's famous chicken and dumplings, with the dumplings hand-made from scratch. KC loved her aunt's dirty rice with andouille sausage and chicken livers. Damien was a huge fan of her bourbon sweet potato casserole with smoked pecans. She topped off the meal with collard greens, peach cobbler, and everyone's favorite homemade biscuits.

Sydney arrived first, an anomaly in their family. As Leona hugged her daughter, she could feel her shoulders sag and when she pulled away, Leona was sure she saw tears on her cheeks,

"What's wrong, baby girl? You seem a little down tonight," asked Leona always the concerned mother. No matter how old Sydney got, she would always be Leona's baby girl.

"I'm okay, Mama. Just tired I guess." Sydney sat down at the table and looked distractedly at her phone. Leona decided to take her at face value. This evening was definitely not about the latest drama in her daughter's life.

Both KC and Damien arrived at the same time and the four sat down to eat. Leona said the prayer and the delicious meal began. Damien, KC, and Sydney were all nervous about the dinner. They all wondered what had they done wrong and were eager to hear what Leona had to say.

As they ate, the group made small talk about the happenings at the funeral home and town news, but they still had no clue as to why they were assembled. Leona decided the best way to start the conversation was to dive right in.

"I wanted you all here tonight so I can share some important news. Richard and I are officially a couple. We are thinking about moving in together." There was a stunned moment of silence before everyone began to offer their congratulations.

Leona looked directly at Sydney. "Sydney, I need to know how you feel about this," she asked.

"Mama, I want you to be happy and if being with Mr. Richard makes you happy, then I'm excited for you. But moving in together is a big deal. What will the people at the church say? Mr. Richard is a deacon." Sydney wanted her mother's happiness, but tongues liked to wag in a small town.

"We will try to keep our business private, but at this point I've survived more scandal than most of the women in Hollywood. My husband of forty years cheated on me, I was almost conned out of thousands of dollars by a man pretending to be my long-lost brother-in-law, and my funeral manager almost sold our family business right out from under us! This town has had plenty to talk about when it comes to Leona Williams. They will hardly blink an eye about two adults cohabitating." Leona hadn't meant to rehash the past, but she wondered how much of Sydney's concern was about Richard and her living situation or the fact that Leona had finally moved past Jimmy. Sydney had been a Daddy's girl plain and simple and she still mourned her father. Leona hoped that she would eventually accept Richard and grow to love him as she had.

Sensing the tension between mother and daughter, KC tried to lighten the mood. "Aunt Leona, we are so excited for you. We haven't seen you this happy in a long time. You're glowing," KC added with a smile.

"My new relationship status is only half of my announcement. I am officially retiring effective at the end of the year. I also have drawn up papers to leave you all equal shares in Williams Mortuary. I expect you to work together as a team. With your respective talents, you will go far."

They were all overwhelmed and quiet, but Damien spoke up for all of them.

"Miss Leona, we love you and are excited for you and Mr. Richard. You both deserve some happiness. But most of all we appreciate the confidence you have in us. I promise; we won't let you down."

As dessert was served, they continued to talk about future plans and the business. Damien and KC seemed excited for their new roles as owners, but Sydney was quiet and sullen, adding little to the conversation. When they all rose to leave, Sydney hung back, waiting to speak to her mother privately.

"Mama, are you selling the house, or will Mr. Richard move in here with you? This is your and Daddy's house." Sydney tried to hide her tears. She could not imagine her mother and another man living on in Grace Lane. This would always be her childhood home, the last place her beloved father had last lived.

"No, baby; this is my house, left to me when your daddy passed away and who lives in it is MY decision. It makes more sense for Richard to move in here—it's bigger than his and has far more amenities. Maybe later we will move into those new luxury townhouses in the new 55+ community they are building on the riverfront. Right now, we just want to travel and enjoy ourselves. I've lived somebody else's dream for almost fifty years. It's time to live for myself." Leona paused to let her words sink in. "Your daddy is gone and he's not coming back."

"I know that, Mama, but you act like our life was so horrible, that you didn't love Daddy—" Leona raised her hand to silence her daughter.

"I loved your father for forty-two years. Gave him the best years of my life—sacrificed my education, my own plans, and dreams. I was supposed to go Meharry and study dentistry. I even gave up my relationship with my family because he never really cared for them. I supported his business and his dream, preserved his legacy even after he died. He gave me this house and a whole lot of heartache. I know this is hard for you to accept but I've found someone who loves me the way I should be loved. After Terrance broke your heart, it was all I prayed for, that you would find someone to love and cherish you. God blessed you with your happy ending. Now, He's blessing me with mine." Leona's words came out with more force than she intended, but she needed her daughter to understand that she needed to live her life her way.

"I'm sorry, Mama. I didn't mean to upset you. There's just a lot going on right now. I'll see you tomorrow." Sydney quickly exited before the tears came. She didn't know how to react to the thought of her mother living with a man who wasn't her daddy or to her mother's retirement. Sydney felt as if her whole life had been turned upside down in the last week.

Leona watched her daughter through the window as she got in her car. She had expected Sydney to be unhappy about her and Richard moving in together, but there seemed to be something else deeper troubling her. Leona sighed and began to clear her table. If it wasn't one thing, it was another.

Sydney let herself into her large empty home. Jamie had texted her that he, Dad, and Morgan were having dinner at the local diner. She walked out to her studio where she had been hiding out every night until Avery fell asleep. She would then slip quietly into their California king, hugging her side of the bed with her back to her husband. This was a far cry from most of their marital nights where they were usually slept tangled up together changing positions whenever the other shifted.

As she opened up what had recently become her nightly bottle of wine, she decided to call her cousin Vanessa. Usually, the first call would be to KC, but the state of her cousin's marital life was as tumultuous as her own. At Mama's, KC had quietly confided in her that she and Troy were also on the outs. Vanessa's cheery melodic voice immediately made her feel she made the right decision.

"Hey, girl! I was just getting ready to call you. You've been heavy in my spirit today. How did the meeting about the painting class go?" Vanessa and Sydney had gotten into the habit of talking every few days, filling each other in on their lives.

At that comment, Sydney began to weep and pour out the events of the past few days, ending with Leona's dinner announcement. She just wanted to talk to somebody who didn't view her as vapid and vain woman who only cared about shopping and appearances. Basically, she needed someone who didn't judge her. Vanessa was sympathetic and tried to console her cousin, but she was used to the bubbly upbeat person who made her laugh constantly. She was instantly concerned because Sydney sounded so depressed. They ended the conversation with Vanessa promising to call her tomorrow. When she hung up, she knew exactly what she had to do.

CHAPTER 11

What You Do in the Dark ...

"Yo, KC, WE got a problem," shouted Damien through the phone.

"Didn't you tell me I had a man to embalm? Ain't no dudes back here; just four ladies. Did your husband mess up and pick up the wrong body? You know they don't always read those toe tags."

"Good morning, Damien. How are you?" replied KC dryly. It was only 7:50 am and she hadn't had her dose of caffeine yet.

"I'm stressed the hell out. Where is the body of Thomas Newsome? Based on your description, I expected a big strapping football player, not some thick chick with double D's! I bet they mixed these bodies up at the hospital. Mr. Newsome probably laying right there, waiting to get picked up. Let me pack this lady up and call the hospital." Damien hung up and started to prepare to put the woman back in the body bag when he noticed a strange bulge under her hospital gown. After further investigation, Damien discovered that the bulge was a penis, taped down to the deceased's leg. Mr. Thomas Newsome had actually transitioned into a woman.

When Damien shared this news with KC, she thought back to the Zoom call she had with the family regarding Thomas' service. His sister Daphne, who resided in Houston, was on the call with two cousins who lived in Smyrna, GA. She was his closest living relative as Thomas had never married or had any children. Neither Daphne nor the cousins had mentioned Thomas' transition, so KC decided to initiate another Zoom call to discuss her findings.

"Good afternoon, ladies. I won't take up much of your time, but some things have to come to light that desperately need to be discussed," KC stated, hoping someone would start the conversation.

"What's going on, Ms. Watkins? Was everything alright with the insurance policy?" asked Daphne Newsome, immediately concerned.

"No, the policy was good. This is about Mr. Thomas. When was the last time you saw him in person?

"It had been a while since I'd been home, or he'd been here. I don't understand, Ms. Watkins. What are you saying?" Daphne was terribly confused.

"I know exactly what she's trying to say, Daphne," answered one of the cousins. "Thomas wasn't Thomas anymore, he was Tanya. When we saw him or when he came here, he was a she. Tanya had been on hormones for five years."

"Yes, Daphne," interjected the second cousin. "Tanya was afraid to tell you, so she pretended to still be a man. When she came to our Taco Tuesdays, she was always dressed to the nines, with her blond hair looking fierce!" The second cousin smiled, recalling their visits fondly.

"Blond hair? My brother dressed as a woman? This is insane!" Daphne was near tears. "I don't understand. Every time I spoke with him, he was Thomas, not some Tanya."

"So, you're saying you never saw him dressed as woman. You didn't know he was transgender?" asked her cousin gently.

"Well, we used to play dress up when we were kids, but that's where I thought it ended. My God, he was a football player in high school. My brother wasn't gay!"

"No, he wasn't. He lived his life as a woman. His friends and coworkers all know him as Tanya."

KC felt like she was caught in the middle of a bad family drama. She attempted to re-direct the arrangement conference by offering to integrate Thomas/Tanya's lives into one memorial. Daphne was reluctant to see her brother as Tanya but was convinced by the rest of the family to let her brother live his truth.

On the day of his viewing, KC went to inspect the body and was mesmerized by Tanya's transformation. After looking at the pictures of Thomas that Daphne provided all week, she could barely see any traces of him in the woman who lay in the casket. Hormones had changed the texture of Tanya's skin and her hair was long, flowing, and blond thanks to a hair weave and color. The only real lingering male characteristic was a slight Adam's apple that was barely detectable. Also Tanya's hands and feet, while polished and bejeweled were far larger than the average woman. Unfortunately, she had succumbed to a heart attack, partially due to the hormonal treatments.

In the end, KC and the family created a program and Memorial DVD that showed Tanya's journey and the happiness she found along the way.

Vanessa navigated her black BMW SUV into Sydney's driveway. She was not expecting the large opulent home. Upon ringing the doorbell, a fair-skinned young girl with a long curly hair pulled in a ponytail answered the door, a taller young man with same coloring standing behind her.

"Hi; is Sydney around? I'm her cousin Vanessa. You guys must be Jamie and Morgan." Vanessa extended her brightest and most engaging smile. Sydney's twins were exactly how she described them.

'Yes, she's here, but who are you? We've never met you. How are you my mom's cousin?" Morgan was friendly but curious about her new relative.

Vanessa appreciated the open and easy nature of the children and shared how Sydney and she had met doing her father's funeral.

"Wow, yeah! She told us she met some of our cousins. You look just like our Mom-Mom, only younger. Mom's outside doing her painting again. You can go out there," offered Morgan, the twins' official spokesperson.

As Vanessa walked through Sydney's home, she marveled at how beautiful it all was. It was apparent that her cousin and her husband were quite successful. She made her way through the modern, blinding white kitchen and through the double French doors to the courtyard that contained a large kidney shaped pool surrounded by stone pavers and a patio with requisite outdoor kitchen, pizza oven and a large stone fire pit. But the jewel in the crown was the almost completely glass studio, which reflected light off the pool.

Vanessa spotted Sydney working diligently on a painting, her worn jeans and t-shirt covered in paint and her flowing mane in a messy top knot. What Vanessa wasn't expecting was her cousin's obvious talent. The painting she was working on was that of a handsome man standing behind an elegant seated woman with a little girl leaning into toward her. Upon closer inspection, she realized that the woman is indeed a young Leona, making the little girl Sydney and the powerful man Jimmy Williams.

Vanessa tapped lightly on the door. A stunned Sydney turned and shrieked with delight. She put her brush down and embraced her cousin, careful not to get paint stains on Vanessa's beautiful red silk kimono, which she wore over a black cat suit.

"What are you doing here? You should have let me know. I would have made food and cleaned up my messy house." Sydney was ecstatic to see Vanessa. The two had made plans to get together later in the month but hadn't finalized anything.

"I was led to come. You sounded like you needed a friendly face and I needed an excuse to come visit with my family."

"I'm so glad you did. I just opened this bottle of wine. Please come; sit with me." The two spent the next two hours sipping Riesling and talking. Vanessa asked Sydney about the painting she was working on.

Sydney smiled wistfully. "It's from a photo we took when I was little. Daddy had a photographer come to the house to take a family photo, but I was scared of the photographer and wouldn't pose for him. Daddy sure was angry, but I always loved the picture."

Eager to hear more about her life, Vanessa asked Sydney all about her childhood and teenage years, both curious and a little envious in hearing about her younger sister's charmed life. They talked late into the afternoon. Vanessa felt drawn to Sydney, as they were both innocent pawns in their family's awful chess game.

Later, Avery came home and made his way to the she shed after hearing the laughter and the sounds of Sydney's favorite neo-soul.

"Hello," he stammered, shocked by the presence of a stranger with his wife.

"Avery, let me introduce you to my cousin, Vanessa. I told you about meeting her at my uncle's funeral. She came for a surprise visit from Charleston. Vanessa this is my husband, Avery."

"Avery, it's great to meet you. I feel like I already know you. I've heard so much about you," exclaimed Vanessa. She jumped up and gave him a warm embrace that he awkwardly returned.

The always gracious Avery wasn't sure how glowing the commentary had been about him given the cold war that was going on in their home. "I hope it was all good," said Avery sheepishly.

"Of course, it was! Syd sings your praises all the time." Vanessa, always the therapist, noticed the uneasy exchange between the couple.

"Are you ladies hungry? I don't mind cooking."

"No, it's cool," replied Sydney icily. "We're going to order something. If you could make something for the twins, that would be great." Feeling dismissed and very much like the third wheel, Avery excused himself and went back to the house.

"A little chilly, isn't it?" remarked Vanessa.

"No," answered Sydney. "I'm still upset with him regarding the whole Chloe situation. I feel betrayed and like I'm the only one upset. He has no problems sleeping these days."

"Well, maybe you'd be able to clear the air if you were both talking and not sleeping back-to-back. Let's touch base tomorrow. I need you to go and relax. Take a warm shower, collect your thoughts and talk to your husband. It's time to clear this negative energy. I'm staying at Beauvoir Mansion Inn and I'll call you in the morning." Sydney knew her cousin was right and agreed to at least try.

Later that night, Sydney was the first in the bedroom, taking Vanessa's counsel. Her normal go to would be to introduce sex into the equation, hoping it would make things better, but tonight, taking her cousin's advice, she asked Avery if it was okay for them to get into bed just to talk.

So happy to break their stalemate, Avery immediately began to apologize. "Babe, I'm sorry. I know I should have said something to you—," Sydney silenced him with a look.

"Please let me explain why I was angry. My first marriage wasn't a partnership. We never looked out for each other, only for ourselves. But in you,

I felt I've found my lover, my best friend, and my partner. We were and are a team. I just didn't feel like we were playing on the same team in this situation. I love how you love all of our children. You are truly an amazing father. But there's no them without us having a strong foundation. We have to come first."

"But, Sydney, you know I love you. I didn't mean to make you feel as if I betrayed you. I was caught in the middle. I begged Chloe to tell you."

"I know, but we have to communicate with each other. You're right, it was Chloe's story to tell, but you could have given me a heads-up. I was completely blindsided by what I walked in on and the person I'm closest to in the world didn't tell me. I was devastated, but not because Chloe is gay, but because neither of you shared it with me.

"It's not your job to always please me or shield me from everything. Sometimes, you will have to share disappointments and hurts and bad news with me, but it will always hurt less because it's coming from you— the one I trust with my life. Is this making any sense?"

She paused to give her words a chance to sink in. Avery looked at his wife of fifteen years and knew for far too long he treated her as if she were glass. He needed to change his approach if he wanted to keep his marriage healthy. As he reached for his wife and then held her tight, they both realized how much they meant to each other. While sex was not on either's mind tonight, something far better was in store—togetherness.

Tre parked his car in front of Nine's aging clapboard house that was badly in need of a paint job and grabbed his backpack full of cash. This was his favorite part of selling weed for Nine—pay day. Tre was about to re-up on his supply and Nine would pay him his cut. Tre was going to get the new Yeezy Turbo boost sneakers and a new jacket he had his eye on at the mall.

"Yo Money! What's good?" Tre always tried his best to fit in.

"Hey, Young Blood—it's all you. What you got for me today?" Nine was impressed at how good Tre was at trappin', the slang term for drug dealing.

In response, Tre pulled out a bulging wad of cash. He had made over $4,000.00 in sales in the past week, and Nine paid him a 20% cut.

"Now, that's what I like to see. You on your hustle. I need to talk to you 'bout a new business venture." Nine's eyes were gleaming from both marijuana and excitement. "I wanna start selling wet." "Wet" or PCP was marijuana soaked in embalming fluid. Nine explained that the white biker gangs controlled all of the PCP sales due to their ability to obtain embalming fluid. Nine wanted in as more and more young people liked the psychedelic high that the combination produced and extended amount of time the drug kept the user high.

Tre was confused and said as much. "Okay, that's cool. But where are you going to get embalming fluid from? Can you just buy some?" he asked.

Nine laughed, "You funny young blood. Unless you own a funeral joint, you can't buy it. But that's where you come in. Your peoples own a funeral parlor. That's why I told you to stop by my house. I knew you'd be an asset to our crew. Figure it out, young blood. Imma need two to three cases a week until we get shit running. Cuz if you don't, Imma have to get in that ass. And when I'm finished, I just might bust a cap in ya old man's ass for not raising you right. He used to slang with my unc—he know what it's hittin for."

Tre had no idea how to gain entrance to the funeral home. He had been there a few times with DJ or his dad, but never really showed an interest in the business.

Nine looked at Tre menacingly. "You need to make that happen, young blood." Nine's word left little to the imagination.

A troubled Tre stopped by his cousin's house to talk. While playing Call to Duty, he told DJ about his conversation with Nine and asked for DJ's help.

"How am I supposed to help?" asked DJ distractedly.

"We get your Dad's keys, go in, take the fluid, and get out. No one will ever know." Tre hadn't worked the logistics yet, but the plan felt solid to him.

"Hell, man! My dad sleep with those keys and my mom don't have keys to the place. You need another plan."

"Shit," Tre exclaimed, putting his head in hands. "Wait a minute; we can ask the kid to take his mom's keys. She ain't gonna notice and I know she'd never suspect him."

"Naw, man, not my cousin. He's just twelve. Jamie ain't built like that."

"I don't have choices—he said he would shoot my dad! This dude is serious."

"Should thought about that before you got in this shit," DJ was both scared and disgusted by Tre's predicament.

"Bro, you helping me or what?" Tre asked again. DJ was reluctant but agreed to help his cousin. "I'll talk to Jamie and we'll figure something out."

DJ came into the kitchen after Tre left. He sat down at the table while his mother was cooking at the stove. She turned around and noticed her son's forlorn look. Concerned, Clarissa asked him why he was so glum.

"It's nothing, Mom, just got some stuff on my mind. I'll work it out. What you doing home so early tonight? I hardly ever see you or Dad anymore—everybody always on their hustle."

Clarissa stared at her baby, not a baby anymore, and immediately felt guilty. *What am I missing out on? I haven't been home to even cook my boy dinner in months*, she thought.

She began to ask questions about school, girls, and eventually his friends. She felt she came up short as he denied having any problems and gave her stock answers. She wished she could discuss this with Damien. Clarissa wondered if Damien had a chick on the side. He was never home anymore and while Williams was busy, it wasn't that busy. They hadn't had sex in months and that hadn't happened since she was pregnant with their son. She was so excited, feeling empowered by her new business that she hadn't realized how much she was truly sacrificing.

Things had been tense all week at the Watkins house. After Syd's revelation about the crematory purchase as well as Avery's bombshell about the state board, there was nothing but polite chatter surrounding the children and schedules. KC was hurt that her husband would make such a large purchase without consulting her or at least mentioning it in conversation. Unlike Syd and Avery, theirs was not a marriage where finances and assets were combined. Troy was sometimes borderline paranoid that she would share his financial status with her family. The notion was ridiculous considering that his business was quite profitable. He once admitted that he felt he didn't measure up to the Williams' family. Of course, it didn't help that when her father was alive, he would constantly compare him to her former fiancé' David, a CPA with a profitable business and plenty of assets. What her father didn't know was that David had been on the down low and that KC had caught him having sex with the church's male youth pastor. So much for assets!

KC got in her silver Cadillac SUV and turned her satellite radio to the gospel station. A true preacher's kid, the sound of anyone making a joyful noise unto the Lord lifted her spirits. She always looked forward to Fridays. Both she and Sydney took turns leaving early to pick up the kids from school. Langley Academy, the premier private day school in the area, had instituted an independent study program for its sixth through twelfth graders; hence, the early dismissal on Fridays. The cousins took turns picking up the kids. This week was KC's turn to get them and then Sydney would do Tianna's thick hair and give the kids' lunch. KC would usually take the girls for a Friday night sleepover, while Sydney would keep DJ and Jamie. The result was a group of kids who were as close as siblings, exactly the way she and Sydney were raised.

As usual, the atmosphere at the Samuels home was full of laughter, music, and fun. The kids were watching videos in the great room while Sydney sat at her kitchen island busily typing on her laptop, probably online shopping, KC surmised. KC slid into one of the bar stools at the island and sighed.

She could hide her mood from most, but her sister-cousin knew immediately something was wrong.

"Hey, Kay-Kay; what's going on?" asked Syd, concerned.

"Just everything! Troy and I are really going through." She looked around to see if Tianna was listening, but she and Morgan were looking at something on the phone and squealing. "I'm so angry that he didn't tell me about buying Harleigh Crematory. Who keeps something that big from their wife?"

"Well, Kay; you haven't been exactly sharing with him either. You didn't share with him your appointment to the state board or that application you put in at Gupton-Jones College of Funeral Service for the mortuary science instructor's position."

KC was stunned that her cousin even knew about the position.

"Don't look so shocked. They called to check your references. Don't worry. I gave you a glowing reference," laughed Syd. "And you haven't told him the most important thing—that you don't want a baby. Maybe it's time you both come clean."

KC knew that Sydney was right, but she was scared about what might happen when they finally put their cards on the table.

At that moment, Tianna bounded over. "C'mon, KC let's go! We're going to miss the mall."

"Alright, ladies; let's get going. We've got shopping to do."

As KC and the girls pulled up in front of the Watkins' home, Morgan realized that she had left her overnight bag at her house. Seeing Tre's car, KC told the girls to go inside and for Tianna to get changed while she picked up Morgan's bag.

The girls went straight to Tianna's room where she changed and then headed to the family room to watch TV and wait for KC. On the mahogany coffee table in the family room, they discovered several sandwich bags full of marijuana and the small baggies used for sales. The young girls were intrigued by the drugs and paraphernalia laid out before them. Morgan was first to speak.

"Ooh, Tianna; this is weed! I saw some once in Kendall's room! Who does it belong too?"

"It's Tre's. I've seen him with it before." She picked up the bag and smells it. "Yuck; it smells like a skunk."

At that moment, Tre came up from the basement game room and was infuriated that they had discovered the stash he had carelessly left out. He never heard the girls enter the house. He quickly gathered everything and shoved it in his backpack with the exception of the bag that Tianna was still holding.

"Gimme that, Tianna!" He attempted to grab the bag out of her hand, but she was far too quick and took off running toward the stairs, with Tre hot on her heels.

"You play too much, Tianna! When I catch you, I'mma slap the shit out of you!" Tre was right behind his sister on the stairs with Morgan running behind, scared by his menacing tone. Tre grabbed at Tianna's shirt, attempting to stop her, but she lost her footing and fell backward down the winding staircase. Morgan ran to her cousin, screaming her name.

"Tianna, Tianna, are you okay?" As Morgan bent over her, Tianna remained still. "Please wake up, Tianna, please," she begged. Tre stood over his sister, terrified. He then picked up the bag that had fallen out of her hand and ran outside. Morgan didn't want to leave Tianna but needed to retrieve her phone from the family room to call her mom.

KC pulled into the driveway and saw Tre pacing back and forth, talking on his phone. As she got out of her car, she heard him crying.

"Dad, please you gotta come now! Tianna, she, she fell, she's not moving!"

KC didn't need to hear another word and sprinted into the house. A crying Morgan was relieved to see her.

"Yeah, Mommy; Auntie just got here. Okay I'll tell her. Auntie, my mom called 911 and they are on the way."

KC sank to the ground next to her stepdaughter, who had regained consciousness and was crying.

"Moomm, my arm hurts," she sobbed. KC kept wiping away her tears and carefully rubbing her shoulder.

"It's okay, baby; I'm right here." KC started to cry herself, as she heard the sirens grow nearer.

Coley and Tyriq were sitting in the morgue, contemplating their next move. A month ago, the men were talking, complaining about the cremation situation, and the state of affairs at Guiding Light.

"Rissa lying, man! She told me Damien was down with this funeral home thing, but she got me embalming, impersonating him for the state board dude and now we can't even take bodies to the crematory. I heard that he's going to run things at Williams I saw him moving his stuff in Miss KC's office. Man, I ain't feeling this shit at all." Coley wasn't one to complain, but he had been working non-stop at both funeral homes.

"Yeah, and she promised me some extra money for those Muslim cases but I ain't seen a dime. And these unembalmed bodies are starting to smell." While that conversation had taken place a month ago, nothing had changed.

Guiding Light hadn't taken any cremations to Harleigh Crematory since Troy Watkins had assumed ownership. Troy had been getting trained as the crematory owner and operator and was constantly in the office. Troy knew both Coley and Tyriq from Williams and would have had plenty of questions, especially when he saw Damien's name on the cremation permits.

"You got that right," agreed Coley. "That one in the corner been here for almost two months. She made me take some of the old cremated remains in the basement at Williams and put them in urns and give them to folks. What we gonna do?"

Tyriq was texting someone and then began to smile as he read the reply. "My man Lamar just hit me back. He works over at the Lawnside Crematory. He said we could bring the bodies over there. He works the night shift and he'll cremate these if we break him off."

"Damn, Lawnside is like almost an hour away. We gotta ride with these stinkers. What time can we drop them off? And can we trust this dude?"

Coley was happy that they had a solution but was afraid it would come back on them.

"Yeah, he's alright. He was my cellie in Clayton County. He's good people." Tyriq was confident that his friend wouldn't let them down.

"Okat; we'll see." Coley was skeptical but hopeful.

In the end, their trip went off without a hitch and two days later he even provided them with cremated remains and counterfeit paper-work. Tyriq reported the successful mission to Clarissa who was extremely pleased. Unfortunately, two weeks after that, when Tyriq reached out to Lamar, he was disappointed to find that his former cellmate had reverted to his old ways and was fired from his job due to his sticky fingers.

"Dude, this sneaky mofo's put cameras in the retort room last weekend. Caught me taking off some old lady's ring. Shit, that bitch couldn't use it no more. I was gonna give it to my shawty, but they made me give it back. Sorry, man. They were also asking about those bodies I did for you. Be careful, man," he told Tyriq.

Tyriq was distraught. They had a new cremation to get rid of immediately. What were they going to do now?

Sydney ran into the Maxwell Regional Medical Center frantically searching for her daughter and cousin. She hated hospitals as they always reminded her of her father's death. She finally located Morgan looking scared, seated in the waiting area.

"Baby girl, are you okay?" The usual unflappable Morgan threw herself in her mother's arms, crying uncontrollably.

"Mom, what if Tianna dies?" she cried.

"Baby, she's going to be fine. Where's auntie?" At that moment, a shaken KC rounded the corner. As she approached her cousin, she did the same thing her niece did, flinging herself in her cousin's arms. Sydney comforted KC as best she could.

"How is Tianna?"

"She's stable now. She has a broken arm that they will need to perform surgery to set. She also has a concussion. Morgan, what happened? How did Tianna fall?" Morgan looked down, a little apprehensive to tell the story.

"Mom, when we got to Auntie's house, Tre was down in the game room and he left stuff on the table."

"What kind of stuff?" asked KC.

"Drugs, Auntie. He had a big bag of weed.... I mean marijuana. Tianna picked it up, and then Tre came upstairs, and he was chasing her trying to get it back and they ran up the steps and he grabbed her. Then, she fell down and Tre ran and got his bag and ran outside."

Both women were horrified at the story but before they could ask any more questions, they were interrupted by the arrival of Troy and Avery. The two men met in the parking lot.

"KC, what's going on, how's Tianna? Tre said there was an accident and T was hurt?"

"Oh, Troy!" KC moved closer to her husband as he wrapped his arms around her. "I left the girls to go to Sydney's to pick up Morgan's overnight bag. When I got back, I saw Tre talking to you and Tianna was at the bottom of the steps. She fell." Troy looked angrily at KC releasing her from his embrace.

"Why would you leave the girls alone? So you could go hang out with your cousin?"

A flash of anger appeared on Sydney's face. "Wait a minute, Troy; you're way out of line! KC just came to pick up Morgan's bag—she didn't even get out of the car. She wasn't gone fifteen minutes. Ask your son what happened since he was there!" She was livid! The nerve of him blaming KC.

"Stay out of this, Sydney; it's bad enough I feel like you the third person in our marriage as it is!"

Sydney was shocked into silence by Troy's words but only momentarily. "What the hell is that supposed to mean? You better watch how you talk to me. I'm not KC!"

Avery stepped in between them, attempting to play the role of peacemaker. "C'mon, now is not the time for arguing back and forth. We need to concentrate on Tianna."

But Troy was not to be reasoned with. "Naw, man what YOU need to do is handle your business and put your smart-ass wife in her place before she gets dealt with!"

"Dealt with? Aww, hell... naw, bro, you can't talk to my wife like that! I'm from Detroit, born and raised and I don't get down like that! You need to change your tone before YOU get dealt with!"

No one had ever heard Avery talk like that. The two men locked eyes for a moment before Troy turned away and Sydney pulled Avery to the other side of waiting room. In fifteen years of friendship, the two had hardly ever had a cross word. Tensions were definitely running high.

Sydney and Avery sat down away from Troy and KC. A wide-eyed Morgan was sitting next to her mother, texting frantically. Her brother wasn't going to believe that their dad just went triple OG on their uncle.

"What was all that, you from Detroit?" In spite of herself, she smiled.

"No one, not even family, is going to talk to my wife like that, I'm sorry," Avery said, sounding more like himself. He looked so serious it actually warmed her heart.

"We are going talk about this later tonight and I'm going to definitely need you to use your Detroit voice," she said seductively. Even Avery had to smile at that.

On the other side of the room, however, things were a bit more hostile.

"KC, I know I came on a little strong, but our daughter was my only concern."

KC quickly interrupted him. "Perhaps you should ask your son about OUR daughter. I don't believe this was an accident."

"What do you mean? Are you saying that Tre had something to do with Tianna falling?"

"Look at him; he's pacing, and he hasn't let go of that backpack since we left the house." They both turned to look at Tre who was furiously texting in the corner. As Troy went over to talk to his son, Damien appeared, asking about Tianna.

"How's T doing?" As he filled him in on the details, Damien noticed that Tre seemed preoccupied and nervous.

"What's up with Tre? I think we need to holla at him."

"Yo, son, let me rap with you for a minute, outside."

Tre looked nervously from his dad to his uncle.

"Aww, Pop, I gotta go to the bathroom. I'll be right out." Tre hustled to the bathroom and went into the empty stall. He opened up his backpack and took the two large plastic bags and flushed their contents down the toilet. He shook his head, knowing that Nine will be upset, but right now Tre was far more afraid of his dad than Nine.

Tre left the bathroom and joined his father and uncle in the parking lot.

"Yo, Dad, I'm sorry what happened to T, but you know how clumsy she can be."

"Was she clumsy or did something happen?" he asked and Tre looked down guiltily.

"Yo, son, you need to let us know what happened. Look at me when I'm talking to you. Did you hurt your sister, yes or no?" Damien's tone was aggressive and firm.

"Naw, Unc, we were just playing. You know how clumsy T can get. I wouldn't hurt my baby sister."

"So what's up with this bag? You been holding it kind of tight." Damien grabbed at the bag as Tre tried to maintain his grip. But he was no match for Damien, who grabbed it and unzipped it quickly. The empty backpack still held the strong pungent order of marijuana but was empty. "Smells like you had some bud in there? You selling bud now, Tre?" asked Damien.

"Naw, Unc—I don't get down like that. I had a little for myself, but it's gone now." His eyes shifted from his father to his uncle. "Since T is staying overnight, can I go home? It's getting late and I'm a little hungry."

"Yeah, go ahead. I'll check on you later," said Troy.

Gratefully, he headed to his car, happy the inquisition was over.

"Man, are we going to even talk about what just happened," Damien asked.

"Dude, don't even start. I know the boy smoked a little weed, but I know he ain't slangin and he definitely didn't hurt his sister. He don't need to sell no dope. We give him everything he could ever want or need."

"My daddy was the richest man in the county and I still did what I did. You need to watch your boy before he gets in too deep."

"Damn, man; I thought you were my boy, but you sound more like your cousin and your sister. I guess you're more Williams than I thought."

"Whatever, dude. These streets are mean, even in Maxwell, and kids get caught up. I don't want that to happen to Tre; that's all I'm saying. I'm glad

Tianna's okay. I'll check in with y'all tomorrow." As he watched his friends' retreating figure, Troy realized he had a lot to think about.

Vanessa was at her hotel, sitting out by the fireplace, drinking a glass of merlot reflecting on her motivations for her relationship with Sydney. She was glad when Sydney mentioned that Leona was out of town. She had spoken to her a few times, but the conversations were stilted and generic. She knew Leona still wasn't comfortable with her or their relationship.

As she stared at the fire; she thought of its power. The flames were both life-sustaining and destructive, a lot like family. She wanted Leona to be released from the guilt and shame of her rape and resulting pregnancy so that they could forge some type of relationship even if it was without formal definition. She wanted to learn more about her mother and the woman she was. Vanessa found it was far easier to grill an unknowing Sydney than penetrate Leona's steely reserve.

Vanessa had a lot of good friendships and one failed marriage, but no real familial ties to speak of, and she craved that more than anything. She especially felt a kinship to Sydney but yet was slightly jealous of her. She had grown up in a house of privilege with two parents who doted on her. Both women had wanted a sibling growing up and at least Sydney had KC and eventually her brother, but Vanessa felt empty on that front. She also knew Sydney was struggling with her own identity. Vanessa hoped that maybe they could find themselves together.

Coley and Tyriq were both upset about their cremation situation. They were afraid to tell Clarissa because, as of late, she'd been increasingly stressed out and testy about anything regarding Guiding Light. As they were discussing the situation in the increasingly odorous morgue, Coley came up with what he saw as a foolproof solution.

"Man, let's just put the one of the bodies in the casket with someone else—like that guy who's being directly buried on Thursday. His family just viewing him, and then we taking him to cemetery."

"What in the hell are you talking about?" Tyriq stared at Coley as if he had three heads.

"Mr. Jimmy always put the guts in the bottom of the caskets of the autopsied bodies. He'd treat 'em with that white powder and wrap them in newspaper. Nobody ever knew and they didn't stink. We could just put the body under the bed of the casket, cover it good. I know they won't notice."

"Coley, that sounds dumb and crazy," said Tyriq, shaking his head.

"You got a better idea? Rissa gonna flip if she sees these bodies still back here. We gotta do something quick."

In the end, Coley's disturbing logic won over and the two men placed the body to be cremated in the bottom of the casket of a decedent who was only being viewed and buried. Both were nervous and insisted on working the service alone. Clarissa was happy to oblige. She was behind in her work at Williams and folks were starting to complain. Coley and Tyriq acted as pallbearers since the deceased had few relatives. They asked the cemetery workers to assist and they tipped them $20 a piece instead of the usual $5. The men were quiet in the hearse on the way back to until they reached the funeral home where they gave themselves a congratulatory high five. Crisis averted.

CHAPTER 12

Sins of the Father

PRESTON JEFFERSON HAD been a fireman in the neighboring town of Caleb City for twenty years and was married to his wife, Denise, for just as long. After years of a tumultuous union, Preston and Niecy decided to part ways. Although he relocated to Birmingham Alabama, he remained close to his only child Porsche. A few years after relocation, Preston met a white woman named Anne and they too had a twenty year relationship but without marriage or children. Preston loved his drama-free existence with Anne and the couple lived a satisfying life. Porsche visited often and while she wished her parents had stayed together, she appreciated the care and love her father found with Anne. Anne saw to it that anything Preston desired he was given. They had a condo, a boat, and two new cars all in his partner's name.

When Preston died suddenly of an aortic aneurysm, Williams Mortuary was called to handle his final arrangements. Sydney made an appointment to see the family but was totally confused when she received a phone call from both the estranged wife and the live-in girlfriend. They each made plans for the arrangement conference at different times.

"Clarissa, didn't you already book an appointment for the Jefferson family? Who is this Anne Levin?" The vital statistics information was the same, but the informant's names were different.

"Anne Levin sounded like a white woman. She kept saying she was arranging a funeral for her "partner." Denise Jefferson was a straight hood sister who said she was calling about her husband. Sounds like you're going to have an interesting afternoon," laughed Clarissa.

"Right? I'm sick of them already. But if they think I'm going to entertain ideas from both of them, they are mistaken. I'm calling the daughter, Porsche. Maybe she can be the mediator." Syd was fed up with all of the back-and-forth and decided that they should all meet at one time in one space. After two days of cancelled arrangements and hostile phone conversations, the family agreed to a face-to-face meeting.

When Sydney sat down at the conference table to meet with the family, she felt like she was at a divorce proceeding with both women on opposite sides of the room with their respective "camps." Team Niecey comprised Niecey's two sisters, who each took turns rolling their eyes at Anne, Niecey's best friend and of course her and Preston's daughter, Porsche. Niecey clutched in her hand the couples' rumpled and tattered marriage license.

Team Anne consisted of the meek and mousy Anne, a bespectacled brunette, who kept wringing her hands and sniffling, her equally mousy daughter, and her brother, a shorter, balding version of his sister. They all looked terrified and huddled together, unsure of their next move.

"Look, I don't even know why she's even here. Pres was my husband and I plan to bury him at our church and then have a full military burial with honors. Pres was in the Navy," Niecey explained to no one in particular.

"Mama, everyone knows what you want, but Miss Anne should have some input. Daddy was with her for almost twenty years." Porsche ignored her aunts' continual eye rolling and her mother's murderous glare.

Grateful to be acknowledged, Anne spoke in a whisper. "Preston loved the sea. His favorite time was on Saturdays when we took the boat out. He wanted to be cremated and his ashes scattered at sea." She looked down at her lap as tears ran down her cheeks.

"He ain't never said no shit like that when he was with me. I couldn't even get him to take me on that boat ride at Lake Lanier that the church gave. Besides, it don't matter what you want—he's still my husband. Should have gotten him to marry you instead buying some damn boat." Niecey's sisters both high-fived at their sister's last remark.

"Well, my mother is the beneficiary of Mr. Preston's policy. All $250,000 dollars of it and where we come from, money talks and bullshit walks," proclaimed Anne's daughter, not quite so mousy after all.

There was a chorus of "hell naws" and "no she didn't" coming from Team Niecey. Sydney knew things were about to go left and looked to Porsche as the voice of reason before she began to speak.

"Listen, I know that both of you have your own thoughts and wishes for Mr. Jefferson's home-going, but we need to come to a compromise. He obviously loved you both because he shared so much of his life with the two of you. Porsche, what would you like to happen for your dad?" asked Sydney.

Porsche, who had seen the dynamic between the two women, carefully considered her words. She was frustrated, but eager to be the peacemaker and honor her father.

"Daddy never told me what he wanted, but I know he'd want something dignified and special. His whole life was spent in service to others and I would like his home going to reflect that. I would like for him to have a service so his friends from Caleb City and Birmingham can pay their respects. Then, we can entomb some of his ashes in the military cemetery and take the remaining cremated remains to sea. Daddy was never good at making decisions—that's why he never divorced or married either of you. He'd appreciate a split decision," Porsche said ruefully.

Both women were unhappy but realized that they each never pressed the issue and handled their business with Preston or bothered to have the hard conversations, which may have enlightened them about his thoughts concerning his last wishes. Later that afternoon, Syd thought about the situation and it made her think about her own family and what she did and did not know about them. Given the recent events with her own daughter, Sydney knew that even close family concealed pertinent information about themselves. After talking with Vanessa, she decided to explore this further in a fun and creative way.

Sydney had been working tirelessly all week on her latest family gathering. She had decided to throw a sip and see for the newest member of the

family, Vanessa. A traditional southern sip and see was thrown to introduce a new baby to family and friends. Syd figured it would work for a new
cousin as well.

Leona usually always held family gatherings at Grace Lane, but Sydney
wanted to change things up. She sent out a virtual invite and asked everyone to meet around her fire pit for a night under the stars. She spent days
planning her soiree and finally decided she would do pizza night. She hadn't
understood why Avery had insisted they install an outdoor pizza oven, but
it quickly became something that the kids loved to do and definitely came
in handy for this occasion. Sydney decided to elevate the experience by
hiring local chef named Asia who would cook the pizzas and provide farm
to table fresh adult ingredients such as arugula and shrimp.

One of the main things that Syd wanted to do was to unpack what she did
not know about each member of the family. For most of her adult life, she
thought her family's history was an open book, but when her father died
and his secret life with Lula Mae was exposed, she realized there was much
that remained hidden. Even meeting her cousin Vanessa seemed cloaked in
secrecy. Since her uncle's funeral, Sydney found her mother more reserved
and distracted, like something was on her mind. Even though the two
seemed to get past their awkwardness following Leona's announcement,
Sydney still felt like something was going on with her mom. She feared
another revelation was on the horizon, but she had no idea what it could
be. Hence forth, the need for this gathering. Maybe some family bonding
might open the path for communication.

Sydney also decided to make it a multi-generational affair. She realized that
it was important to understand the kids as much as the adults. Sydney also
wanted this event to be an ice breaker between her and Chloe. They hadn't

had any conversations since their confrontation, just a few generic "check in" texts. Other than Avery and Vanessa, Sydney hadn't told anyone about Chloe and Blaze. She purposely invited the two as a couple and was excited when they sent back "yes' on the RSVP.

As everyone arrived, they were greeted with a cocktail or a mocktail as well as an apron with their name embroidered on the side. Laid out on the large patio around her pizza oven there was a beautiful bounty of vegetables, meats, and cheeses. After a quick tutorial from the chef everyone began building their pizzas. It almost became a competition with who was going to make the best pie.

As they waited for the pizzas to cook, Syd decided it was time to introduce her game. She paired up the most unlikely couplings, but this was intentional. She explained that the game entailed the two partners sharing something about themselves that they felt no one knew; a hobby, an interest, or a fact that they hadn't discussed with the family. At first, the participants were skeptical, after all they were a close family who knew a lot about each other, but Syd explained this was to be a bonding experience with one another. Afterward, they were to share the new-found facts with the group. Everyone got their partners name and began to pair up. In the end, she realized it would leave her and Troy paired together. This would be the first time the two had spoken since Tianna's hospital stay. The guys had seemed to work out their differences, Troy admitting that he overreacted and Avery apologizing for losing his cool, but he and Syd hadn't interacted since then.

Leona was a little unnerved at being in Vanessa's presence. She had questioned her daughter as to why a formal party was needed to introduce Vanessa to the family. A Sunday dinner would have done just fine in Leona's mind. She had talked to Vanessa several times since her arrival, but Leona

242 |Lady Undertaker II : The Embalmer's Blues

kept the conversations brief and basic, full of pleasantries and questions about what was going on in Vanessa's life.

Arriving at Sydney's home for the festivities, Leona could see what obviously had to be Vanessa's influence, the patchouli candles lit everywhere, the bundles of herbs used as table decorations and the soft new age music playing in the background. Sydney's parties where always full of designer finery, opulence, and jazz. But what struck her most was how comfortable the two women seemed with each other, laughing and joking, acting more like sisters than the cousins they were supposed to be. Sydney had even begun to copy Vanessa's bohemian style with a bright red patterned silk kimono paired with her favorite jeans and Hermes sandals. Her brown tresses were in their natural curly state and pulled up in messy bun. Her daughter never went anywhere without her hair not blown out and flat ironed.

Vanessa approached her with a hug that left her vaguely uncomfortable and every time she looked her way, she felt her piercing stare. Leona had yet to share Vanessa's parentage with Richard or any member of the family. Leona, who was used to masking her emotions as well as any veteran stage actress, knew this would be a strained evening for her.

Vanessa and Damien circled each other warily, with Damien secretly glad that he had been paired up with the guest of honor. While they had never met prior to this event, Damien was instantly intrigued by Vanessa's beauty and calm, inviting demeanor. Since his troubles with Clarissa, he hadn't looked at or felt anything for any woman. But Vanessa intrigued him. From her premature gray hair and youthful face to her colorful bohemian outfit, there was something about her that made him want to know more. As they shook hands formally, Damien noticed the soft melodic sound of her gold bracelets and the scent of her lavender perfume. He also knew that he had held her hand a little longer than necessary.

"I'm Vanessa, Leona and Sydney's cousin. I've heard a lot about you from Syd." Vanessa felt herself grow warm as she stared into his hazel eyes. He and Sydney only vaguely resembled each other, but they had the exact same eyes.

"I'm Damien, Sydney's brother. And I haven't heard enough about you." Damien's stare was penetrating, making Vanessa blush.

"Well, everything she said was true; you are quite handsome and charming. So, what's your secret fact that you're keeping from the group? You look like a man of mystery," she said flirtatiously. Not one for random banter with a man clearly in a relationship, Damien Moore had the ability to bring women out of themselves.

"That's to keep you guessing," he laughed. "Okay, so I have a black belt in Jeet Kune Do karate. I've been practicing for seventeen years. I always felt I lacked discipline, so karate helped me focus and channel my aggressions into a more manageable form."

Vanessa was impressed and asked him several questions about karate, which he answered knowledgably. After chatting for a few minutes, he turned his attentions to her.

"Okay; so now it's your turn. Tell me all of your secrets."

She laughed, but quickly turned serious. "I recently had the chance to meet my birth mother. It was a long-time dream of mine. I've known that I was adopted since I was twenty-two." She looked around nervously, hoping that Leona was out of earshot.

"How did that go? Did she accept you? Do y'all get along?" He was interested in family situations that were out of the norm—it reminded him that he was not alone in his alternative upbringing.

Vanessa shrugged and looked sad for a moment. "It's a work in progress. She just has to get used to the idea of me. For fifty-four years, she had tried not to dwell on the child she gave up. I didn't expect it to be easy on her. But it's alright; I'm extremely patient." Vanessa smiled trying to convince herself with her own words.

Damien was thoughtful. "Wow, you're fifty-four? You definitely don't look it. We're the same age. I hope things work out with you and your birth mother. Even though I knew Jimmy was my father since I was a kid, I never really found a space in his life. I don't think he could ever reconcile how his family and I fit together." He sighed. "Do you want me to share that with the group? It's kind of intimate."

She was instantly grateful for his understanding and discretion.

"Let's just say I recently met a long lost relative." He shook his head in agreement and touched her hand as their eyes locked.

Clarissa was relieved to be paired with Avery. In her opinion, it was the only kind thing Sydney had done for her in a while. Avery was literally the only adult member of the family who consistently treated her kindly, instead of merely tolerating her presence. Maybe it was because he, too, was an outsider. Avery dove right in, talking about his childhood as a foster child, something that only his wife knew.

"I guess it's not a secret, but I have trouble talking about my childhood. My mother left when I was a kid and my dad tried his best to keep us together, but he was a long-distance truck driver. I ended up in a group home and then finally with my foster mother, Mrs. Hannah Leiberman. She was a retired Jewish music teacher." Avery paused, waiting for Clarissa's reaction.

"You have no reason to be ashamed. Do you keep in touch with your foster mom?" asked Clarissa. She was surprised by Avery's admission. She figured he came from a family with money and status given his success.

Avery sighed. "She passed away a few years ago. Morgan's middle name is Hannah, after her. She taught me how to believe in myself, the value of hard work, and how to play the piano. I guess I appreciate the piano lessons the most because it's how I met the love of my life." He smiled, referring to his chance encounter with Sydney in hotel lobby as he played the hotel's piano years ago. She was captivated by his talent and it was the beginning of their courtship.

He also shared that his childhood made him relish his children more. He had few real happy childhood memories and he was determined to make sure all four of his kids' lives were full of them. As he smiled proudly glancing over at his wife and children, Clarissa realized what Sydney saw in him. Avery was a genuinely good person who appreciated what he had in his wife and family. Again, she sourly wondered how Sydney could be so lucky!

"Okay, Clarissa; it's your turn. And please don't tell me anything about Damien—he's one of my closest friends," he said jokingly.

Clarissa was so touched that he shared something so personal she decided to share something she too kept close to the vest. "Well, I want to be a business owner; I want something of my own, a legacy to leave my son that has nothing to do with the Williams." The words came out in a rush and she then looked around immediately to see if anyone had heard her.

Avery was equally surprised by her admission. He had obviously underestimated her as he thought Clarissa's main interests were gossip and getting Damien to the altar.

"I get it, Clarissa. The Williams family can be a hard act to follow. When Syd and I were first married, I constantly thought I had to prove myself. When I started my own company, I was so nervous. What if I wasn't successful or didn't turn a profit? What would they all say? Thank God it all worked out, but I spent many a sleepless night, worrying."

Clarissa was excited to hear that someone else understood how intimidating the Williams clan could be.

"Well, if you need any help or advice, please feel free to ask. I have a young woman in my company who just works with potential clients on business development. She can listen to your ideas and help turn them into real plans. I understand about building something for yourself. After my family, my business is my greatest achievement and blessing. God has been good to me," he said reverently.

"Thank you so much," answered a grateful Clarissa. She was appreciative of the offer and more that someone saw some type of potential in her.

Chloe was sure her mother was still mad when she saw that she was paired with Deacon Richard. Other than hello and goodbye at family dinners and church, the two had never had a conversation of any kind. Deacon was happy to start the conversation with his little known fact. He had recently solidified his relationship with her grandmother and that she was even planning to retire so they could travel together.

"Are you serious?" Chloe inquired. "Does my mama know?" Chloe couldn't wait to share this with her sister.

"She might. I know your grandmother spoke to her, KC, and Damien recently. I have found my second chance at love, Chloe. I feel so blessed and honored to have a woman like your grandmother to share my life with. I want to travel the world and spend the rest of my life with her. Finding someone to love and share your days with is everything." Deacon Richard was positively beaming.

Chloe looked at Deacon Richard with new eyes. She had originally planned to share something mundane but decided to go for it and share something real.

"Blaze is my girlfriend and we're in love," she whispered. Chloe knew that telling him meant he would probably share with Mom-Mom.

Deacon Richard looked at her with kind eyes and no judgment. "Love is love and I'm happy that you've found it, no matter whom with. The world is lonely out here by yourself."

Chloe's eyes welled with tears. She had no idea how understanding and sweet her grandmother's beau actually was. She hoped that her grandmother would be as accepting.

"Well, after all this you're going have to start calling me something other than Deacon Richard, don't you think?" he quipped with a smile.

Syd tentatively approached Troy. He was sullenly sitting by the fire pit, as apprehensive as she was about this game.

"Hey; how's it going?" she asked with a weak smile. Troy returned her smile with an equally half-hearted effort.

"I'm good," he replied. Troy was obviously still salty about their waiting room blow-up.

Syd knew she'd have to start off this conversation. "I wear glasses and nobody knows. Since I've gotten older, I can't see a lick, so I carry them around, but never put them on in front of people."

Troy looked at her unimpressed. "So what?" Troy replied. "I'm sure KC and Avery have seen you in your glasses."

"Nope, no one has ever seen me with them on." Sydney had considered contacts, but they irritated her eyes.

"Well how do you see, read, or paint?" He was amused that she was too vain to wear glasses in public.

"I squint a lot. I mean, what if Avery doesn't like me in glasses? For so long, looks and appearances was all I cared about. I dye my hair, hide my glasses, and act like I enjoy wearing high heels when all I really want to wear is a pair of flats. I'm trying to change on the inside and show people I'm more than just a chick who likes designer labels. But it's hard, so here I am, showing you my glasses." Sydney didn't realize that her secret was less about her glasses and more about the inward makeover she'd been trying to achieve.

Troy laughed out loud at that one. "Girl, that man would love you if you were blind with a cane and a dog. Besides, people who really know you realize that there's more to you than just your looks or the stuff you buy. You're a good wife, mother, and funeral director. And that isn't going to change if you wear glasses. Okay; so let's see you in these glasses."

Sydney turned her back to the party, pulled out her glasses and put them on. They were Gucci, of course.

"Syd, you still fine," he laughed. But he realized behind all that swagger and confidence was someone who was as insecure as the rest of them and like himself, longed to be seen as more than what she appeared. "You should keep them on," he encouraged.

As Sydney inquired about his hidden fact, Troy became uncharacteristically shy. "Well, when I was young, I wanted to be a rapper, so I read an article about the rap game. The author said you had to study poetry to be a good rapper, so I started writing poetry. I kept at it even after my rap dreams had faded."

"Dang, Troy, that's so cool! We should have an arts night; you could recite your poetry and I could show my paintings. It would be so dope!" Troy wasn't expecting Sydney to be so interested.

"Hey, it might be cool; I've seen some of your work—you pretty good and I'm not into art like that. Imagine how good you're going to be when you wear them glasses," he joked.

The two total opposites laughed heartily at Troy's joke. Though they spent a lot of their time at odds, Troy and Sydney found that evening that they had more in common than either had ever dreamed.

"Yeah, yeah," she retorted laughingly. "And you better write KC one of those poems."

Kendall ran over and jumped in her grandmother's lap, very much like the little girl she still was.

"So what's going on, baby?" asked Leona.

Kendall laughed, "Nothing, Mom-Mom. This will be quick because I have no secrets. I'm an open book! Just check my Instagram," she joked.

"Ha, darling! Everyone has secrets. Let's see. Are you dating someone special?"

"Dating? No, I wouldn't call it dating. Well, not really."

"Well, are you dating more than one person?" Leona gave her granddaughter a sly smile.

Kendall blushed, but answered "Maybe."

"Well young and foolish is quite alright, but safety first, baby. Make sure you use a condom!"

"Dang, Mom-Mom, of course I do. I'm not crazy, just enjoying being young and single!" Kendall wasn't ready to discuss her sex life with her grandmother.

"Don't think your Mom-Mom has forgotten those days. I used to sneak your Pop-Pop into my dorm at Spelman many a night! "

"Mom-Mom, we're still doing that," she laughed. They both cackled at their memories.

"Well we can't share that with the group because," Kendall and Leona laughed as they exclaimed in unison, "Harris women don't tell!"

Short one person since Tre declined to attend tonight's gathering, the twins were paired together with Blaze. They stared curiously at Blaze, with Morgan as usual, breaking the ice.

"We're Morgan and Jamie! Is Blaze your real name?"

"No," she answered truthfully. "My real name is Brianna."

"Cool! So you're my sister's friend?" Both twins looked at Blaze expectantly. Blaze decided to tell her truth.

"Yes, I'm her girlfriend." She wasn't sure if the twins knew what she meant.

"Like you're gay? Chloe is gay?" As most young people their age, they knew more about modern sexuality than their parents.

"Yes!"

"Wow, I didn't think Chloe was that cool," said Jamie.

Blaze laughed at Jamie's remark. "Chloe's cool; just quiet. Are you guys okay with that?" She hoped that her girlfriend wouldn't be angry that she shared their relationship with her siblings. Since they received the invitation from Chloe's mother, Blaze had urged Chloe to be more open and "out" to her family. "Your mother wouldn't have invited us if she wasn't okay with it," was Blaze's thought on the situation.

"Of course. You seem pretty cool," Blaze smiled. She loved that kids were so open to everything.

"So, what's you guys' secret?"

Morgan and Jamie looked at each other, debating on how to explain their secret.

"Okay, so it's our parents—they really embarrass us. They are always touching, kissing, and holding hands in public—it's humiliating. At Jamie's soccer game, my friends said they were actually kissing. Dad even posted a picture of Mom in shorts and hashtagged it #hotgirlsummer. Do you know how embarrassing that was? Our mom is not a hot girl; she's a mom! We just wish they would stop. They act like their young, but they're not!" Morgan's speech was impassioned while her twin shook his head in agreement.

Blaze started to crack up. She wished she'd had those kinds of problems when she was growing up. These kids had no idea how fortunate they were to have parents who still loved each other.

Tianna was happily teamed up with Grandma Belle. After admiring her dress and the beautiful drawing that Sydney had sketched on the pink cast she still wore, Belle expected her secret to be something along the lines of what she wanted for Christmas or a boy she had a crush on. She was shocked to hear her blurt out that she was afraid of her brother and that KC might get mad and leave them.

"Sweetie, KC isn't going to get mad and leave you. She loves you and your dad and Tre." Belle tried to be reassuring and calm, but her mind was racing. What was going on in the Watkins house?

"Tre' is really mean to her and to me too. The only one he's afraid of is Dad."

"Tianna, has Tre' ever hurt you? Or threatened to hurt you or KC?" Belle held her breath, waiting for her granddaughter to answer.

"I can't talk about it, Grandma Belle. Can I go check on my pizza?" Tianna seemed eager to escape.

"Alright, baby. Let's go see about these pizzas." A disturbed Belle was glad to distract her granddaughter, while she mentally prepared herself for the talk she desperately needed to have with her daughter and son-in-law.

DJ and KC sat chatting easily. The teen admired his aunt as she was always so interested in his life, asking questions and being supportive. He really didn't understand why Tre didn't like her.

KC casually asked what his secret was but like her mother, was not at all prepared for the answer.

"Tre sells drugs, Aunt KC, and he's in trouble. The guy he sells for is a bad dude. He beat down some guy in front of me, him, and Jamie. I'm scared, Aunt KC." She noticed that DJ was trembling as he spoke.

"It's okay, sweetie. I'm actually not surprised. I knew something was going on with him. I'm going to take care of this; don't you worry." KC wanted to seem adult and in control, but she was as scared as DJ was. A sheltered kid all her life, she had no idea about drugs and street life.

"Please don't tell him that I told. I don't want to be a snitch, but wrong is wrong."

KC assured him she would keep his confidence. "But DJ, we have to think of something to say when our turn comes."

"Okay, Aunt KC; you can say I'm afraid of the dark because I am. But what will I say about you?"

KC chuckled. "The truth, sweetie; I never learned how to ride a bike. My dad always had me studying and learning bible verses! I can recite most of the New Testament, but show me a bike or roller skates and I'm clueless."

"Dang, Auntie; that's crazy! But no worries, I'll teach you." The pair laughed and high-fived.

Once everyone had completed their assignments and sat down to enjoy their pizza creations, they casually went around the large rustic table with everyone sharing their new insights on the others. There was laughter, some tears, and lots of questions for new couples Leona and Richard and Blaze and Chloe.

It was truly a magical night for the family. Vanessa ended the evening with a heartfelt prayer about the depth of understanding for each other. She recited a well-known quote by Leonardo Da Vinci, "The noblest pleasure is the joy of understanding."

As everyone began to gather their things to leave, Chloe pulled Blaze aside and whispered and nodded in the direction of her parents. Blaze smiled, kissed Chloe quickly, and said her goodbyes.

Chloe stood by waiting for her mother to see her guests off before she approached her.

"Mom, can I crash here with you guys? I know Kendall's going to stay over. We need to talk, and I've been missing you guys, especially you, Mom. I need my family more than I even care to admit." Chloe had felt lonely and adrift the last few weeks. She, her mom, and Kendall shared a unique bond and everything seemed out of sync when that bond was weakened. Sydney grabbed her daughter and held her for a long time.

"I would like nothing more."

Tre and DJ met up to discuss their situation Monday afternoon, with Tre picking up his cousin after school.

"Man, you missed a cool night on Saturday with the fam. Felt like we all got closer. And we made these bomb ass pizzas. Aunt Syd hired this chick to bake them for us—," but Tre interrupted DJ's story.

"C'mon cuz, that family shit ain't my thing. Bunch of fakes trying to act like they care. It's all good though. But I gotta get at that funeral home and that fluid. We gotta get lil man to get those keys this weekend. Nine ain't playing with me. I owe him money and he says he will get at my Pops when's he's not even looking." The usually -acting Tre' seemed genuinely frightened.

"Alright, man. It's just that Jamie, he's a just a kid…." He trailed off, deep in thought about what this meant for him and Jamie. Vaping and drinking a few beers was bad enough but stealing from their parents and breaking into the funeral home was in a whole other league.

"I got you. I'll get him to do it," DJ knew he could convince his younger cousin to do anything.

Tre breathed a sigh of relief. The tight rope he was walking might finally disappear.

Saturday came sooner than anyone expected. DJ had spoken to Jamie and explained that he needed him to get his mom's keys and they would do the rest. Saturdays were usually Syd and Avery's date night. The twins would snicker at their parent's excitement for the evening. The couple usually made an attempt to dress up and impress each other. For Sydney, this usually meant heels and a clutch. It would be fairly easy for Jamie to secure the keys, which Syd had left in her Louis Vuitton work tote. His greatest dilemma was to get away from the girls. Tianna and Morgan were planning what movie they would all watch that evening and expected Jamie and DJ to join in the festivities.

To his great relief, his sisters Kendall and Chloe popped in as they sometimes did on the weekends. They decided to watch the Beyoncé "Lion King" special, with the girls making it easier for him to slip out with the guys. Jamie called out that he was hanging out with DJ. The girls barely acknowledged him for all the giggling. He quickly slipped out and slid into the backseat of Tre's car, handing the coveted keys to DJ.

"I'm telling you, KC I'm not trying to hear this crap about my son. First Damien, now you saying Tre is selling drugs. My son ain't no thug." Troy's voice was controlled, but KC could tell by his demeanor that her husband was angry.

"I have no reason to make this up! He's in trouble with some bad people and could get himself killed. You have to believe me," cried KC. She felt guilty about betraying DJ's confidence, but this was far more serious that her nephew being perceived as a snitch.

"Okay, KC, if this is true, who told you?" Troy was frustrated and was sure the information came from Sydney.

"DJ told me at the party last weekend. He said that the head drug dealer, or whatever he's called, had beaten another man up in front of DJ, Jamie, and Tre. They're good kids, honor students, and shouldn't have ever seen anything like that."

"And since DJ said it, it has to be true?" Troy sighed and sat back on the sofa. The quiet Saturday night watching Netflix was now out of the question. "I'll talk to him when he gets home tonight. I'm sure DJ and Jamie got the whole thing confused."

"Dammit, Troy, you need to call that boy now! You can't wait until later. Later might be too late!"

"Alright, alright. I'll call him now." Troy called his son's phone, but it switched immediately to voicemail. He tried again, this time leaving a terse message for Tre to call him ASAP. Troy looked at his wife's worried expression and realized that he too was worried.

The three boys were silent, only the sound of Money Bag Yo's rap filling the car. Upon arriving at the funeral home, Tre cut the music and the lights. The funeral home was dark except for the outside lighting. The boys decided to enter through the employee entrance at Jamie's suggestion. He shared that there were less cameras placed there. His mom usually used it when she was late or wanted to avoid folks.

DJ insisted that they leave Jamie in the car as the lookout. He was to call them if he saw a car or the police. Tre fumbled with the keys, finally getting in using the flashlight on his phone to light the way. DJ knew his way around the funeral in the dark as he'd been coming here since he was a toddler. He felt sick to his stomach breaking into what had been his childhood playground. They quickly reached the locked storage closet inside the morgue where the chemicals were stored. It took them almost ten minutes to go through all of Sydney's keys to find the right one. Upon opening the closet, they grabbed the boxes, unsure they were taking the correct chemicals, but something was better than nothing. Sweaty and full of adrenaline, the boys quickly carried the boxes to the employee entrance, ready to make a clean getaway.

At just that moment, the hall light came on as Ronnie, the night clean-up man, approached the boys. A Williams Mortuary employee for over forty years, Ronnie was past retirement age, but was loyal to the Williams family. They had buried both his wife and son and countless family members over the years, most for almost nothing. The funeral home was his life and its staff his extended family. He took his job very seriously.

"Who's there? What y'all boys doing in here? DJ, is that you?" Ronnie immediately recognized the young boy from being in the morgue with his dad.

"Yeah, Mr. Ronnie; it's me. Just getting some stuff for my dad. We were just leaving."

Ronnie looked at the boys with skepticism. "Son, your daddy was just here 'bout an hour ago and he never said anything 'bout you coming. I'm going to just call him to check."

The boys traded terrified glances. This whole plan was about to blow up in their faces if Ronnie contacted Damien.

"Yo, old man, you don't need to call nobody. My cuz said we getting stuff for his dad; that's it and that's all," Tre advanced menacingly toward the older man.

"Boy, I don't know who you think you're talking to, but you better back up!" Ronnie wasn't used to young folks talking back to their elders. *Someone needed to teach this one some manners*, he thought to himself.

"Naw, old man; you better back the fuck up." Tre pushed the box up against Ronnie, causing him to lose his balance. The elderly man fell to the ground hitting his head on the glass table in the hallway. Bleeding and stunned, Ronnie lay on the floor as Tre moved closer, kicking him with force.

"I told you to back up; now I gotta hurt you," said Tre, now fully enraged.

"Stop, dude; let's just go okay?" pleaded DJ. He grabbed at Tre's shirt, but he threw him off, continually kicking and taunting Ronnie.

"This old fool gonna call your dad. I can't let him do that." Tre stepped on Ronnie's phone, which had fallen out during the scuffle. "Can't call nobody now, can you, old man?" He kicked the older man a final time, causing a series of moans to escape from Ronnie's bloody mouth. DJ was weeping silently, watching the scene in horror.

"Help me drag him in the storage closet, DJ," Tre yelled. But DJ was rooted to the spot, having a complete meltdown. Mr. Ronnie was a nice man who always told him stories of his own grandson who was DJ's age. *This shouldn't be happening*, he thought miserably.

Both boys turned as the employee entrance opened. They both expected to see Jamie, but it was Damien's angry face that confronted them, with a scared Jamie right behind him. The boy had called his uncle when saw the lights go on and heard yelling.

"What the hell are you doing?" He looked at his son, clearly disappointed. "You two, go get in my car and don't move." DJ and Jamie both ran away, clearly upset and relieved to be away from the violent scene. "What are we doing here? Son, you need to put the box down."

"Unc, I'mma need to leave with this box, so you gonna need to step aside," Tre said and gripped the box tighter.

"Naw, son, it's not going down like that. Put the box down so I can tend to this man whose blood you have on your shirt."

Tre advanced closer with the box still in hand. "I'm in a situation. I gotta give this dude this embalming fluid or there's going to be a problem. Let me by, Uncle Damien."

Damien was unwavering, staring right in the young man's eyes.

"Can't let you do that, son. Those bottles have serial numbers, which can trace back to this funeral home. I'm sorry."

Tre was unmoved by his uncle's speech. He pulled out his small caliber .22 and raised it toward Damien. "Don't make me shoot you, please!"

"You don't have heart enough to shoot me, but since you a man with a gun now, go ahead, shoot your shot. Go ahead!" Damien was almost taunting the boy, whose hands were trembling, barely able to keep the firearm steady. Tre decided to make a run for it but as he got to the door, gun in hand; he was confronted with his worst nightmare—his father.

"Troy Tavius Watkins, III, just what do you think you're doing?" Troy's booming voice filled up the room.

Tre dropped the box in shock, as his father in one fell swoop, grabbed the gun from his hand and slapped him in the face. Rubbing his stinging cheek, Tre stammered as he tried to explain.

"I, I was trying to protect you, Dad."

"How? By breaking into the funeral home and beating up an old man?" Troy gestured toward Ronnie, to whom Damien was rendering first aid. "Boy, you don't have to protect me from nobody. Now, tell me the whole story." He and Tre walked outside as the story began to unfold.

Inside, Damien realized that Ronnie needed an ambulance for his injuries. After calling 911, he leaned over and whispered to the injured man.

"I'm sorry that this happened to you, Ronnie, but you didn't see who attacked you. Do you understand? I'm going to take care of everything, but you never saw the guy, got it?" Groggy and in pain, Ronnie still knew not to cross Damien.

"Yes, son, I understand. He pushed me down and I never saw his face."

"Good man. Hold on; the ambulance is coming right now." Soon, the funeral home was ablaze with lights and sirens. Troy had put his son in his SUV and driven away. Damien stayed and answered the emergency technician's questions. He explained that Ronnie had been ambushed by someone who had broken into the funeral home. Unfortunately, Ronnie never saw his assailant. The police asked the injured man a few additional questions and Ronnie was then taken to the hospital for treatment of his wounds. The EMT assessed that they would probably keep him overnight but that he should be fine.

The police asked Damien about the security video, but he explained it would have to be retrieved from their security company. He assured them he would obtain the video and make a formal complaint in the morning. Damien secured the building and got back in his car. He leaned his head on the wheel; the events of the night were taking their toll on him. The boys were silently staring at him, just waiting for him to explode.

"I just don't know what you two were thinking—y'all are good kids. I'm so disappointed in you both tonight. This is our family business, our legacy. We don't steal period, and especially not from family." Damien stopped talking, unable to find the words to express the anguish he felt. He did everything he could to keep his son away from the streets and the drug game, and tonight he felt as though he failed him.

But right now, he knew he had to call Sydney, Avery, and KC to apprise them of the situation. A breathless Sydney answered on third ring.

"Hey, bro; what's going on?"

"Hey, baby girl; we have a big problem. Are you and Avery together?"

"Yes, we're in the city at STK Steakhouse. We just finished dinner." Sydney hoped her brother's call had nothing to do with the funeral home. This was her night off and she was enjoying the ambiance of the restaurant and her husband's company.

"Sorry, sis, but you're going have to cut that short. This is an emergency."

"Damn, D; you're scaring me. Are the kids alright? Is Mama okay?" Her annoyance at being interrupted quickly turned to fear.

"Nobody's hurt but nothing is okay. Please just hurry up. We'll meet at your place." He hung up and made the same phone call to KC. She, however, asked him about Troy. She said her husband quickly left the house after receiving a phone call and hadn't returned. Damien explained that she would understand when she got to Syd's. He contacted Troy last, telling him to meet everyone at Syd's but to drop Tre off at home. This was a conversation that he didn't need to be present for.

The girls were surprised to see all of their parents arriving at the house around the same time. They were also curious at why DJ and Jamie appeared so glum. Damien took control of the situation, sending the boys to the pool guest house while the parents talked in Sydney formal living room.

"What the hell is going on, Damien?" Sydney looked worried and held her husband's hand tightly.

Damien relayed the night's events including the hospitalization of Ronnie. Each parent's reaction was different. KC began to weep at hearing Ronnie's extensive injuries, Avery had turned pale when his son's involvement in the situation became apparent, and Troy was just ashamed, not making eye contact with anyone. But Sydney was livid and finally exploded.

"I can't believe this shit!! That thug had my babies out there breaking into the funeral home to steal our embalming fluid? First, he's disrespecting KC; then he's throwing his sister down the steps, now this!"

An angry Troy was about to start defending his son when his wife stopped him, "No, Troy, don't you dare defend him! She's right—DJ has never been in trouble before, and dammit, Jamie is a child! Tianna told my mother that she's afraid of her brother, that he's cruel to her, and that he threatened her if she told the truth about her fall. Now he's selling drugs and beating a man so badly that he's in the hospital. He needs help, Troy."

"Humph, he needs to go to jail," Sydney was definitely not letting this go.

"Whatever, Sydney!" Their recent truce was definitely over. "You and your perfect children and fucking perfect life. Nobody in this family ever does anything wrong. I guess it wasn't your precious son who stole the keys."

"Yes, but to help YOUR drug-dealing thug son stay out of trouble," she spat back.

"Stop it, Troy," yelled KC. "I'm sick of you bashing my family when something goes wrong in your life. We aren't perfect, you aren't perfect… no one is. But what we do is support each other. Now, either we can work together as family to get through this or you can leave now! Your choice." KC took her seat, her hands trembling. Troy was so shocked by his wife's outburst that he sat down.

Damien figured this was his chance to take control of the volatile situation.

"Look, we've got to devise a plan to deal with this situation and keep everybody safe. I've already spoke to Ronnie and he's going to keep quiet, but the police are expecting me to turn in the security video. There are no cameras at that particular entrance, but you can see Tre's car on the street. Tre's going to need to turn his self in tomorrow and say he was in the funeral home and he was startled by Ronnie. He was scared, he pushed the old man, he fell, and Tre ran out. Ronnie will go along with that story. But it's going to cost us. Once his family finds out, they are definitely going to want cash, and lot of it." Damien had thought up the story on his way over. If Ronnie or the funeral home didn't press charges, the whole thing might blow over.

"I don't like this plan of yours, D," stated a very angry Troy. "Why does my son take all the blame? As I see it all three of them broke in, but only Tre is the only one going down for it."

"Man, this is not the time to get in your feelings about your son. DJ and Jamie tried to help Tre out of a bad situation because he's selling drugs. Tre tried to steal boxes of our embalming fluid and put an old man in the hospital. He needs to take responsibility because this is his mess, plain and simple. Now, either we tell the whole truth and he does three to five at Phillips, or we do it my way and maybe he gets probation or time in a juvenile facility. Your call, bro."

Troy put his head in his hands at the mention of the Phillips State Prison. He knew that hard time would only make his son's problems worse. Damien's plan still didn't sit well with him, but he couldn't take the alternative.

Taking Troy's silence for acquiescence, Damien continued with his plan of action. "I say we draw up a settlement agreement. Syd, contact Mr. Hendrickson and get his law firm working on something immediately. We need to make sure Ronnie is compensated and silent. Troy, you need to reach out to Tyrone Pickney from 6th Street since y'all used to hustle together back in the day. He's uncle to this cat that Tre's working for. Smooth things over with him. We don't need some low-level street punk having beef with our family. Avery, you are on research. We need a good strict military school for Tre and a good criminal attorney. The school should be somewhere near enough that he can visit, but far away enough that he won't know anybody. He needs a clean start. Look, it's been a long night. Let's get these kids home and get together tomorrow afternoon for a progress report." Everyone stood up and dispersed silently, but Sydney stopped her brother and hugged him hard.

"Hey, baby girl, what was that for?" When Sydney released him from the embrace, she had tears in her eyes.

"You remind me so much of Daddy. You took charge just like he would in a crisis. I'm just so proud of you."

As Damien went to get his son, he realized he too had tears in his eyes.

The following day, the family sans Troy and Tre gathered at Syd's for an update. Each set of parents had chastised their sons in their own personal way. Syd and Avery had a long talk with Jamie about the theft of his mother's keys and about not sharing some of the events that had led up to that night. Jamie profusely apologized and was put on a month-long punishment. They did also tell him that they were proud that he had called his uncle. Things might have been worse if he hadn't.

Damien took a similar approach with DJ. As he listened to his son explain how he just wanted to help his cousin stay out of trouble, Damien was secretly proud of DJ. He wished he'd had someone to look out for him growing up. DJ apologized to him and later to his Aunt Syd for not taking better care of Jamie. Damien made him sit out half of the track and field season as punishment. He wasn't happy but he accepted the punishment. Damien also went to the police with the video clip, which only showed Tre's car on the scene. He had wanted to share the whole incident with Clarissa, but she was up and gone before he had even woke up. Something was definitely going on with her, but Damien was far too preoccupied with his own family drama.

KC arrived looking worn out. She explained that Troy had taken Tre to meet with the lawyer Avery had found. The attorney figured that they would release Tre into his parents' custody as he was a minor. Syd had reached out to her former roommate and Municipal Court judge Didi Roberts. While she would have to recuse herself from the case, she assured that her colleagues would be fair since Tre's family was so well-respected in the community. Avery also emailed them that morning a list of boarding schools to check out. KC had also insisted that Tre go stay with relatives in light of Tianna's fear of her brother. She was glad Tianna had stayed at Sydney's last night as things were far too volatile in their home.

A bright spot for Damien was another encounter with Vanessa. Sydney had convinced her cousin to move out of her hotel and stay in her modern guest house. Sydney had shared with Vanessa the previous night's drama and she had offered her advice on how to talk with her young son. Vanessa was sitting out by the pool when Damien came and sat next to her. After a few moments of witty banter, Vanessa gently broached the subject of DJ and Tre. She listened as Damien talked about his son and at times his own childhood. She was intrigued by his personality and attracted to his smoldering good looks. He stared so deeply at times she thought he could see her soul. Unfortunately, Vanessa had to excuse herself to take a phone call from a patient. When she returned, she found he had abruptly left. However, on the table next to her glass of wine was his number scribbled hastily on the back of a business card with the message—"Please call."

Mondays were always busy at Williams Mortuary, but this Monday was different. The buzz was not about new death calls or funerals, but about the real story behind Ronnie "accident." There were several wild stories circulating, none even close to the truth. KC, Sydney, and Damien tried to conduct business as usual, but all three were deep in their feelings. Damien dropped in on KC to check on her and ask her a favor.

"Hey, cuz. Can you look into who owns that new place Guiding Light? And who's the supervisor over there? I heard some crazy stuff about them and I'm just curious who's in charge." He stood there expectedly, not ready to share the information he'd heard about Tyriq.

KC sighed, still worn out from the weekend's events. "I guess you want me to do this now?"

Damien turned on his mega-watt smile. KC shook her head and logged into the state's website. "You could have done this yourself, you know. It's public record."

As the information flashed across her screen, KC frowned and continued to scroll. As she got to the end of the record, her frown turned to shock.

"What's up? Who's the owner?"

"Well, apparently you are. You and Clarissa Moore."

CHAPTER 13

When Your Luck Runs Out

AN EXCITED CLARISSA was in her car, rapping loudly along with Megan Thee Stallion. She had just made the largest funeral arrangement of her short career. The Jones family had called her regarding the loss of Jerry Jones. "Big Jer," as he was known by friends and family was a long-distance truck driver from Maxwell who died in a fiery crash in Kentucky. Jerry kept his family afloat with the proceeds from his profitable trucking business.

Mama Jo was devastated at the loss of her one and only son and the family breadwinner. She, her daughters, and their children relied on heavily on Jerry for everything. So distraught at his death, she had been confined to her bed. Her daughters asked Clarissa to come to their home to make arrangements.

Clarissa was shocked and a little out of her element when they led her to Mama Jo's bedroom. Propped up on pillows with a soiled nightgown and a bonnet, the matriarch sobbed throughout the process and barked orders.

"Mrs. Jones?" Clarissa asked tentatively.

"Yes, baby, it's me. Don't you go calling me anything but Mama Jo! You family now that you handling my baby's home going," the elderly woman explained. "You sit down right here, so I can hear you good." Clarissa was forced to sit edge of the bed as the only other available chair in the room was Mama Jo's potty chair.

The entire Jones family had seemingly gathered in the small dingy bedroom to be a part of the arrangement conference, each with opinions of their own. Nieces, nephews, and cousins lined the walls, staring intently at Clarissa. The family wanted the best of everything for Jerry and surprisingly had the means to pay.

"I need my baby boy to have the best! I want a gold casket like Michael Jackson had and he needs a horse and carriage just like James Brown. He ain't gonna see it, but he'll be riding in style."

"That's right, Mama. And we need at least four limousines. My friend's daddy had a stretch hummer limo. Y'all got those?" asked one sister eagerly. The other nodded in agreement.

Clarissa was overjoyed at all of the upcharges she was able to bill for. In the end, the funeral was almost $18,000.00. She was determined to have all the staff present and sold the family on a two-day affair. This service would have the town talking for sure.

As she arrived home, with all the details and plans she had swirling in her head, she barely noticed that her house was totally dark, but Damien's Escalade was in the driveway. Still humming, she turned on the lights throughout the house and she stopped at the kitchen to put her things down on the counter. It was then that she heard Damien's voice.

"Do you have something you'd like to share?" Damien sat in the darkness, a glass of bourbon sitting on the table in front of him.

"Shit, Damien; you scared me. Why are you sitting in the dark like some crazy person?"

"I scared you?" He laughed mirthlessly. "That's interesting because I thought a boss bitch like yourself wasn't scared of anything."

"Bitch? What the hell are you talking about?" Clarissa had a sinking feeling in her gut but tried to act natural.

"You want to tell me why Clarissa Moore is the President of Guiding Light Funeral Home and Damien Moore is the licensed funeral director and supervisor? I don't know this Clarissa Moore. I do know Clarissa Dickson. But let me stop talking and let you explain."

"Damien, I… I can explain. Wait a minute; where's DJ?" She needed to stall for time and really didn't want to have this conversation within earshot of her son.

"He's with his family. Don't change the subject." He began to tap his fingers rhythmically on the wood table.

"Damien, I've wanted to talk to you for some time about this." She told him everything, from starting the business eight months ago to her current funerals. She was proud of her accomplishments in spite of his anger.

Things got heated when he questioned how his name became involved and she told him about Coley impersonating him for the state board inspection.

"Are you fucking serious? That half-wit signed my name to a legal document. I could lose my license behind this shit!"

"He's not a half-wit; he's a damn good embalmer. You taught him well because his work looks good. Look, I'm sorry. I wanted to share this with you, but things haven't been that great between us lately."

"Naw, Rissa our shit been crazy for a while. And here I thought you were dipping out on me. Actually, I wish that had been the case. If you had told me about this half-assed idea, I would have told you that Miss Leona signed over the funeral home to me, KC, and Syd two months ago."

"What? Why didn't you tell me?" Clarissa stared in astonishment at her partner. How could he have kept something so important from her? She wondered when their union had become so disjointed.

"I'm finally going to carry on my father's legacy the way it should be. KC, Sydney, and I are going to make a perfect team."

Clarissa, unable to conceal her disgust, exploded. "Once again, you're choosing them when this would have been about you and me and our family's legacy." She was near tears, fighting to stay calm.

Damien shook his head. "You just don't get it, Clarissa! There's no legacy because there's no us anymore. We're not running a business together and we aren't getting married."

Openly crying now, Clarissa asked the question that she already knew the answer to. "Doesn't any part of you still love me?"

Damien looked away, knowing that the next statement would forever change their lives. "Rissa, I will always have love for you, but I'm not in love with you. Haven't been for a long while."

Clarissa slumped in her kitchen chair, unsure that her legs would hold her. "So, what happens now? Are we splitting up?"

"Splitting up? I ain't worried about this relationship right now when both our livelihoods are at stake. The state board is on to you. KC provided me with the information. This could affect her as well since we are cousins and business partners. Sydney filed the paperwork last week, making me the supervisor and as soon as it hits the board they are going to know because even you must know I can't be supervisor at two different places." Damien began to pace floor, deep in thought regarding his next move.

"I'll have to file a report with the state ASAP since clearly the signature on file isn't mine," speaking more to himself, than to Clarissa.

A panicked Clarissa was clearly upset about the thought of him informing the state board and the potential closing of her business. "Wait a minute, Damien; you don't have to do this. I'm sure we can work something out. Maybe Sydney can be the supervisor at Williams. I've got employees and funerals. People depend on me." In a last ditch effort, she stood up and reached for him, seductively in an attempt to change his mind.

Damien recoiled at her touch. "Naw, sister; that ain't working this time. My name and my reputation mean more to me than a piece of ass." His rebuff stung as she moved away.

"Please give me a few weeks. I'll work this out! I just have one service next week and then we can work on shutting it down."

Damien stared at her dumbfounded. "Girl, you don't have weeks. This is going to blow up in a few days. Shut that place down now. Pack up the files, lock the doors, and shut off the phones. Did you pick up the body yet? Take any money?"

"No; I just made arrangements tonight. They haven't even signed the contract yet."

"Good; just send the case to Williams. I'll take over and it will be okay." His dismissive attitude regarding her and her business infuriated her.

"What! This is my case and I'm not giving it to them!" She was enraged at the mere thought. "It's just a burial—the guy can't even be viewed. It will be a small service and then off to the cemetery. We can handle it!"

"Whatever, yeah I'm sure you and 'your staff' will handle it," retorted Damien, using air quotes sarcastically. "After that one it's over. I'll give you some cash to get out of town till this all dies down. There's going to be an investigation and you will be arrested for fraud if you get caught."

Never once had Clarissa thought about the ramifications if the truth were to be found out. She figured naively that Damien would be happy about having a funeral home of his own. She even thought he might be impressed that she was able to pull it together on her own.

"Gimme some cash? What about our life? What about our home? DJ needs to stay in Maxwell for school...," she was silenced by his hard look.

"I have this house and I will keep it. DJ will stay with me. You made this mess, so you'll make this sacrifice."

"I can't live without my son! Where will I go?"

Damien's eyes held no sympathy and his voice was steely as he answered her. "I don't really care where you go, but I suggest you go north."

Damien turned and walked away but left her with a few parting words. "DJ is at my sister's, spending the night. I figured you needed some time to get yourself and your things together."

It was when she heard the door shut that her hysterical sobbing began.

Damien got in his truck and backed out of his driveway. He felt as if the weight of the world was on his shoulders. He wouldn't even let his mind think about what came next. He knew his son would be devastated at his mother's departure and Damien wasn't sure he had what it took to be a single parent. But he couldn't risk DJ getting caught in the crosshairs of this fiasco.

As Damien drew closer to Sydney's home, he knew he didn't have it in him to put on a poker face for the family. Even though the love had been gone for some time, he was hurt by Clarissa's actions and her betrayal still stung. Damien couldn't imagine a life that didn't include Clarissa in some way, shape, or form. Instead of parking in Sydney's circular driveway, he maneuvered his truck to the side entrance near the guest house. He got out and tapped softly on the door. Vanessa's face registered surprise and then pleasure.

"You up for some company?" he asked.

"Always," she replied softly, as she fully opened the door and let him inside.

Early the next morning, Avery, while working out on his Peloton saw something that felt like a mirage. Vanessa and Damien slowly exited the guest house, walking toward his car hand in hand. He kept his head down to try and avoid being seen through the gym's glass windows. However, he couldn't help but notice the intimacy between the pair. He knew he should mind his own business, but he couldn't wait to tell Sydney about this new development.

Later that morning, as KC was getting her coffee from Lola's, the local coffee shop, Damien slipped in behind her.

"Morning, Cuz," said Damien brightly.

"Hey, D; how is it going? You're awfully chipper this morning. How did you make out with Mrs. Moore?" quipped KC.

"Here you go… about that, cousin. I need to talk to you before we go into the building." Damien's voice and demeanor turned serious.

He bought her coffee and added a dozen of the girls' favorite honey buns to their order. He recounted the evening to his cousin and shared his desire for Clarissa to leave town.

"D, do you think she'll do it?" KC was not as convinced as him about Clarissa's ability to do the right thing and shut down her operation.

"What choice does she have? That's why I need you to keep this under wraps until I can figure some things out."

"Are you bribing me with this honey bun?" asked KC, jokingly.

"Absolutely not, State Board lady. I have a whole dozen for you to enjoy," laughed Damien.

KC hesitated but reluctantly agreed. Damien assured her that Clarissa would dissolve the mystery business. KC hoped he was right for everyone's sake.

KC, still unsettled by the conversation she had with her cousin, entered the funeral home and was greeted by overly friendly Clarissa.

"Hey, girl; good morning!! What's happening?" drawled Clarissa.

"Not much," answered KC dryly. "And you—how are you?" countered KC, trying to pierce her with a stare.

"You know, girl, easy breezy. Are those honey buns from Lola's? I can smell them from over here!"

KC clutched the honey buns closer to her. "Yup, they sure are," answered KC, who kept walking and didn't offer to share. As she finally reached to the sanctity of her office, she was puzzled by Clarissa's good mood. She didn't seem like a woman who had just broken up with her man and had to close her business and leave town.

Meanwhile, back at her desk, Clarissa too, was surprised. The nicer of the two girls, KC, was usually pretty talkative, but obviously that heifer, Sydney, was rubbing off on her. *No matter*, thought Clarissa, *I got shit to do.*

Clarissa had no intention of closing her business before the Jones service. Once everyone, including Damien, saw how tight this service was, they would see that her business was viable. She took out her phone and called the Georgia Horse and Carriage Company to place the order.

Leona placed her bags on the settee as she slipped out of her sweater coat. She appreciated all the energy of a bustling household full of children and grandchildren, but she also treasured this time of day and the solitude it brought. No one wanted anything from her or had a problem for her to solve. She had just gotten off of a red eye flight from California with Richard. The two had spent a romantic two weeks on Catalina Island and had attended the annual Catalina jazz festival. They thoroughly enjoyed all of the performances as well as the laid-back lifestyle. She confessed that it was something that she could get used to. Leona had worked tirelessly for the last forty years and she was determined to do something different.

As she moved to the kitchen, the doorbell rang. She could not imagine what Richard could had left behind as he had only departed twenty minutes earlier. She was shocked to see Damien when she opened the door.

"Hey, Ms. Leona! How was your trip?" asked Damien. He gave her a warm hug.

"Simply wonderful. I was in awe of all that California had to offer. And Richard was an exceptional travel partner. We had a ball. How are you? Did you miss me?" teased Leona.

Damien recounted the past weeks to her with great detail. Without telling her about Clarissa's ownership of Guiding Light, he did tell her that their relationship was over, and they had decided to go their separate ways. Leona was full of questions, but mostly her concern was for DJ and how this would affect him.

"We haven't told him yet. It's going to be hard on him, especially since she's planning to leave town and stay with relatives."

Leona expressed surprise. "She's leaving her son behind? That doesn't seem like Clarissa at all." Leona stood up and began to busy herself with making coffee.

Damien was a little nervous at this line of questioning, so he decided to change the subject. "We'll have to find a new office manager."

Leona sighed and shook her head. She always knew that this relationship would negatively affect the business somehow, but truth be told, it was no longer her problem.

He hesitated when he came to the subject of Vanessa, but he knew he had come to the house for a reason. "Ma'am, you know we haven't always seen eye to eye, but things have gotten better between you and me in the past few years. I believe we've come a long way…"

"Damien, you're making me nervous! What's going on?"

"I've been talking a lot to Vanessa…"

Leona interrupted. "She's still here?" She had hoped that Vanessa would return to Charleston and life back there.

"Yeah, she's been staying at Syd's for the past two weeks. They are becoming quite close. We've spent some time together and well, she has shared some things with me…"

Fidgeting, Leona continued to make the coffee. Without looking up she offered "I'm not sure what she has shared, but I think you should keep it between the two of you."

Damien was not surprised at her response. "I think so many secrets have been holding this family back for years. Long and short, Sydney needs to know who Vanessa really is." Damien stood up ready to end the conversation. He knew they wouldn't see eye to eye on this subject.

"Damien, sit down. Let's talk about this," sighed Leona. She was devastated that Vanessa had shared their story.

"Nah; I'm good, Miss Leona. We don't need to talk, just please do the right thing. You've been pulling the strings forever, but not this time. Sydney and Vanessa deserve to know the truth." Damien, seeing Leona's expression of fear, reluctantly sat down. In all his years of knowing Leona Williams, he had never seen fear in her eyes.

The two spoke in depth about the situation and Leona came to understand why he was so impassioned

"I know you're not happy with me," said Damien. "But this is for you as much as it is for the girls. You need to put these old demons behind you. My father, Lula Mae, and what happened to you when you were 18—it's overwhelming. I want you to have a fresh start with Mr. Richard. Miss Leona, I love you like a mother, probably even more than my real mother because you believed in me and gave me a chance, despite my lineage. Most women wouldn't want any part of me, let alone leave me part of their business and accept me as family. Any good son wants his mother's happiness and that's what I want for you. That's' all."

Resigned and full of emotion by what he had shared, Leona quietly agreed.

As the Watkins household rose, the normal sounds of the four were silent, almost muted. Tre was in his room packing his second duffel bag full of sneakers and his favorite sweats. He pulled out a picture that captured his parents and Tiana. He couldn't believe how the last weeks had unfolded. After turning himself to the police for Ronnie's assault, he was charged as juvenile for misdemeanor assault. The expensive attorney his father had engaged was able to get the charges reduced, providing Tre attended anger management therapy and attended a court mandated military school. Tre had been packing for several hours, preparing for the long journey. As he began to wrap up the photo and place it in his bag, his father walked in.

"Hey, son; you ready?"

"Almost, Dad," answered Tre. Once in the car, Tre wanted to address the awkwardness in the air. "Hey! I really want to say I'm sorry."

"Sorry about what, Tre?" responded Troy. He was curious if his son even knew the implications of his actions.

"First about Mr. Ronnie. He didn't deserve that. I just got caught up." The two men talked candidly for the next three hours until they arrived at Fort Mitchell Military Academy.

"Son, one thing I can tell you is that you are responsible for what you do and don't do. You need to take this time to grow and learn. I'm here and I will always be." With an embrace, the two men parted. Troy stood watching his son enter the intake room and realized he could use a dose of his own advice.

Four days later, it was show time for Clarissa. While she didn't consider this her last funeral, Clarissa knew that even if they had to take a break while everything got sorted out, this would be the funeral to beat. Even with Williams' reputation for excellence, none of their services were as well orchestrated or intricate as Big Jerry's home going. The service was taking place at an old time Pentecostal church on the out skirts of Maxwell, far away from its suburban main streets, giving it that hometown country feel. The choir of the Jericho AME church was in their mourning robes—somber black, with red piping. The old church was packed with over 200 mourners, some spilling out into the church yard and the parking lot. People had come far and wide, to show their love for the charismatic young man.

Clarissa thoughtfully had blown up several pictures of Jerry throughout his life, which flanked the casket and decorated the small plain church. Having found a website that offered discount caskets, she purchased a less expensive dupe of the famed Promethean gold casket. She had also ordered all white floral arrangements full of roses, hydrangeas, and lilies. The flowers matched the family's attire of all white and gold.

She had also hired a young lady from Atlanta to do a special musical selection for the family. Accompanied by the choir, her rendition of "Total Praise" had the whole church in an uproar with several saints catching the spirit as well as Mama Jo needing the attention of the nurses' unit. There wasn't a dry eye in the congregation.

The Guiding Light team was resplendent in their black, and the golden casket gleamed as it moved down the aisle, Tyriq at the front and Coley on the back end. Attendants Dorinda and Layla assisted the family, while Clarissa led them out, clad in a brand-new fitted Michael Kors suit that she had purchased yesterday at Nordstrom's, black wide brim hat and pearls, her hair straight down her back.

While Big Jer's death was tragic, the service itself was quite uplifting. Clarissa invited the mourners to join them the next day at the Harleigh Cemetery for the final portion of Jerry's special home going service. She was proud of her staff and the service they provided. She was certain that they would garner more business from this service.

The team was assembled early the next day, hyped for the final portion of the home going. Each spoke of accolades that Guiding Light had received for their professionalism, both in person and on social media. Tyriq's brother had managed to discreetly take an artistic looking photo of the casket going down the aisle, with only the backs of the staff. He had posted it and gotten over 400 likes overnight. Clarissa gathered the team before their departure.

"Guys, I'm so proud of y'all. We did the damn thing!" As everyone high-fived and fist-bumped, she continued, "Just want y'all to know you're the best team ever—thank you for your dedication and loyalty. Today, they saw what we can do and will continue to do—give excellent service!"

There was a large shout as each team member went to their assigned duties. Tyriq and Coley took a final look at the casket, checking the seal. Each nodded at the other, both silently acknowledging that this was almost over.

A block from the cemetery, a black tractor trailer truck appeared at the end of the Kroger parking lot. The gleaming truck held the 1,800 lb. carriage, as well the trailer, which contained the horses. The pallbearers had followed from the funeral home and assisted with the transfer. The large casket was expertly lifted from the hearse to the carriage with the aid of eight pallbearers. Clarissa had thought of all of the extra details including having extra men on hand due to the weight of the deceased.

"Man, what do I need these white gloves for?" asked one of the pallbearers, a cousin of Big Jer.

"You ain't never been nowhere? The gloves are for the pallbearers, fool. Just put 'em on and shut up—let's get this show on the road," answered another pallbearer.

Once the glass doors closed to the carriage, the horses started to move at slow but steady pace toward the cemetery gates.

As the carriage reached the cemetery gates with Clarissa and her staff walking solemnly behind t, they realized an extra fifteen cars had joined their already lengthy procession. In military precision, a full jazz band merged into the processional, directly behind the carriage. They played a low funeral dirge as they marched in their matching gold and black uniforms. The family was moved, particularly Mama Jo, who was surprised by the addition of the band. As she clapped and waved, the children took turns pushing her wheelchair.

The band slowly changed the tempo as they moved closer to the grave. They began a resounding rendition of "When the Saints Came Marching In." The family was in high spirits, lifted up by the joyous music. All was well until the cymbals began their crashing interlude. The sound was so piercing and disturbing that the horses began to buck. The driver strug-gled to remain in control, but the frightened horses began to gallop off the paved roadway, attempting to break away from the carriage. The car-riage's wheels became caught in the trench that separated the paved road and cemetery grass causing the entire carriage to come crashing on its side. The driver was pinned under the carriage wheel, his legs crushed by its weight, and the casket had come flying through the glass doors. The casket itself appeared to be in bad shape as the lid looked like shattered glass. More importantly, the casket had opened revealing not one but two arms hanging over the side of open lid.

As the mourners approached, the screams began. A man's charred arm was clearly recognizable, but the smaller arm, clad in pink satin certainly was not Big Jer. The shrieks began to rise as Mama Jo fainted in all the commo-tion. To add insult to injury, the cell phone cameras had come out, record-ing the entire fiasco. As the nurse attended to Mama Jo, all that could be heard was, "Get Miss Clarissa; Get Miss Clarissa!"

Seeing the pandemonium and hearing several loud and angry calls of her name, Clarissa panicked. No longer feeling like a boss, but more like a fugi-tive, she decided to run. As she backed out quickly, the crowd turned into a mob and chased her car. Clarissa sped out the back entrance of Harleigh Cemetery with the mob close on her heels. The last thing she heard amidst the chaos was the sound of a revived Mama Jo wailing and her daughter screaming, "Imma kill that bitch." She knew she had to get away quickly before the authorities arrived.

On her way through town, she saw the sheriff and two deputies as well as two ambulances speeding in the opposite direction, presumably on their way to the grisly scene. She quickly dialed Damien's number, but it went straight to voicemail. Damnit, Damien, she cried, where are you? On her third try, he picked up.

"Where are you?" he questioned.

"I'm driving! Everything just went crazy on my funeral, the horses...."

Damien quickly interrupted her. "I already heard. Sydney had a service at Harleigh today too and she just called with the whole story. I thought it was a small service. How could you have been so stupid?"

"Please. I already know I messed up, but, D, the sheriff was on his way!" She was crying openly and was clearly devastated.

"I know; he's there already and they are throwing your name around. Sydney has our guys trying to help the fire department get the carriage off the driver's legs, but it's clear that there are two bodies in that casket. What the fuck were y'all doing?"

"I don't know how that other body got in there. Coley and Tyriq take care of that stuff." She knew how lame an excuse that was the moment it came out of her mouth.

"Yeah, and not a license between the two of them. But we don't have time for that right now."

"Should I meet you at home so we can talk?"

"No, don't go anywhere near the house. There's a motel out on R532 called the Skylight Inn. Park around the back and wait for me. And, Rissa, stay in the car and don't answer your phone." Clarissa put the hotel's address in her GPS and set off.

Damien sat at his desk paralyzed. He knew this was going to be bad and he wasn't so sure he wouldn't come out unscathed. He dialed his sister's number for an update.

"Hey, bro! This shit is getting crazier by the second. Apparently, Coley, Tyriq, and that ignorant Dorinda work for this crap show too. They got the carriage up, but the poor driver didn't look too good. The sheriff and his deputies opened the casket and there was a charred body which was of the deceased, whose service was today. But under his body in the bottom of the casket was an older woman in a pink gown. Nobody knew who she was, and Tyriq is screaming that they should call Clarissa. What's Clarissa got to do with any of this? The deputies just hauled their asses away. Aww, shit; here comes *Channel 7* news. How the hell did they get here so fast?"

Damien's heart sank at the mention of the news. "Sydney, clear out of there NOW! We don't want to be tied to this in any way. Come back to the office right now and don't say a word. I'll explain everything."

Damien quickly grabbed his jacket and headed for his car.

Clarissa sat in her car in back of the Skylight Inn, looking horrified at the post on social media regarding the funeral. One user got the entire accident on video complete with her own ratchet commentary. Unfortunately, that was one of the better posts. She couldn't believe that the whole thing had gone down like that. But the most distressing thing of all was the second body in the casket. Who was that? Could Coley and Tyriq really be that stupid? Her thoughts were interrupted by a small black car, which she didn't recognize, pulling up next to her. Damien rolled down the window and told her to get in the car.

"Whose car is this?" Clarissa asked.

"Don't worry about it," he answered in disgust. "It's got a clean registration and insurance. In the trunk is a bag with some of your things and some of your jewelry and makeup. I'm checking you into the motel. Stay inside and I'll order you food. Don't come out and don't call anyone. As a matter of fact, give me your phone."

"My phone? I'm not giving you my phone!"

"I could care less what's in your phone, but they can track you with it. I need you to lay low until I get this mess straight. They took Coley, Tyriq, and Dorinda into custody. How long do you think it will be before they implicate you and me in this mess?"

"What are you going to say if the police question you?"

"I'm going to tell them that we came home, and you were gone. Your stuff was missing and your car was gone. I'll get Troy's homeboy to get rid of the car. I need to get the cash and then you've got to bounce."

"Damien, I'm so sorry. I know I was wrong to have tried to do this without consulting you. I just wanted something for us. I wanted you to be proud of me." That was probably the most honest she'd ever been with Damien in their seventeen-year relationship. Damien looked at her with sadness in his eyes.

"I was always proud of you; you're a great mother and a good friend. We just grew apart. I'm sorry too, Rissa, more than you'll ever know." Damien kissed her softly on the lips and exited the car to check her into the motel.

Coley sat, sweating in the interrogation room. He'd never been in a police station before in his life. The deputy came in with a pad and pen. He sat down and sighed heavily. The deputy had sized him up and knew he was the weakest link and would break easily.

"Mr. Smith, or should I call you Coley? How long have you been working at Guiding Light Funeral Home? And in what capacity do you work there? But most important where are your employers, Clarissa and Damien Moore?" He had tons of questions and Coley wanted to take his time to provide the best answers. Coley was scared and knew he should ask for a lawyer, but he had little money for an attorney. He hoped if he was helpful, they might let him go.

"Damien isn't my boss; his girlfriend Clarissa Dickson runs the show. We all work at Williams Mortuary together. Clarissa came up with the idea of running our own place." The deputy was busy taking notes.

"So, Coley, are you a licensed funeral director?"

Coley put his head down and mumbled, "No, sir."

"So, this Ms. Dickson is the funeral director?"

"Nope, she's just a secretary at Williams, but she saw all the Guiding Light families and ran the whole thing. I just pick up the bodies and worked the services."

"I see. Exactly what does Damien Moore do?"

"He doesn't do anything," clearly frustrated at the references to Damien. "I've never even seen him at the funeral home. Clarissa is in charge." Again, the deputy was furiously taking notes.

"Coley, you need to talk to us about those bodies. Why were there two bodies in that casket? Your buddy Tyriq already told his version of the story and it doesn't look so good for you, my friend. But I want to hear your side of the story."

Coley started to panic—he knew that putting those cremation bodies in the caskets was originally his idea. "Look, if I tell you the whole story, could we make a deal or something? I don't want to go to jail."

"Well, that depends on what you have to say."

"Okay," he said, resigned to what came next. "It all started when …."

The sheriff deputies had discussed how they would divide and conqueror between the three suspects. The deputies who spoke to Dorinda and Tyriq got very little in the way of answers from the two of them. Both asked for legal representation and remained silent. Dorinda did, however, tell them to speak to Clarissa Dickson, as she was in charge. As they met with the sheriff to update him, the deputies recalled Coley Smith's statement as well as the other two. Nobody could tie Damien Moore to the funeral home except by the paperwork that was on the State's website. The sheriff, who was a close friend of Leona Williams, had called the Williams Mortuary to speak to Damien Moore, but he was told that he was unavailable and would return the sheriff's call as soon as he was able. If they didn't hear from him by morning, deputies were going to pay Mr. Moore a visit to the address they had off his driver's license.

"Maybe we'll get a two for one since they're supposed to be a couple." The others nodded because they all came to one conclusion—a warrant for the arrest of Clarissa Dickson aka Clarissa Moore needed to happen immediately.

Damien came back to the funeral home to find the staff glued to the television in the conference room. Most of the metro Atlanta area stations were carrying the grisly tale complete with video of the actual crash and Coley, Tyriq, and Dorinda being taken into custody. Channel 7 also had an exclusive interview with the grieving Jones family representative who named Clarissa Moore as the director with whom they made funeral arrangements. Everyone was staring at him curiously and some were even whispering. Damien walked into his sister's office, finding her and KC also glued to the TV.

"What the hell is going on, D?" exclaimed Sydney, full of questions regarding the "Horror at Harleigh," as it was named by the news media. Damien looked at his sister, ready to answer her questions when he was silenced by KC.

"Syd, I know a little more than you do, but the long and short of it is Clarissa started her own funeral home called Guiding Light and managed to convince some of our loyal employees, mainly Coley, Tyriq, Dorinda, and Layla to join her."

"What?" cried Sydney, "Those disloyal bastards! And Clarissa, she sits at our table, works here, and then does something this messed up."

"It gets worse, Sydney. She forged Damien's name to get the business started," stated KC.

Sydney was seething. Many years ago, she liked Clarissa, even called her a friend. How could she do something so underhanded?

"Where is the heifer—she needs a beat down," replied Syd angrily.

Damien shrugged his shoulders. "They say she left the scene. Her phone just goes to voicemail."

Syd just shook her head. "What a coward!" She was also shocked that Clarissa was smart enough to think of something with this ingenuity. *I guess we taught her well*, she thought ruefully.

"What are we going to do? It's only a matter of time before the press and the authorities start asking for Damien," she added, suddenly scared for her brother.

"Too late," said KC matter-of-factly. "The sheriff has called twice already, and the State Board administrator has already called about an emergency meeting being convened in the morning." KC sighed. "You know I'll have to recuse myself."

Sydney grabbed her phone. "We can't wait for any of that to happen. D needs a lawyer right now and not that old ass Mr. Hendrickson. She quickly dialed her husband. There were no loving pleasantries as Sydney cut straight to the chase. "No questions, Avery; we need the best attorney you know."

Already knowing the situation, his only question was criminal or civil. She replied both.

Not in his usual take-charge mode, Damien sat there looking defeated. As he listened to his sister arrange for the attorney to meet him at the sheriff's office at 10 am, he knew he had to get to Rissa and make sure she was ready to leave as soon as her got her the cash.

Damien rose quickly. "I've got to get to DJ. I don't want him to hear this out on the streets or on the TV. And I need to be ready to talk to the sheriff. It' has been a minute since I've talked to a sheriff," he remarked dryly.

"I'm leaving, too, D. Somebody's got to go talk to Mama. She's been blow-ing up my phone," said Sydney. Mercifully, Leona had taken a few days off after returning from her trip with Richard.

"Mine too! I'll go with you. There is definitely strength in numbers," remarked KC.

"Dang, that makes going to see the sheriff seem easy," said Damien with a chuckle, as they all gathered their things to leave.

Damien parked his car in back of the motel and quickly jogged to Clarissa's room. He had asked for a room in the corner, out of the way. He was glad he had gotten rid of Clarissa's red Nissan Maxima. The car was far too noticeable. He knocked on her door and a tearful Clarissa answered, with only the glow from the ancient TV lighting the room. One look at Damien's face said it all.

"This is bad," she sniffled tearfully.

"Yes, it's pretty bad, Rissa." He gave her as much as he knew himself. The driver of the carriage was in critical condition, Mrs. Jones had to be hospitalized due to stress, and he had heard that they had released Tyriq, Dorinda, and Coley on their own recognizance.

"What if he dies?" questioned Clarissa.

Although Damien was thinking the same thought, he tried to reassure her. "C'mon, we can't think like that. This ain't going away, Rissa, but you need to!"

"Where?" asked Clarissa.

"Anywhere, dammit, just not here. The sheriff has already called for me. My lawyer has me going there tomorrow morning and you need to be long gone. I'll get the cash for you, and you need to get at least 300 miles away."

"Can I see DJ before I go?"

"Hell no! I know the sheriff is watching the house and I don't want our son to have to lie to the cops if they ask him if he's seen you. We'll figure the rest out as we go. I'm sorry, but this how it's going down."

Clarissa knew he was right, but her heart ached at the thought of not hugging her baby one more time. "Please tell him I love him so much. Take care of my baby, okay?" The tears were following freely and she could barely catch her breath.

Doing something he hadn't in a very long time, Damien took Clarissa into his arms and rocked her gently, kissing away her tears. "Don't worry; I got you."

Damien slipped into his house, disheartened by the sheriff's deputy parked outside. He knew if they planned to arrest him it would have happened outside his home. They were probably watching for Clarissa. He found DJ in the family room playing his Play Station 5 online with Jamie. *Thank goodness for video games and kids who don't watch the news*, thought Damien.

"Hey, lil' man; I need to talk to you for a minute. Finish up your game and meet me in the kitchen." Damien walked out and went to find himself something to eat as he was literally running on fumes. Seeing the leftovers from last night's dinner reminded him of how hard a task lay before him. DJ came in and flopped in the chair, eager to hear what his father had to say.

"Hey, Dad! What's going on? You look kinda tired and sad. Everything okay?"

Damien stared at his son. He was growing into a compassionate young man. He hoped that this situation would not change him.

"Look, son. I have to tell you something that's going that will be hard to understand. It's about your mom. You know that your mom loves you more than anything. She did something to make us proud of her, but things went terribly wrong. No matter what people say, she's a good person and she shouldn't be blamed for other folks' decisions."

"What's going on, Dad? Where's Mom? Is she okay?"

"She had to leave, son, at least for now." DJ's eyes welled with tears as he listened to the events that would change all of their lives.

Damien awoke at 5:30 am eager to slip out before DJ rose. There would be no school for any of the Williams family children today due to the scandal. His son had cried for a while, but finally fell asleep, with Damien by his side. The deputy on duty saw him leave and probably radioed for another car to follow him. As he pulled into the boxing gym on Center Street, the deputy parked across from the gym. They probably figured he was going for a morning workout, but nothing could be further from the truth. Damien had come here to meet his brother-in-law who trained here twice a week. The two often came together to spar. Damien always chuckled to himself when it came to Avery and boxing. He'd been a super middleweight in college and kept boxing to stay in shape. Damien had seen him beat guys half his age. He was actually respected, even feared in the gym, clearly much different from what was in his home life. As usual, he was already there, warming up on the speed ball. He stopped his workout, surprised to see Damien.

"Hey, bro! What's going on? I didn't think you'd feel up to working out today. Sydney filled me in on everything. I'm sorry about Clarissa. I didn't see her doing something quite so extreme," offered Avery.

"It's okay, man; nobody saw this coming, especially me. Can we talk out back for a second?" Out back was where more personal conversations took place. If two guys went out back, the other patrons gave them some space. Damien launched right in, pressed for time.

"I'd appreciate if you kept this to yourself, but I need to borrow some money, but it has to be cash. I got Clarissa stashed at the Skylight Inn. She needs enough to get out of town and lay low till I can sort this mess out.

She's my son's mother and I can't see her go to jail, even if she deserves it. I got $5K at the house but she's going to need at least $20k to ride this out."

Avery was deep in thought. "I have $25K in the safe at home. It's yours and if you need more, I'll get it."

A relieved Damien was overwhelmed with gratitude. He and Avery were pretty close, but this was next level.

"Bro, you'll never know how much this means to me. I'll get it back to you in thirty days. Damien knew his words were inadequate to express his true feelings. Avery just smiled.

"No, don't worry about when you give it back. We are family. If we can't count on each other, who can we count on? Be back in fifteen minutes. As Avery set off for his home, Damien asked him a parting question

"How are you going to get $25k past my sister? Don't you think she'll notice it missing?"

Avery laughed ruefully. "You don't really think I'd let your sister know we have $25k in cash lying around in the house?" Damien cracked up thinking maybe Avery wasn't as whipped as they thought.

At 10 am, Damien and his attorney were in the sheriff's office, answering a slew of questions regarding Clarissa and Guiding Light Funeral Chapel. His attorney had instructed him to tell the sheriff of the couples' recent break-up and his lack of knowledge regarding her whereabouts.

The sheriff explained that Coley had given a statement detailing the events surrounding the Jones funeral, the accident, and the identity of the second body found in the casket. Apparently, Coley and Tyriq placed the body of the late Lorraine Mason in the casket with the remains of Jerry Jones because they hadn't been able to use the town's only crematory at Harleigh Cemetery. Since Troy Watkins had purchased it a few months ago, they had been unable to complete any cremations. Coley explained that they knew Watkins from Williams' Mortuary and was afraid he would find out that they had been routinely forging Damien Moore's name on cremation documents.

Damien expressed his disbelief and listened in amazement as the tale continued to unfold. Coley also confessed that he stole old cremated remains from Williams and presented them to the families of the deceased at Guiding Light as their loved ones. The sheriff's office was in the process of notifying all of the Guiding Light clients about the fraudulent activity. The family of Lorraine Mason had already retained legal counsel.

Damien was relieved to see a text from Avery that his mission had been accomplished. Avery was able to get the money and even delivered it and an untraceable burner phone to Clarissa at the Skylight Inn. It would have been far too dangerous for Damien to do it himself. Avery personally watched her drive away, away from Maxwell and the craziness she had caused.

The lawyer Avery had recommended was thorough and came with plenty of paperwork supporting Damien's innocence. He shared documents, clearly showing the forgery that had taken place regarding the State Board. He had sworn statements from the inspector that the gentleman he met at Guiding

Light was not, in fact, *the* Damien Moore but the man who was arrested at the Harleigh Cemetery scene, which corroborated Coley's statement.

The sheriff asked a lot of questions, but in the end, thanked Damien for his time and asked him to let his office know if Clarissa reached out to him or DJ. The lawyer assured him he would.

Avery had recommended a top-notch PR firm in Atlanta, which prepared written statements regarding the situation, basically pointing out the importance of using a reputable, licensed funeral home and always checking your funeral director's credentials. Both he and Sydney made statements on behalf of Williams Mortuary, even alluding to the fact at Williams', one of the directors was also a State Board Member. Williams' Mortuary offered to help the victims bury or cremate their loved ones free of charge.

Sydney loved the good press and was delighted that they made Damien out to also be a victim—the handsome honest funeral director and single father who was duped by an illegal firm and his unscrupulous ex-girlfriend. He even had more than a few ladies, calling to make pre-arrangements and asking about his marital status! But Damien only seemed to have eyes for Vanessa. Syd had spotted his car a few times well after midnight.

As the holidays approached, a new type of normal started to take hold for the Watkins family. KC and Troy seemed to have adjusted to being family of three instead of four. Tianna was thriving in her new role as an only child and even Troy appeared to be happier since his son's departure. He still made the trip twice per month to visit Tre. When he returned, he would sometimes be moody and melancholy, but would return to normal after a few days. KC felt as though her husband still suffered with guilt for what his son had done and that he hadn't been able to stop him from selling drugs. Though their household in general was happier, the couple was still struggling with their problems from the past year. KC decided to have a date night to clear the air and try to get them back on track. She put extra time in her appearance, actually applying a little makeup and putting on a new outfit. Troy was appreciative of the efforts she made.

"Girl, you look good!" exclaimed Troy.

"Thank you, babe," KC answered, smiling. The couple decided to try one of the new restaurants on Main Street. They choose an Italian Soul Food called Manella's where they enjoyed one of the best meals they'd had in years. The night was full of wine and laughter. KC felt hopeful for the first time in years. As they drove home, they reminisced about old times and the early years of their marriage and courtship.

"Kay, can I ask you something? Do you even want to have a baby? You know it's not too late. I've been reading articles about older women having babies all the time." Troy stopped seeing the look of pain on KC's face.

"Oh, Troy," KC began. "I love you but no I don't want to have a baby. I'm forty-six years old and I have so many things I'd still like to accomplish, but a baby isn't one of them. I agreed to be a mother to your children the day I married you, but we never discussed having our own."

Troy interrupted his wife. "Babe, I always assumed we both wanted a child, something that we would have together."

"Dang, Troy, we have our life, our love, our marriage together—isn't that enough?"

Troy looked straight ahead, concentrating on the road.

"I guess it isn't," replied KC sadly. "Tell me something, Troy. Would you have married me if I told you that I didn't want children?"

Troy was quiet at first, choosing his words carefully. "I loved you then and I love you now, but I really wanted more children. I missed Tre and Tianna's childhoods because Sharisse and I couldn't get it together. I wanted a second chance to do right, give my kids everything I couldn't because we were struggling."

KC shook her head in disbelief. There was no way she was planning to have a baby so that he could have a do-over. "I was offered a teaching position at Gupton Jones College of Funeral Service. I'll be teaching Anatomy and Physiology."

Troy said nothing as he maneuvered the car into their driveway and shut off the engine. As he exited the car, he looked at her and shook his head. "Maybe you can pencil me and Tianna in between classes."

So much for date night!

In the weeks to follow, the sorted tale of Clarissa and her band of merry men and women began to unfold. It was clear that all of them, while misguided, were highly motivated to do more than their current positions in funeral service. As a result, Williams Mortuary started a mentorship program that allowed employees to learn different aspects of the business as well as further their education in funeral service. The program became so successful that it was introduced to other funeral homes in the area as a remedy to the problem of unlicensed activity in funeral service. The program's motto—"Do It the Right Way!"—was a rallying cry for the state's professional association. They hoped it would take hold all over the nation. Sydney, KC, and Vanessa worked on this project together and it proved to be bonding experience, especially for Vanessa and KC.

A new after work ritual had developed between the women with the trio gathering at Sydney's home for cocktails and conversation. Today, it was Vanessa's turn in the hot seat.

"Okay, Nessa; spill it. What's going on with you and D? I've seen his Escalade outside a few times this week."

KC chimed in. "Yup and I caught him in his office on the phone the other day and that boy was blushing!"

Vanessa smiled coyly. "I've been counseling him. He's going through a lot and I hope I'm aiding in the healing process."

"Counseling? That's what we are calling it?" teased Sydney playfully.

KC laughed. "More like that Sexual Healing," sounding a lot like her husband.

"Sister Watkins—shame on you," remarked Sydney, poking fun at her usually strait-laced cousin. The new KC was far more outspoken and in control.

"I do have my memories," she said demurely

"Look ladies, I'm going to just say this. What's happening is special. We have a good vibe and he really needs this right now." She smiled like the cat that swallowed the canary.

"Whatever, Nessa. I know that smile. Y'all screwing!!" Sydney wasn't sure how she felt about the relationship, but her brother definitely deserved some happiness. The situation with Clarissa had put him under undue stress.

"Sydney!" she cried in mock horror.

"Okay, ladies, as much as I want to continue this conversation, I have to pick up the girls from debate practice," saying so, KC gathered her things and started to leave, only to be surprised by Leona at the door.

"Hey, Auntie, look at you; that outfit is fabulous." Leona was clad in a silk Givenchy track suit and matching loafers, her hair impeccable, as always.

"Are you going to pick up our babies?" asked Leona

"Yes, Auntie. Those kids are in every afterschool program known to man." Leona laughed and hugged her niece. She truly missed being in the girls' everyday lives.

As she walked into the kitchen and saw Vanessa, she realized her presence was more permanent that she had previously thought.

"Leona, you're absolutely glowing," remarked Vanessa.

"Yeah, Mama. Is that Givenchy? I know that doesn't come in my size—I wonder if I ordered two of them," mused Sydney jokingly. Both ladies laughed. Leona smiled at the two and their comfortable banter and was reminded of her earlier conversation with Damien. She figured there was no better time than the present.

"It's nice to see that you two have gotten so close. I guess I'm just surprised—you two couldn't be more different.

Vanessa countered, "Not so odd; sometimes opposites attract. We're like missing puzzle pieces to each other," staring directly at Leona.

"I see. There's a reason for that," said Leona more to Sydney than Vanessa.

She turned to Sydney her voice serious. "I came here to share something with you, something I should have told you a long time ago."

Vanessa felt a sense of tension and excitement, realizing that the moment had finally arrived. Over the next hour, Leona revealed the story of her rape and the fact that she was Vanessa's birth mother. Sydney was incredulous but empathetic, grabbing her mother's hand through her own tears. Vanessa just listened silently. In the end, Sydney embraced her mother, comforting her. She then turned to Vanessa, grabbing her sister; they held each for a long time.

Sydney turned to both women, saying, "I'm sorry this happened to you, Mama, but I'm glad you told me. Your story makes me admire and love you even more. And I'm glad to have my sister."

Leona looked at her two daughters and realized that perfection was no longer her only goal. She knew that she needed to be transparent and open to both her daughters if they wished to embark on this portion of their journey free of burden or regret.

Two Years Later

LEONA WAS BUSY overseeing the caterers and florists as they set up the tables in her garden. Like everything she did, she needed this to be picture perfect. She smiled to herself at how she had arrived at this particular moment. After Richard and she had decided to rent one of the new luxury townhomes in Maxwell's newest 55+ community, Leona had struggled about what to do with her Grace Lane Mansion. Sydney was vehemently opposed to her selling their family home, but Leona didn't think it prudent to keep the house as a shrine to her late husband.

It was during a brain-storming session with her, Vanessa, and KC that they came up with the idea of using the stately mansion as the site of a community service center. While they all had individual thoughts, Leona came up with the idea of a wellness and crisis center for rape victims. The Sarah and Elise Beaumont Wellness Facility offered counseling, legal services and wellness therapies for rape victims and their loved ones. All of the women from Leona to her granddaughters volunteered at the center in some capacity with Vanessa working as the center director. While the center had been open for almost a month, today was its official grand opening. Dignitaries, community leaders, and clergy were all invited to the celebration.

At first, her Grace Lane neighbors were not happy about the traffic and attention that the center had brought to their upscale enclave, but Leona was quite persuasive when a cause was near and dear to her heart. Leona convinced them that the center would be an asset to the community. From the positive press to the women whose lives were being changed, Leona's Grace Lane Mansion would leave a legacy for years to come.

The center also gave her and Belle a purpose to their days. Leona worked in administration, while Belle was head of hospitality, giving clients and their families comfort with her delicious food. Both women found great satisfaction in their work and enjoyed each other's company daily.

KC and Tianna arrived in matching mother-and-daughter dresses, ready to help with the day. Tianna had sprouted overnight from a needy little girl into a beautiful teenager. With all of the changes in their lives over the past two years, the bond between the two had grown stronger, with Tianna officially calling KC "Mom." They immediately pitched in to help Leona, with Tianna running off to help her beloved Grandma Belle in the kitchen.

"Where is that handsome husband of yours?" asked Leona. She hadn't seen Troy around in a while.

"Tre is shipping out overseas today. Troy wanted to spend some time with him before he left." KC's face clouded over at the mention of her stepson. Tre had graduated from Fort Mitchell Military Academy and enlisted in the Marines. He came to visit a few times but there was still a coldness about him that made KC uneasy. Both she and Tianna were always relieved when the infrequent visits were over.

Unfortunately, the events of the last few years had taken a toll on the Watkins' marriage. While KC's professional life had flourished—she had recently been voted as chairman of the Georgia State Board of Funeral Service—her personal life was in shambles. She and Troy barely spent any time together and when they did, they argued incessantly. KC knew Troy was disappointed about her not wanting a baby, but she couldn't understand why he constantly criticized everything she did. They had recently started couples' therapy, but the sessions left the couple angry and even more distant. KC prayed things would get better, but she was discouraged by the state of her marriage.

Troy hoisted the last of Tre's duffel bags into his truck. He felt a swell of pride seeing PFC Watkins stitched onto his son's backpack. Tre had done a complete turnaround since the incidents of two years ago. He excelled in basic training and was an expert marksman. Troy was impressed at his maturity and growth. While they had repaired their relationship, Troy wished the family could be as forgiving.

"I'm going to miss you, Dad. I wish I could have spent some time with Tianna before I left. She's getting so grown," he remarked wistfully. He and his sister had been close as children, but there was a divide between them now. Tre secretly blamed KC and her family for his sister's attitude toward him. He had learned to suppress his emotions during his time in the military, but his rage was still there, lying just beneath the surface. While Tre had appeared to change on the outside, he still battled his old demons.

"I'll tell Tee and KC you asked for them." Troy tried unconvincingly to make his son believe that his wife would be interested in his farewell. KC and Tre would never be close—his wife had made that plainly clear. Troy was unhappy in his marriage and no matter how hard he tried, this was a situation he couldn't fix.

Tre laughed mirthlessly. "We both know KC is probably happy that I'm leaving. It's okay, Dad. She isn't ever going to forgive me. It's cool." Tre didn't really care if he and his stepmother got along, just as long as his dad was in his corner. A life without KC would be just fine with him.

"Come on Private Watkins, let's roll before you're late for your flight."

DJ carefully backed his Aunt Sydney's Range Rover out of the driveway. He and his cousins were on the way to the center to help out with the day's festivities. He was always excited to drive his aunt's car—not just because of its luxury, but because she trusted him with something so expensive. There was a time in the past years that he thought he would never regain his family's trust, but he tried to live up to the promises he made his dad to be a better man. He hoped he had succeeded.

"Bro, do you think your dad will buy you a car before you leave for school?" asked Jamie. DJ had been accepted at several colleges but had been offered a basketball scholarship to Georgia State University. He would be graduating in a few weeks and then off to summer training camp for freshmen team members.

"I hope so, but you never know with my dad. Doesn't really matter because freshmen can't have cars and there's nowhere to park in the city," answered DJ. He really could have cared less, for the thing he wanted most for graduation wasn't going to happen. DJ wanted more than anything for his mom to come home and attend his commencement service. Clarissa called him every once in a while, but the conversations were short and perfunctory. She asked about school and sports and, of course, about his dad. DJ had no number to reach her and she didn't know about his girlfriend, Kayla, the prom, or his scholarship. More than anything, he wanted to talk to her and ask her why she left him behind without as much as a proper goodbye. He struggled with the feeling of abandonment and clung to his Aunt Sydney as a second mother.

"I know when it's our turn to go to college; we are getting as far away from home as possible. No Maxwell, no Atlanta! We are outta here," declared Morgan, her twin shaking his head in unison. Now almost fifteen, the twins had separate lives, but were still very much in sync.

"Aunt Vanessa went to UCLA. I would love to go to Cali," said Morgan, dreamily.

DJ tensed at the mention of Miss Vanessa's name. She and his dad had a secret relationship that only they believed was a secret. DJ had seen the way they looked at one another, smelled her lavender perfume in the house, and had once seen them kissing in his dad's office at the funeral home. He wondered if Miss Vanessa was the reason his parents split up. For this reason alone, he'd never warmed to her, always polite but that was all. And as far as DJ was concerned, that was all it would ever be.

Chloe and Kendall arrived at the Center at exactly the same time. So much had changed over the last few years for the young women. Chloe had graduated from Emory over a year ago with honors and had recently passed the Georgia Bar Exam. She was currently clerking for her godmother, Judge Deidre "Didi" Roberts, her mother's best friend. Chloe also did *pro-bono* work for some of the women at the Center, who often needed legal assistance but had little money or resources. However, the most exciting part of her career was the time she spent working with Avery in his business. Chloe and Avery were both surprised at her natural acumen when it came to mergers and acquisitions. She managed to catch loopholes that Avery's legal team had missed!

Kendall had also started her professional journey by graduating from Spelman College and mortuary school simultaneously. She was almost through her year-long internship and preparing to take her State Board Exam. Kendall too loved working with family and was utilizing her psychology degree by starting a new grief program for young adults who had suffered a loss. She had even started dating a young man from the group, who had recently lost his father.

However, the biggest change in the sisters' lives was their new living situation. Blaze had abruptly left Georgia after being awarded an Arts Council Fellowship in New York State. After a few months, Chloe realized the distance was more than the couple's relationship could stand. She and Kendall decided to move in together and relocate back to Maxwell. They were able to rent a townhouse near their parents' home and maintain their independence while still being close to family. Living with her sister was a perfect way for Chloe to get over the heartache of her break-up with Blaze.

"Over to the left a little, babe," instructed Sydney. She was overseeing the final hanging of her painting, "Sister" which featured a group of women of all ages, colors, and faiths comforting each other. This inspiring abstract work was the focal point of the Center's main entrance. Avery, clad in worn jeans, a work shirt, and a tool belt, was dutifully completing the installation. He took pride in his wife's work, which had grown from a hobby and pastime to an actual business. Together, the couple had launched a company called Notre Amour, which merchandised Sydney's art on stationery, bags, notebooks, and other types of gift items. What had started as a small online gift website had blossomed into a brand that was carried in major upscale department stores and boutiques. They were scheduled to open an art gallery and boutique combination later in the year. Notre Amour was French for "Our Love" and was the basis of their brand. After the recent life changing events, Avery and Sydney felt their love had grown stronger. Both finally felt contented and confident in themselves and their marriage.

Avery's presence had sustained Sydney in dealing with her mother's revelation regarding her rape and the fact that Vanessa was her sister, and not a distant cousin. At first, Sydney was excited to have another sibling, but that excitement turned quickly into anger, resentment, and, at times, jealousy. Sydney was angry that once again when her parents' secrets were revealed, the family was now supposed to accept things—no questions asked. She even felt a bit jealous at first of her mother and Vanessa's budding relationship. With time and a family therapist, Sydney and Vanessa's relationship had gotten back on track and were working to restore the closeness they once felt.

Avery had listened to her rants, her fears, no matter how irrational, and never judged. He dispensed sound advice and unconditional love. Sydney would forever be grateful for his patience and love.

Avery came down from the ladder and stood next to Sydney, surveying their work. "Looks pretty good, don't you think?" he asked, putting his arm around his wife.

"Team Samuels all the way," she replied with a smile.

Vanessa sat nervously in her office, combing through paperwork, trying to make sure everything was perfect for today's grand opening. For as long as she had waited for this day to arrive, she couldn't believe she was suffering from opening day jitters. The planning, long hours, and sweat equity were about to unveil her dream to the public—a wellness facility where folks from all walks of life could be helped. However, Vanessa's real hesitation lay in what the words of Leona's welcome address would bring to light. She was set to reveal the story of her own rape and introduce Vanessa to all as her daughter. It had taken two long years, but she and Leona had forged a familial bond, talking daily and dining together a few times a month. The rest of the family had grown to accept her presence and she was included in all family functions and outings. But telling their truth in public would be different. After years of staying firmly planted in the shadows, she and her birth story would now take center stage. The idea was both exhilarating and terrifying.

Vanessa's phone began to buzz, signaling an incoming text. She smiled when she saw that it was Damien.

"Just breathe, Van. U got this. I'll be right there for you when it's over. Forever D."

As their relationship progressed, Vanessa marveled at Damien's uncanny ability to know exactly the right thing to say to make her feel safe and protected. Their coupling was, however, not without its problems. Vanessa knew that in some degree DJ, Leona, and even Sydney disapproved of the relationship. But they shared a bond that neither fully understood but seemed impenetrable. Vanessa sighed and smiled to herself. She had come to Maxwell to explore her roots but had found love and, eventually, acceptance. She found herself excited for the next chapter and what it would bring.

Damien studied his reflection in the mirror of his truck. He knew everyone would be looking for him as Leona had wanted him up on the stage with her and the girls. As he stared at his reflection, he couldn't believe how much gray hair he was getting and how much older he looked. He chalked it up to his life and the stress of the last two years. The fiasco with Clarissa and Guiding Light had cost him nearly everything—his livelihood, his savings, and his freedom. Even though no criminal charges were filed, Damien was still named in the lawsuits levied against him, Clarissa, and Guiding Light. His lawyers had avoided a lengthy and costly trial by offering out of court settlements. The families' greed won over their need for justice, and they all happily settled out of court. While Damien avoided the negative publicity, he lost all of his savings, having to even take a second mortgage on his home to pay his debts. Both Leona and Sydney offered to loan him the money, but his pride would not allow him to accept their generosity. He was grateful that Leona had started a college fund for DJ when he was born. At least, his current financial situation wouldn't derail his son's future.

Damien tried not to be bitter toward Clarissa, but it was an uphill battle. He tried at first to keep Clarissa informed about everything happening in their son's life. However, she seemed preoccupied and distant when he reached out, often not answering his calls or texts and very rarely contacting DJ at all. He couldn't imagine why Clarissa was ignoring her son as she had always been an attentive and loving mother. DJ alternated between anger and depression regarding his mother's absence. He seemed to take some of that anger out on Damien, especially when it came to his and Vanessa's relationship. Damien hoped with time his son would grow to accept Vanessa, but they had a long way to go. He was always going to be there for his son, but Damien hoped to find some happiness of his own.

As he approached the ceremony, he hoped that Leona's revelation of Vanessa's parentage would be positive. She had become such an important part of his life and he looked forward to their future together.

Clarissa studied Sydney's Instagram post carefully. It seemed like a lifetime ago that she was a part of the Williams' family. Her life in Maxwell felt like a hazy, distant memory, as if in a dream. She stalked the pages of the Williams' family social media for glimpses of her son and Damien. Though the story of Guiding Light and her hasty departure was no longer breaking news, she longed to see if she was mentioned in every news article or social media post. But what she really wanted to know was if her son and

316 |Lady Undertaker II : *The Embalmer's Blues*

Damien were happy, if her presence was missed. Looking at the family's social media accounts, it appeared that life for the Williams' had moved on. She even noticed that Damien was in several photos next to Sydney's cousin. She wondered if they were seeing each other. Even after the past two years, her feelings for Damien had never faded. She was as in love with him today as she had been eighteen years ago.

Clarissa was so engrossed in the post, and her memories she barely heard the soft cries coming from the other room. She rushed into the room only to find the baby standing up in her crib, her bright smile lighting up the room. Clarissa reached for her daughter and held her close, delighting in her smell and soft skin. The little girl, named Dominique, was eighteen months old and was the light of her mother's life. Having her made the pain of leaving DJ behind a tad more bearable. She started to dress and prepare her for daycare.

Dominique was the result of the last night that Clarissa and Damien were together in the Skylight Inn before she fled Maxwell. As Damien comforted her, their interaction turned sexual. She had hoped that he would feel their connection and maybe even want to stay, but he got up, dressed quickly, and left without saying a word. Two months later, when she realized she was pregnant, Clarissa was overjoyed. She ended up staying put in Philadelphia due to her pregnancy. It was there, in the city of Brotherly love that she found her new job—ironically as a secretary at a local funeral home. The work was familiar and her boss was a young unlicensed funeral practitioner who started her business with her sister. Their business, Peaceful Memories Mortuary, was nothing like Williams Mortuary, which was exactly why Clarissa liked it. These women had lots of new and creative ideas and treated Clarissa like an equal and an asset. She often worked funerals and occasionally saw families. She was sure that here she could implement some of her ideas and grow as "funeral service professional."

Though she longed to tell Damien about their daughter, part of her felt like keeping the baby a secret was revenge for him making her leave. As she looked into Dom's pretty brown eyes, she whispered, "Someday soon, sweet girl, you'll meet your daddy and big brother. It's just a matter of time."